D1021923

PHOENIX FLAME

Books by Sara Holland

Havenfall
Phoenix Flame

———

Everless
Evermore

PHOENIX FLAME

SARA HOLLAND

BLOOMSBURY

NEW YORK   LONDON   OXFORD   NEW DELHI   SYDNEY

BLOOMSBURY YA
Bloomsbury Publishing Inc., part of Bloomsbury Publishing Plc
1385 Broadway, New York, NY 10018

BLOOMSBURY and the Diana logo are trademarks of Bloomsbury Publishing Plc

First published in the United States of America in March 2021
by Bloomsbury YA

Text copyright © 2021 by Glasstown Entertainment

Bloomsbury books may be purchased for business or promotional use. For information on bulk purchases
please contact Macmillan Corporate and Premium Sales Department at specialmarkets@macmillan.com

Library of Congress Cataloging-in-Publication Data available upon request
ISBN 978-1-5476-0382-4 (hardcover) • ISBN 978-1-5476-0383-1 (e-book)

Book design by John Candell
Typeset by Westchester Publishing Services
Printed and bound in the U.S.A. by Berryville Graphics Inc., Berryville, Virginia
2 4 6 8 10 9 7 5 3 1

All papers used by Bloomsbury Publishing Plc are natural, recyclable products made from wood
grown in well-managed forests. The manufacturing processes conform to the environmental regulations
of the country of origin.

To find out more about our authors and books visit www.bloomsbury.com and sign up for our newsletters.

To Grammy—thank you for believing in me
from the very beginning

A BRIEF INTRODUCTION TO THE ADJACENT REALMS

⟞ Fiordenkill ⟝

Most of Fiordenkill is encased in ice and frost. Ethereal in its beauty, Fiordenkill sparkles with ice bridges and palaces of packed snow. It seldom sees the sun, but the sky is bright with auroras and thousands of stars. Soldiers ride on wolves, and great bears roam the woods; enchanted fruits grow on the trees, immune to the frost encasing their bright skins.

But beauty can hide secrets, and Fiordenkill is no different, its darkness concealed beneath the glittering ice, in the shadows where the brilliant starlight doesn't reach.

⟞ Byrn ⟝

The massive world of Byrn swelters under the heat of two suns and three moons. Enormous, long-lived storms batter the deserts, the roiling seas, and the lightning plains, so that the ground seems to shift constantly beneath one's feet. Millennia of elemental magic, unleashed without care for the consequences, have ravaged the world and left most of it uninhabitable to Byrnisians.

Years ago, the Silver Prince used his immense magic to tame the storms and erect a wall around his city-state, Oasis. For a time, he ruled in peace, keeping the storms at bay. But now the lightning, hurricanes, and burning wind batter at the wall, and the people grow discontented. So the Prince has begun to cast his sights elsewhere . . . to Havenfall and all the other worlds to which it connects.

⟶ Solaria ⟵

Little is known about Solaria, a tiny, sealed-off world that is a hotbed of powerful, highly volatile magic with a blazing golden sky. Solarians can take many shapes, and they can walk in any world without sickening. But one of their powers—the ability to bind magic to matter—has been weaponized against them. A magical trade has sprung up, with Solarians held captive and forced to use their magic to enchant objects for trade. Each enchantment strips away a bit of a Solarian's soul, which is then trapped in the object alongside the magic.

The doorway to Solaria remains closed, but with the soul trade now out in the open, many believe its people should no longer be considered enemies at Havenfall.

⟶ Haven ⟵

Haven is what we know as the human world. It is the only realm without natural magic, which is why the people of other realms call it Haven—a safe place, a neutral place. The existence of other worlds has been kept secret from humankind. Humans can't live in the other Realms; their biology prevents them from surviving conditions outside of Haven.

~ *Omphalos:* The Inn at Havenfall ~

All the realms intersect at Havenfall, through a series of doorways connected by tunnels hidden beneath the Rocky Mountains. These doorways have been guarded by a long lineage of Innkeepers dating back as far as anyone can remember. There is a radius around the doorways within which people from all realms can breathe safely and not sicken, as people usually do in worlds not their own.

The Inn at Havenfall was built on this spot, as was the town of Haven—so named because, to the people of the realms, the town and the inn represent our whole world.

There used to be many more worlds accessible from the inn, but over the centuries some doorways have closed due to the inscrutable forces that govern the realms. Only the doorway to Solaria has been sealed shut on purpose, for the protection of the Last Remaining Adjacent Realms.

~ The Annual Peace Summit ~

On the longest day of our year, Fiordens witness a blazing, multicolored aurora in their dark sky, and Byrn undergoes a simultaneous eclipse of its three moons. This is the solstice. On this day every summer, travelers can pass safely through the doorways into the Inn at Havenfall— the neutral realm that serves as host to them all.

During this special time, the inn holds its annual peace summit, where delegates from all the realms negotiate trade and political agreements by day and dance in the ballroom by night to celebrate the diversity and unity of all the inn's guests.

THE KNIGHT TRAVELER
A FIORDEN FAIRY TALE

ONCE IN THE LAND OF Myr in the world of Fiordenkill, there lived a knight and a lady who fell in love and promised to never part. The knight was often in danger, defending the capital from the beasts that roamed the forest. So his lady gave him a pendant of ice and stone imbued with healing magic.

After that, though he crossed sword with claw countless times and suffered many injuries, the pendant healed him and sustained him, so that as long as he wore it he would never fall.

One day a great plague swept through the city, and the lady fell ill while her beloved was fighting beasts in the woods. Having poured all her magic into the pendant, she had none left to heal herself and perished.

Without her, the knight was heartbroken, lost. Every street in the city was awash in memories, every tree in the forest freighted with grief.

Upon hearing their story, sadness filled the gods. One—the bird-shaped god of death and flight—cried tears of bright metal over the pair's lost love. They couldn't bring the lady back, but they could offer escape. This metal— called phoenix flame—was said to allow passage between the worlds. From the tears, the knight forged a suit of armor.

Armed with the pendant and the phoenix flame armor, the knight left Myr, left Fiordenkill, and vowed never to let harm come to anyone under his care ever again. He wandered through all the worlds, and he slayed monsters and protected the innocent in every one. But he never came back to Fiordenkill.

Whether he died in another Realm or found new life there, no one knows. But wherever he trod, the fabric of the world grew thin and weak, a wound in the world.

1

HAVENFALL IS MY HOME.

I test the words out, whispering them to myself as I walk slowly down the grand staircase toward the ballroom. My high heels sink into the gleaming red carpet; my painted fingertips glide smoothly against the polished oak of the railing. Music—the strange, otherworldly strains of the Elemental Orchestra, sounds shaped of metal and wind and flame—floats up from the ballroom, muffled and mixed with laughter and the clinking of glasses. A smoky-sweet smell suffuses the air from the candles clustered on top of every flat surface, the same candles throwing nets of dancing light up onto the paneled walls. Their warm gold glimmer contrasts with the velvety dark night outside. No moon, but so many stars that they look like salt grains spilled across indigo silk. The mountaintops all around us are faintly visible against the sky, craggy peaks of even deeper darkness.

Tonight, the magic of Havenfall is almost tangible in the air. Willow has pulled out all the stops to signal to the delegates that this will be a night to remember, the night the new peace treaty—one that doesn't carve Solaria out as the enemy—is to be signed. This is what the Inn at Havenfall is meant to be, a place of peace and togetherness. Connection.

Omphalos.

I come to a halt at the landing overlooking the first floor, my hands subconsciously tracing the subtle carvings of trees and wolves and mountains set into the banister. Below, the open door of the ballroom spills yellow light and smiling, tipsy delegates. Music floats up to the rafters.

For the first time in what seems like a lifetime, the mood inside the Inn at Havenfall is jubilant. We defeated the Silver Prince. We're safe. The Silver Prince is gone—we beat back his attempt to wrest Havenfall from my hands. Marcus has woken up and seems to be doing better every day, even if he's not totally back to his old self. Brekken is here at Havenfall, safe. He made it back from Fiordenkill. At last, things are starting to go according to plan.

Yet I don't feel safe, not yet. Looking down at the ballroom, at the people laughing and dancing, my skin feels itchy, my heart unsettled. This place, the *omphalos*, represents so much: the peace summit that's happened every summer for centuries; safety for people from every world; and a home for me. A future.

"Peace at Havenfall," I whisper to myself, trying to inject confidence into the words I don't really feel. That's the goal. That's why I need to succeed tonight. It's been a long couple of days of meetings with the delegates of Fiordenkill and Byrn, nailing down the language of the peace treaty which will bring Solaria—at least officially—into the fold with the other allied Adjacent Realms. It took a lot of talking and frustration, but we finally landed on language that everyone could agree to. Then Marcus wrote it all out in his elegant handwriting on a sheet of creamy, gilt-edged paper. That paper is now tucked into a velvet folio in a slim leather case at my side. All it needs is signatures, twenty delegates each from Fiordenkill and Byrn.

Ideally, we'd be getting Solarian signatures too—any Solarian input at all, really. But there are no Solarians here, except for Sura, the girl we rescued from the antique shop, who's only a child. And of course the dead Solarian, Bram—if that was even his real name—buried out in the woods beyond the glittering windows. We had Taya up until a few days ago, but by the time she figured out that she wasn't human, the Silver Prince had captured her. And now she's gone, in Solaria.

But I push away that line of thinking before it can drag me down. The Fiorden and Byrnisian delegates have agreed, at least in theory, to make peace with Solaria. Even if the treaty isn't perfect or complete without being able to contact Solaria, it's necessary—Marcus and I will need all the delegates' support once we start making moves against the soul trade in order to save the Solarians victimized by it.

I pull the folio from my bag and open it to read the words of the treaty. Although the last few days of meetings have drilled them well enough into my memory, it's reassuring to read them again.

Byrn, Fiordenkill, Haven, and Solaria, if its people should wish it, with this instrument enter together in accord. The previous Accords, presided over by Annabelle of Havenfall and signed by the representatives of Byrn and Fiordenkill, is hereby revoked.

Let it be known that the people of Solaria are once again welcome at the Inn, and that Solaria is to be considered a peaceful Adjacent Realm alongside Byrn, Fiordenkill, Haven, and any other peace-seeking world as may yet be discovered.

It's time.

As my foot steps off the staircase, the noise and warmth of the ballroom immediately wraps around me, waking up my senses, pulling me in. Even without two-thirds of the summer workers—we sent the humans home after the Silver Prince's attack, dosed with forgetting-wine, for their own safety, in case he struck again—the ballroom is sparkling clean, and the Fiorden and Byrnisian staff is darting around proffering platters of hors d'oeuvres and refilling goblets.

Everyone is wearing their very finest clothes—the Byrnisians in light, airy creations of silk and metal, baring skin in inventive places; while the Fiordens wear angular jackets or sweeping cloaks, rich velvet accented with fur and lace. Willow even talked me into wearing a dress, and I have to admit it's gorgeous—midnight blue satin, with a skirt that hits at my knees in the front and dips low in the back. It swishes, smooth against my legs as I finally gather my courage and head down the stairs, feeling grateful that I insisted on wearing high-heeled boots rather than the strappy heels Willow tried to foist on me.

And jewelry. Everyone wears jewelry, from the traditional gems that the Fiordens stack in the shells of their ears—a unique color sequence for each family—to the Byrnisians' stacked bangles and dangling necklaces of iron, gold, obsidian. Silver. It all flashes around me as I ease into the heat and press of the crowd, like the stars outside have sunk down and settled on our skin.

Which reminds me of my other mission, the one I haven't told even Marcus about. Though I know my first order of business has to be the treaty, tonight also seems like the perfect opportunity to fish for leads about the soul trade, while the delegates are in a good mood fueled by liquor and relief. Relief to be free of the Silver Prince, and to be done with negotiations about the new treaty. Maybe they'll be loose—maybe someone will let something slip.

I weave through the crowd, walking fast and with purpose so no one stops me. Until I find the Heiress waiting at our prearranged spot, beneath the huge antique mirror that spans one whole wall of the ballroom. She grins at me as I approach, drawing something out of the pocket of her black velvet gown.

As usual, she looks regal, like a queen of some far country who is only deigning to grace us with her presence here for the night. She is one of the few people—alongside Marcus and Graylin, Willow, and our head of security, Sal—who is in permanent residence at Havenfall. I'm not even sure what Realm she's from—she doesn't have the scaled cheekbones of a Byrnisian, or the willowy build typical of Fiordens. But I can't imagine she's human either, seeing as she never seems to age. For most of my life, I thought her merely an eccentric historian. She told everyone that she was at Havenfall to write a history of the Realms that never seemed to materialize.

But now I know there's more to her. She unearthed evidence of the soul trade all on her own, and she decided to fight it. There were gaps in her knowledge, yes—she thought the enchanted silver objects circulating through the Realms contained only stolen magic, not stolen souls—but she saw that Havenfall was in danger and took steps to fight the threat, even though she thought it meant going up against Marcus. She even recruited Brekken to help her. She was the one who approached me with a plan for tonight—the idea to squeeze more information out of the delegates. Now she's giving me the means to do so.

"You look lovely tonight, dear," she says, putting a soft hand to my cheek and nodding approvingly. "You ought to let Willow take a crack at you more often."

I blush. "Yeah, I know." But impatience gnaws at my insides. Normally, I'd love to bask in her compliments, but right now isn't the time. "Do you have it?"

The Heiress nods, her hands dropping down to mine so she can press something into my palm. I look down to see a small crystalline vial, stoppered with a cork and containing a clear liquid tinted the faint green of grass. A kind of truth serum, the Heiress told me, an old kind of magic from Tural, one of the former Adjacent Realms whose doorway closed long ago. I haven't the faintest idea how the Heiress came to have this, and she wouldn't tell me. Only how to use it.

"It's not perfect," she tells me now, withdrawing her hand from mine, leaving the vial in my palm. "It will simply make those who partake of it more forthcoming, and they will find it more difficult to construct a lie. But it will not cause them to offer up what they would otherwise keep to themselves. You still need to ask the right questions and coax them to share."

She must see the trepidation on my face, because she pats my shoulder. "You'll do fine. The delegates respect you."

Do they, though? After the fiasco that was Havenfall under my watch, I wouldn't count on that. I held on to the inn, but just barely. I guess the fact that the Silver Prince didn't take over can be counted as a victory, but in the meantime I let half the Fiorden delegation return to their realm early, destabilizing the doors; I heightened tensions between Fiordenkill and Byrn.

The unsigned peace treaty weighs momentarily heavier at my side as the Heiress grips my arm—gentle, but firm—and turns me around so I face the crowd.

"Go."

I take a deep breath and go.

In summers past, this moment—the one where I merge with the crowd of delegates, join the dance—has always been one of lightness and joy.

Still, it's hard to feel too morose amidst all this merrymaking. Music and laughter and the scents of fruit and wine wrap around me as I push deeper into the crowd. The Elemental Orchestra is playing a rearranged version of *The Rite of Spring*, with minor-key Byrnisian flourishes woven into Stravinsky's arrangements. Delegates swirl around the floor, creating a maelstrom of different colors and textures. With everyone moving like this, you could fail to notice that our ranks have thinned at all. You could think that everything was all right.

My uncle, Marcus, is at the bar, chatting up the delegates as he passes out glasses of wine and champagne. I don't think he's fully recovered from being in a coma after the Silver Prince's attack, but right now you wouldn't know it from looking at him. He's animated, handsome, happy. Graylin, his husband, even convinced him to wear a tuxedo. He looks smart—not a wrinkle.

Staying out of his sight line, I lurk by the bar until Marcus steps away, at which point I quickly duck behind the counter, put together a tray of glasses filled with fruit-studded wine, and spike each of them with a dash of truth serum. Straightening up, almost immediately, I fix my eyes on someone who could be my first target. Saber Cancarnette. He's respected among the Fiorden delegation, and his signature on the treaty will carry real weight. Plus, as a fur trader who works closely with the gem miners of Byrn, it seems possible he might know something about the soul-silver.

I stride up to Cancarnette with determination. The Fiorden lord looks slightly taken aback by my approach. His ice-pale cheeks are tinted pink with the influence of wine. Good. Hopefully that'll give me a head start. I smile and proffer my tray carefully.

"Another drink, Sir Cancarnette?" I ask with a bright tone. "Willow and I are trying out new recipes."

Let him think, let them all think, that now that Marcus is recovered I'm back to my previous role, sidelined, a child with nothing to do with the real affairs of Havenfall. It will make it easier to find the truth.

Cancarnette doesn't hesitate to accept one of the spiked glasses. As soon as he does, one of the staff materializes and whisks the tray away, leaving my hands free. I clink my own serum-free glass against Cancarnette's and increase the wattage of my smile.

"To the new peace treaty."

The lord hesitates a moment, his brow wrinkling in confusion or concern, I'm not sure. But then he returns my toast and echoes my words. "To the treaty."

So he's not completely prejudiced against Solarians, then. That's good. I was afraid that the delegates might flat-out refuse to acknowledge the treaty, even as ineffectual as it is now. That gives me hope enough to ask my next question, once Cancarnette's throat has moved to swallow the wine—and the truth serum—down.

"That's a lovely pendant," I say after I've tilted my own glass back. I gesture to the ornament hanging on Cancarnette's chest, a delicate figurine of a bird of prey, an eagle, carved out of pale, marble-like stone, white with blue veins. "Is it a family heirloom?"

I know he is a lover of jewels and precious things, or at least a connoisseur. When Marcus was comatose, one of the first Innkeeper duties I carried out in my uncle's stead was overseeing a trade negotiation between Cancarnette and a Byrnisian merchant—Fiorden furs in exchange for Byrnisian jewels. Most of their talk went right over my head, as scared and overwhelmed as I was. But I remember the hunger in Cancarnette's eyes when he looked over Mima's spread of jewels.

The lord reaches up to trace the amulet with long fingers. "Indeed." Pride colors his voice. "It belonged to my mother before me, and her father before her. Furs are my father's trade, but my mother and grand-father raised eagles for a living."

I'm momentarily distracted as I imagine a Fiorden eagle. All the ani-mals in the great forest of Myr—the Fiordenkill country on the other side of the door—are many times larger than their counterparts on Earth. What must it be like, to face down an eagle with a wingspan as long as a car? To know that it'll come when you call?

"The piece is beautiful," I say admiringly. "You know, Brekken told me a story once about a knight whose beloved gave him a pendant enchanted with her healing magic. And after that, no matter what oppo-nents he crossed or how they wounded him, the pendant healed him and sustained him so that as long as he wore it, he would never fall."

I lift my hand up as if to touch Cancarnette's pendant, and then let it go, weaving wistfulness into my voice. "Do you think such a thing could ever be?"

Cancarnette smiles. "Magic belongs to people, Miss Morrow. The wild gods granted it to us; it runs through our blood. To enchant a life-less object, no matter how beautiful, would be blasphemy."

My heart speeds, as I notice that he's said it's wrong, not that it can't be done. "Of course. Naturally."

"I remember that story," Cancarnette goes on. "But perhaps your soldier left out the part about how while the knight was adventuring, his lover fell ill. Having poured all her magic into the pendant, she had none left for herself and died alone."

I feel myself flinch. "I hadn't heard that part." He's right, Brekken never told me.

"Even had the knight returned the pendant to her, it wouldn't have saved her," Cancarnette goes on, his raised voice showing annoy-ance. "Once magic is torn from you, it cannot be reintegrated, not in the same way. Of course, that doesn't stop the magpies."

He takes a sip of wine, his eyes bright and hazy. I edge closer as the dance swirls all around us, my heart beating fast. Even cloaked in riddles and fables, this is more than I've gotten out of any of the other delegates. "Magpies?"

"Collectors," Cancarnette clarifies, the scorn clear in his voice. "There are some who hoard such objects, believing themselves above the corruption."

"Like who?" I ask eagerly.

The haziness clears for a second from Cancarnette's eyes, and he looks me over skeptically.

"No one you need concern yourself with," he says with a scoff. "Princess Enetta would never grant them a token to come to Havenfall."

"But—" I bite my tongue, frustration mounting. "If binding magic is blasphemous, where do the objects come from?"

I should have phrased it in a more diplomatic, less pointed way, but I sense the Fiorden lord is growing bored with me, with this conversation. My time is running out. And if he knows something . . .

But I've let myself be sidetracked. There are plenty of people from whom I might learn something about the soul trade, but I need Cancarnette's signature on the treaty. I fumble to take it out with the hand not holding my glass, too flustered to think of a smooth transition. "Could I get your signature on the treaty?" I ask, hoping I at least sound winning.

Cancarnette takes the folio. I can see his eyes roving, searching for loopholes or catches.

When he's done, Cancarnette arches one eyebrow. "Isn't that a little premature?" His eyes skate around the room. "How are we to execute a treaty between four parties, when only three are present?"

I resist the urge to remind him that we talked about this in the meetings, if he had bothered to attend. Instead, I point to the line on the page where it says Solaria will become part of the Adjacent Realms *if its people should wish it.* "Marcus accounted for that."

"Well, if the Innkeeper says so." He takes my pen and smiles indulgently as he signs. As he passes the treaty back to me—his signature bold and looping at the bottom—I'm bothered by the sense he isn't taking this, taking *me*, seriously.

At least he didn't refuse outright. I feared that might be the case, seeing as lots of the Fiorden and Byrnisian delegates probably still hate Solarians. They're governed—as I was until recently—by stories of soul-devouring, shapeshifter monsters, fiery-eyed and sharp-clawed creatures who would tear you limb from limb just for the joy of it. Two weeks ago, we were hunting my friend Taya in the woods with knives and guns. But she saved me . . . us . . . Havenfall from the Silver Prince. I admit I was hoping for a little more enthusiasm from Cancarnette.

Still, Cancarnette isn't wrong. This is a hollow treaty, tonight a hollow celebration, seeing as we don't have any actual Solarians here. Not since Taya disappeared into the golden light of the Solarian doorway and the door sealed closed behind her, leaving only a blank wall of stone.

I have no way to reach her, no way to know if she's even alive. There's nothing I can do to help her—nothing at all, except to do my best to make this world safe for when she comes back.

She has to come back, right?

I can't think about that now, or I'll lose heart. I blink and focus on my surroundings, trying to get the image of her face in my mind—her radiant, powerful expression in the moment before she slipped through the door to Solaria—to recede.

But it doesn't, and I feel suddenly claustrophobic, suffocated. Everything is color and music and light and laughter now, but suddenly I feel the aches and pains left over in my muscles from the fight with the Silver Prince. The Prince himself might be gone, but he's taken with him the unconditional trust and happiness I once felt within these walls. Now I know it's possible for enemies to enter here, and everything feels a little warped, a little off, tainted.

It's impossible to know for sure that everyone in this room means us well. I learned my lesson about blind trust, and it came at a cost.

2

THE NIGHT HAS ONLY JUST started, but I need a breather. Before I can think too much about it, I hurry from the ballroom, walking fast but aimlessly down the hall until the noise from the dancing recedes. A moment ago I was nervous but confident; now I feel raw, panicked, like the task facing me is impossible. And the last thing I need is for the delegates to see me freak out. I don't want to go all the way back up to my room, but I think I need to be alone. Fortunately, Marcus gave me a copy of all the inn's keys.

In the small, secure room that Marcus calls the armory, silver glitters all around me, and I feel the weight of souls in the air. A tiny window set close to the ceiling lets in orange sunset light, but only a little. The air is chilly and smells like pine, and it's blissfully silent.

But as soon as the door closes behind me, I realize I chose the wrong place to calm my nerves. It's usually empty in here, but now silver objects stacked on shelves all around me catch and refract the sunlight, turning it strange and cold.

Jewelry—rings and necklaces and bracelets, earrings dripping with jewels, goblets and coins, vases and candlesticks and any other small precious thing you could think of—all of it is here. Once, I would have thought the pearlescent silver beautiful. It still is, but I can never look at the pieces the same way again, now that I know what they're used for. Now that I know the truth beneath the surface . . . that they're black market soul-silver. I can't look at any of it without feeling an overwhelming knot of guilt and dread in my stomach.

I only learned about the silver trade—the soul trade—a few weeks ago. I'd always been taught the same thing about the Adjacent Realms that Cancarnette said a few minutes ago—that only people can possess magic, not objects. But it turns out that isn't entirely true. Someone has been capturing Solarians and binding slivers of their souls, like pieces of string, to silver. The metal can then become enchanted with bits of magic—like Fiorden healing magic, or Byrnisian fire-wielding powers.

It seems silly now that I thought I could find anything out about the soul trade with a few indirect questions tossed casually to the delegates. While we know of some of the human buyers—the Heiress got their names when she was working with them and pretending to be one of them—there are no records of who brought the objects in or out of the other Realms.

Turning around in this small room, I meet the worried gaze of a hundred warped reflections. I want to believe that my beloved Havenfall wasn't the focal point, that the stolen souls didn't pass through here. But if the traders come from Fiordenkill or Byrn, the inn is the only place they can exist outside of their own respective worlds. Byrnisians and Fiordens have been known to leave the safety of the inn's walls and walk into the town of Haven for short periods of time, but they can't go farther than that without getting sick. If the soul traders aren't smuggling silver through the inn or town, they must have access to the Realms somewhere else in order to smuggle the magic between worlds.

Could it really be possible? That there are other ways to enter other Realms? Marcus thinks that the world used to have more doorways, that Havenfall wasn't always the only one. When I was a kid, that possibility seemed wondrous, and I often wished that I would stumble upon a doorway in a janitor's closet at school or in the fallow fields behind my mom's house. But now the idea makes me sick with worry. There's just so much, and we don't know about all of it.

Music drifts in through the closed door. The Elemental Orchestra has started playing a merry jaunt. I should be headed back already. I have a job to do tonight. I can't let myself get derailed so easily going forward.

I take a deep breath and remind myself that this, what I'm doing, is in service to the captive souls. We need to know how the objects are being made, how they are getting into Havenfall, and who's doing it. Maybe it's someone in the ballroom right now.

I reach up to touch a silver vase, not really for courage, more as a reminder of what I have to do. Why tonight is important. Why I have to succeed.

Then I arrange my face into a smile and slip from the armory, pulling my shoulders back as I stride down the hall and back toward the ballroom.

The first thing I notice upon reentering is that *Brekken is here.* He stands by the entrance just inside the ballroom, as if he is waiting for me. I witness the moment he notices me, watch the sweet, startled smile unfurl across his face.

Seeing him is strange—it quiets and amplifies my nerves at the same time. Makes my heart feel light, but also makes it beat faster and unevenly. He looks amazing in a short velvet cape hanging smartly off his sharply angled shoulders—finery he hasn't worn since that first night he arrived at Havenfall. His copper hair is combed back to accentuate his handsome face and brilliant blue eyes.

He smiles softly at me as I get close, pushing away from the wall. "I was just looking for you. I thought you'd be here by now." He must see something off in my expression, because his brow creases in concern. "You all right?"

I nod. "Just needed a minute." Looking into the ballroom, though, I don't know if my few minutes in the armory with the silver objects has helped or hurt my calm. The responsibility—both to execute the peace treaty and to do everything I can to free the Solarians trapped in the silver—feels all the heavier now.

Brekken's hand finds mine. "You can do this."

Startled, I look up at him. "I don't know." The words fall out unbidden.

Brekken steps closer to me. Something has shifted between us in the days since he came back from Fiordenkill, where he'd fled after witnessing the Silver Prince murder his own servant, Bram—the chain of events that set everything off, all the ill events of this summer. I had been angry with Brekken, not knowing where he went or why, even harboring a suspicion—before the Silver Prince's guilt came to light—that Brekken was the traitor. Even though we're safe now and I know the truth that he was trying to help, the weight of that suspicion hasn't entirely dissipated.

Brekken has been careful with me, not like the easy familiarity we had as kids. But the way he's holding my hand—well, that's different from how we were as kids too. He looks at me like he has utter faith in me. It's almost enough to give me faith in myself. Almost.

"Just be your charming self," Brekken says now, raising my hand to brush my knuckles with his lips.

It's a courtly gesture, one that probably means nothing to him, but it still makes my pulse even more erratic.

"Charming, yeah, that's me," I say jokingly, but I don't think the sarcasm comes across with my voice all breathy and trembly.

Brekken squeezes my hand gently before letting it fall. "Shall we?"

I nod, and we make our way side by side deeper into the ballroom. The high spirits of the party guests sweep us up right away. It feels easier to be a part of it, now that Brekken is by my side. I retrieve my tray of spiked wine from the credenza where it was stashed and throw myself back into the politicking.

With Brekken near, his presence drawing me out, I feel bolder approaching two Byrnisian delegates, Lonan and Mima. They break off their conversation—gossip about who was rumored to be slipping into the gardens with whom and which buyers are angling for which bargains—and listen curiously as I give my pitch.

They agree to sign as well, but like Cancarnette, seem to regard it as some kind of amusement. Not real, not binding. But that doesn't matter. All that matters is the signatures on the page.

Three down. Then four, five. The more signatures I get, the easier it is to obtain each successive one, as the delegates see their peers are willing to align with Solarians again.

They'll understand the importance of it once Solarians return to Havenfall, once we start taking down the soul trade. It's been just a few weeks since everything at Havenfall has both turned upside down and clicked into place, hardly any time at all. I feel ashamed that I ever thought Solarians were evil—now that I know they're just people, and many are victims, hunted for their ability to capture magic in exchange for pieces of their soul. The delegates haven't seen the things I've seen.

They don't truly know Solarians like Taya or Nate.

Nate . . . My brother's face flashes across my mind, but I push it away. Last week, I realized everything I thought I knew about Nate was untrue. The boy I thought was my biological brother was actually a Solarian, rescued from the soul trade by Marcus and raised by my mom as one of us. Nate was—is?—Taya's blood brother. And he was not killed by my mother or an intruder ten years ago. He was kidnapped, presumably into the silver trade.

This is another reason why I must find out more about the traders. There's no guarantee Nate's still alive after all these years. I have only seen the tiniest corner of the soul trade, and I don't know how survivable it is. But knowing that he was taken, when I was sure beyond a doubt he was dead, is enough to plant the seed of hope.

He could be out there.

I could find him.

And if there's any way to find him, it will surely be through the soul trade—following the corruption as deep and wide as it goes. Hoping that it hasn't destroyed my brother.

But while I'm occupied scanning the room for another suitably influential delegate to go after, Brekken suddenly leans down and kisses my cheek.

I look up, surprised, to see his face abnormally bright and open, flushed in a way I've almost never seen him. Not since a few weeks ago in the hayloft, his body against mine, his face inches from mine, millimeters . . . I feel heat flood my own face at the memory.

"Brekken," I say, startled, and that's when I see a tumbler of fruity wine in his hand that matches the others on my tray—my tray that I realize now is one glass lighter. Crap. I never told him about the wine.

"I just wanted to dance with you," he says with a grin.

Any other time I'd be thrilled at the prospect, but I have signatures to gather. And I feel bad that he accidentally drank the truth serum. And yet . . . His eyes are shining. And I feel both frustration and worry melt away, bubbly excitement rising in me like champagne. Surely one song couldn't hurt.

I let him sweep me into a dance as the next song starts. It's easy, since his movements are so graceful and self-assured. I let him lead me. Let the fears swirl in my wake like so many dead leaves at the end of the summer.

Brekken leads me into the thick of the dance. Silk and velvet rustle around us, music and perfume and laughter melding in a delirious aura. When we reach a pocket of space on the floor, he claims it, turning and wrapping his arms around me. He's still grinning like he just won the freaking lottery.

"Brekken." I have to stand up and speak close to his ear to be heard, not wanting to shout. Sometimes his skin is cool to the touch, but somehow, wrapped up in him like this—my hands on his shoulders, his around my waist—I'm warm all over. "I'm really sorry. There was a truth serum in that wine. I didn't mean for you to have it . . ."

But I guess I'm not loud enough, because Brekken tilts his head, eyes crinkling with confusion. "What?"

"I—" But then the music kicks up into a faster, lively section, and my words are lost in the cheer that goes up from the crowd of delegates. I give up. "Never mind," I say, loud enough for Brekken to hear. This conversation is better suited for another time anyway, sometime when I have the space and quiet to explain myself.

He grins at me, lifting me off my feet, and we dance; and my worries ebb away again. I'm usually no good at this—which is why I usually park myself behind the bar during Havenfall's nightly dancing. Maybe it's the couple of glasses of wine in me, or the feeling that I finally got somewhere with Cancarnette and the magpies he mentioned. It's not much of a lead, but it's better than nothing. Whatever the case, I feel slightly lighter.

As the gravity of the music swirls us around the ballroom—somehow slow and fast at the same time, other dancers coming together then making way for us like it's all been choreographed—I catch a glimpse of Marcus holding a tall glass of ice, sitting next to Graylin in one of the golden carved chairs lining the sides of the room. Marcus isn't dancing or schmoozing at the bar anymore, and he looks tired, but at least he's here and upright. Marcus has been getting better slowly but surely since the Silver Prince forced open the door to Solaria and threw the inn into imbalance. He's not the same as before, that much is clear, but at least we have him back.

The truth of the matter is that none of us are the same, really. At the beginning of the summer, my uncle took me to task for my closeness with Brekken, now that he was a soldier. He said that paying too much attention to him could look like favoritism, and Innkeepers are meant to be impartial. The delegates at Havenfall have stuck around through chaos and fear and upheaval. I doubt seeing me dance with Brekken is going to faze them, and if it does, well, in all my summers here I've seen them do a lot more embarrassing things with the help of wine.

By the time the song is over, the currents of the dance floor have taken Brekken and me to a corner of the room. Relative quiet falls as the band takes a breather and a sip of wine—normal wine this time. I drop my hands from Brekken's shoulders, self-conscious. But he grabs them before they fall all the way to my sides, and holds them between us.

I feel heat rise to my face and hope I'm not tomato red as his fingers fold around mine. What the Heiress told me floats back into my mind. That the serum only brings out impulses, and truths, that were already there.

"Brekken . . . ," I start, trying to figure out how to break it to him, when he leans forward and cuts off my words with his lips.

My breath catches. Suddenly it seems like all my senses have been dialed up to eleven; and yet, somehow, the world has fallen quiet. My eyes flutter shut, but I still hear everything: the Elemental Orchestra launching into a new, slower, aching song; the low threads of conversation crisscrossing the room like spider silk. The fizz of champagne in glasses, and the late summer wind whispering outside the walls.

And Brekken. Everywhere, Brekken. His hands on my waist, polite and chaste but burning hot and trembling a little. The solidness of his shoulders under my hands, muscles shifting beneath cloth. The scent of him, like an ice wind. And his lips, warm on mine, moving gently at first and then more urgently.

People must be looking, I think. I can feel the weight of eyes on my back. But I don't care. I can't bring myself to care. Brekken's taking over everything—until he breaks away to take a breath, and we realize at the same time that we're surrounded by a circle of onlookers, some smiling indulgently, some looking scandalized. A different kind of heat, one I like much less, rises to my cheeks. I grab Brekken's hands and lift them from my sides.

"Let's take this somewhere else, shall we?" I ask with a smile.

As we head out, I accidentally meet Marcus's gaze across the room, and he doesn't look happy.

Guilt slides in . . . but then it dissipates. I hold my uncle's stare. Without me, the inn would be in chaos right now. Who's to say we would even be here, dancing, if the Silver Prince had gotten his way? We're not safe yet, not by a long shot, but I think I've earned a little bit of freedom. I hold my head high and square my shoulders as I lead Brekken out of the ballroom. Not embarrassed, not scurrying as I once might have.

Let them look. Who I kiss is none of their business. There's only two weeks left in the summit anyway.

Outside, we automatically meander past the gardens and find ourselves skirting the edge of the woods. We don't speak, but we don't need to; the silence is a comfortable one, built up like layers of lacquer by years of friendship.

My breath hitches only when we pass a spot where the undergrowth is slightly trampled, some of the leaves and branches indented. Brekken doesn't know it, no one would even notice unless they were looking closely, but this is the path Graylin and I cut to the clearing where we buried Bram.

Unbidden, a memory sneaks in of Taya, her face in the dark as I emerged from the woods. I tense a little, and Brekken looks down at me, his hand tightening around mine.

"Are you sure you're all right?" His voice is soft, languid.

"I'm fine."

Shake it off. Thinking about Taya when I'm holding hands with Brekken makes me feel guilty. Both of them have claimed a part of my heart. I've loved Brekken since I was a kid, but earlier this summer I thought Brekken had double-crossed me and Havenfall. Marcus was sick, and I had no idea who I could trust. Taya was the only one who seemed to understand. Not to mention those dark eyes, her motorcycle jacket and crooked smile. Of course I caught feelings for her.

When I look at Brekken, though, I can't quell a low, wild excitement deep in my chest—that how he's looking at me now, with tenderness and longing and not a little hunger, is how he really feels. And part of me feels that way about him too.

I tug his hand onward until we're past the woods, away from the inn. We come to a stop at the edge of Mirror Lake. It spreads out before us, reflecting the purple dusk sky. For a moment, we stand side by side in silence, watching the stars slowly make themselves known overhead.

"Did you learn anything from Cancarnette?" Brekken asks at length. The music from the Havenfall ballroom reaches us faintly, spilled from open windows and floating through the twilight, now backed up by a chorus of crickets and frogs.

"A little," I say. "I told him that story you told me when we were little, about the knight and the princess with her healing pendant. But you left out the ending, Brekken." I speak lightly, finishing with a laugh, but the space between us suddenly feels a little denser.

"Did I?" Brekken says. His voice is similarly light, but when I glance at him, his eyes are serious. "Well, who could blame me?" He turns his body toward mine, and I find myself automatically doing the same, like a magnet responding to a lode. "I want to make everything perfect for you."

"Perfect doesn't exist," I say, grinning.

But he doesn't grin back. He looks intently at me. "I disagree."

And he leans down to kiss me again.

This time, without our audience of delegates, things get heated quickly. His hands roam over my back and sides; my tongue slips out to taste his lips, sugar and frost and mulled wine. That reminds me of the truth serum, and the guilt slices through the dizzy want. I turn my face to the side—just a little, our bodies still pressed together—and gasp the words into his ear.

"Brekken, wait."

He freezes immediately, then steps back, concern creasing his face. The evening air that rushes into the space between us feels extra cold, and I reach after him.

"No, don't go, I'm fine—"

"Then what's wrong?" His voice is husky, his cheeks pink and eyes hazy bright.

I don't remember running my hands through his hair, but I must have, because his usually tidy copper locks are messy and wild. He lets me grab the lapels of his jacket and pull him back close to me, but all he does is rest his hands cautiously on my waist.

"That wine," I say, shame and happiness running circles inside me. "It had a truth serum in it. I just wanted to find out if the delegates knew about the soul trade—"

"A serum?" Brekken says. But instead of the shock and indignation I expect, his words carry the edge of laughter. He blinks and smiles at me. "Maddie, I knew that."

The relief that hits me is profound and immediate. "You did?"

"I mean, not before I drank it," Brekken clarifies. "But after that it was fairly obvious."

"And . . ." I wait for him to go on, to reprimand me, but he doesn't. "You're not mad?"

"About using it on me or on the delegates?"

"Either," I say. "Both?"

He shakes his head, his face growing serious. "Once I might have been. But that was before I found out about the soul trade. Now I know we have to end this however we can."

I think of my brother, Nate. A sense of resolve and relief fills me, relief that Brekken feels the same way. "I agree."

He leans in and kisses me again. It's not so wild this time, but tender and slow and serious. Like a promise. I kiss him back, winding my arms around his neck, playing with the impossibly soft hairs at the nape of his neck. I feel like I'm falling through space, but gently somehow. There's no fear in it. Suddenly I know that whatever I decide to do next,

Brekken will be behind me, and that makes me feel so much braver. Like maybe I can actually do this.

"Did Cancarnette tell you what happened to the knight in the story?" Brekken whispers after a few minutes, low and close to my ear.

For a moment I don't want to hear any more. I want to tell him I only want to know if there's a happy ending. But I stop myself. Surely, after everything, I can handle a story. "Just that the lady died from an illness."

"After the lady died, the heartbroken knight wandered through all the worlds," Brekken says. "There were more Realms then, more than we even remember. He traveled them all, and he slayed monsters and protected the innocent in every one. But he never came back to Fiordenkill. Either he perished in one of the other realms or he decided to stay away."

I pull back and stare. "That's a terrible ending," I say, indignant.

Brekken blinks, like he's been caught up in a dream and I just pulled him out of it. "Is it?" he says. "I always thought it bittersweet. How even without his lady, he found life again in new worlds. Perhaps he even found a new love in one of them."

"But it doesn't make sense," I press. "How could he have traveled to other worlds without getting sick?"

Brekken shrugs. "Supposedly he had some talisman that let him pass through. I don't remember exactly. But, Maddie, lots of them have just such a traveler." His hands tighten around mine. "Maybe it's possible. Maybe we've just forgotten how."

"You're drunk," I say, giggling despite the spike of sadness that's just gone through me.

"No, I've had truth serum. And whose fault is that?"

His lips graze my temple, my cheek, and a thrilling, bone-deep want rolls through me.

But . . . I still have a job to do. I can't make out with Brekken here by the lake all night. Even if at the moment, I want badly to do just that. I stop his lips with a finger before they can find mine again.

"I have to get the rest of the signatures," I say breathlessly, hoarsely. "On the peace treaty."

Brekken sighs; cool air brushes my fingers. "All right, then." He steps away from me with a heavy, regretful sigh. "Can I help you?"

"Sure." I try to sound businesslike, even though my body aches like a part of me has been torn away now that he's not touching me anymore. "Talk it up to the Fiorden delegation, so that they're willing to sign when I come round. And . . ." I hesitate, then go on. "I've been trying to dig up information about the soul trade, how the objects got through Havenfall without us noticing. So if you hear anything about collectors, or silver merchants, or magpies, listen close."

With the mention of the soul trade, the lightness drains out of the moment, both of us remembering what we have to do. Our responsibility. Brekken straightens up and combs his fingers through his hair, making it fall back into place. I touch my mouth with my fingertip, hoping my lip stain isn't smeared.

Brekken reaches out to cradle my cheek for one more moment, then lets his hand fall. "All right," he says, turning back toward the inn, his eyes fixing on the golden lights of its windows. "Onward."

3

LATER, AFTER THE DANCING IS over, I head to the kitchen, where Marcus, Graylin, and I have planned to meet and discuss our next steps, as we've done almost every night since the door to Solaria closed and the Silver Prince was banished back to his Realm.

I'm exhausted, my feet sore from dancing—more like chasing the delegates around as they danced—but I feel amped up from the success of the night. Despite being more than a little distracted after stepping out with Brekken, I've gotten almost all the delegates' signatures on the peace treaty, safe in the velvet folio tucked into my bag. I know many of them are still skeptical, but once the treaty is signed and official, hopefully it will ease their concerns about Solarians. It's imperative that they're welcoming, because when we figure out how to free the Solarian souls trapped in the silver objects, we don't want them to face hostility from the delegates.

Especially if we find Nate . . .

I push the thought away, trying not to get my hopes up.

The kitchen is as grand as the rest of the inn—with shining polished-brick floors, huge high windows that show off the night sky, and gleaming copper cookware hanging neatly on the walls, reflecting the cozy light of the lamp Marcus has on the oak worktable. When I get there, he and Graylin are sitting with Princess Enetta, the future ruler of the kingdom of Myr in Fiordenkill. She looks as lovely as ever in a shimmering gold gown, matching gold beads woven into the ends of her braids.

The trio is leaning over a bunch of papers spread out in front of them, and my heart beats faster as I recall what Marcus has been working on for the last few nights. Those are the Silver Prince's papers. Even though he's back at Oasis after his play to take over Havenfall failed, we'd be idiots to think that was the only thing up his sleeve. We can only hope the papers contain information about his intentions, whatever he might do next.

Marcus's smile to me is a little strained, and I wonder if he's still mad at me for kissing Brekken out on the ballroom floor. Or Brekken kissing me. Whatever. But all my uncle does is pull out the counter stool next to him.

"How did getting the signatures go?"

"Great." I let myself feel proud as I pull out the folio and smooth it on the countertop. "A few more to go, but I'll try again tomorrow."

I look down at the Silver Prince's papers, covered in writing in a language I don't know. To each, Willow has stapled a printout of her translation. At a glance, it just seems to be a mundane recount of life at the summit—meeting logs and notes about fellow delegates. But Marcus must have found something else. He looks shaken, his hair mussed and sticking up, which means he's been running his hands nervously through it. Stress curls, my mom used to call them. He palms through the papers too fast to be reading anything, like he's just giving his hand something to do.

"What's up?" I ask, pride giving way to nervousness.

My uncle shakes his head as he pulls one page from the pile. "The Silver Prince talks about meeting his traders outside of Havenfall. He could be referring to legitimate trade from Byrn, or something else. But I'm more concerned by the 'outside of Havenfall' part." He stabs a finger down on the page. "Maybe he was planning to use a proxy instead of going himself, or maybe it's a misdirection, but . . ."

He trails off and hands me the sheet of paper. My heart sinks as I read over Willow's translation.

I haven't enough to travel at the moment, but I will soon. In Haven's winter, I can meet you far away from the inn to discuss further and examine the gemstones.

I pass it to Enetta, reeling inside. "How can that be?"

Far from the inn. No one, except for Solarians, can survive outside of their home world or Havenfall. If I were to step into Fiordenkill or Byrn, I'd sicken and die within hours. The sphere of protection the inn offers extends to the town of Haven—but no farther. That's what makes Havenfall special. Safe—the fact that we guard the only way in and out of Earth.

The Silver Prince shouldn't be able to get in without us knowing, nor survive elsewhere. I watch Enetta's brow wrinkle as she reads.

"It doesn't necessarily mean there's another doorway," Marcus says, and I can tell he's trying to keep an even keel. "He could mean to meet this trader in Byrn, *far from the inn*, though that's an odd way of putting it. Or it could be deliberate. Could be he left this letter so we'd find it in case his plan went wrong." Marcus turns to Graylin. "Have you and Willow found out anything more from the delegates?"

"The elder King of Byrn has agreed to rule in the Prince's stead, since he's still missing from Oasis," Graylin replies. "They think he's in hiding somewhere in the wildlands, outside the city walls."

In the wildlands, or here on Earth, I think.

Graylin exudes calm, the characteristic Fiorden stoicism, but I can tell he's anxious by the way he fidgets with his wineglass.

"Willow is interviewing all the Byrnisian delegates from the summit," Graylin goes on. "Of course, she's not making it obvious what she's doing, but that means she's slower to get answers. So far she says no one appears to know what the Silver Prince might be planning."

"Do we think they're telling the truth?" I ask. "The Byrnisians, I mean."

Graylin tilts his head at Marcus, who is the one to answer. "We can't know for sure. I figure we can run two scenarios, one where they're honest and one where they're not."

Hearing that makes me sad. We never used to ask these kinds of questions, not me or Marcus or anyone. We used to trust the delegates unconditionally—that they meant well. At least I did.

"I hadn't realized the extent of dissent against the Silver Prince in Oasis, and in Byrn more generally," Graylin says, his long, dark fingers drumming the stem of his wineglass. "Of course we know about the nomads, who have never accepted the Prince's rule and are therefore shut out of Oasis. But from the Byrnisian correspondence I have in my library from around the time of his ascension, it appears that there are some who didn't entirely support his rule, even among those who elected to renounce their magic and stay in Oasis."

"Hmm." Marcus runs a hand through his curly hair, leaving it to spring back higher than before. "That's good for us, right? Whatever he's planning to do, the fewer people behind him, the better."

"It could be good." Enetta speaks for the first time. Her voice has a brittle quality. "Or it could mean that absent the responsibilities of the throne, he will feel free to do whatever he wishes, whatever all *this*"— she waves her hands over the pile of papers—"is."

"We know he wanted control of Havenfall," I say quietly.

I remember what he said that day we fought in the tunnels. His vision for the inn. *Not just a crossroads. A throne room. For all the Realms.*

"We still control the doorway," Marcus says. "I've spoken to Sal about bringing more security in, but even with the team we have now, no one's coming into Havenfall who we don't let in. It's a bottleneck."

The words of Brekken and Cancarnette earlier this evening whirl together in my mind. Magpies. A knight who journeyed across the worlds. "What if he does have another way in?"

Marcus's mouth turns down at the corners. "Then why would he need Havenfall at all?" he says heavily. "And it's not as if we can go search the whole world for the Prince, especially when that would mean leaving the inn more vulnerable. I think it's best that we stay on our guard here and hope that whatever he was trying to do, he's given up."

A suspicion is forming in my head. I know I should probably keep it to myself until I'm more sure of things, but I can't stop myself from giving voice to it.

"It seems like a big coincidence," I say. "That everything with the Silver Prince happened just as the soul trade was coming to light." I look around the table; Marcus, Graylin, and Enetta are all looking intently at me, but I can't make much of their expressions. "What if he's involved with it somehow? I've been wondering how the silver traders moved their goods between the worlds without us knowing." I take a deep breath. "We probably should have been watching more closely, but still . . . it doesn't seem likely that all the souls and the silver came through Havenfall, does it? Maybe there are other openings, passageways between

Fiordenkill and Byrn and Solaria. Or even in other places here on Earth."

I turn to Marcus, wanting his support, wanting to be believed. He, more than anyone else, knows how important this is—in general, because it's the right thing to do, and to us, our family. Nate—my brother—was a victim of the soul trade. And he might still be alive. But I don't want to spend all our efforts on Nate—it would be all the more devastating, then, if we didn't find him. Plus, the problem is way bigger than just one Solarian. Still, I can't stop myself from hoping.

"Maybe if we look into the soul trade, we'll learn more about the Silver Prince too," I finish breathlessly.

Marcus's expression is carefully neutral. "Then we run into the same problem. As horrible as the soul trade is, we don't have the numbers or the resources to root it out. Not when it could be literally anywhere. If I could stop it, I would have already."

"But we can narrow down where to look." I glance at Enetta. "I was talking to Lord Cancarnette earlier, and he said something about magpies. People who collect magical artifacts. That must have something to do with the trade, right? If we got their names, if we investigated them . . ."

"I've heard tell of the magpies too," Enetta says. Her voice isn't harsh, but it isn't exactly warm either. "But the rumors I've heard point to powerful people in our country. Influential ones. And relations with Havenfall are strained enough as it is. The Fiorden delegation will not appreciate being asked by the Innkeeper to spy on their own, as a favor to Solarians."

My breath sticks in my throat. I want to argue, but I know Enetta is right. Half of the Fiordenkill delegation left the summit early a few weeks ago, angry and afraid because they found out a Solarian was on the grounds and I hadn't told them. An unprecedented early departure, and it was my fault. I want to remind Enetta that they were never really in danger from the Solarian—Taya wouldn't have hurt anyone—but that isn't the point. The keeping secrets and telling lies is where I went wrong.

"I know how important it is to stop the soul trade," my uncle says gently. "I've been fighting it for years. But the Silver Prince is the more immediate threat. He almost killed you, Maddie."

"Yeah, I remember."

It's hard to keep my voice even as the memory creeps in. But as scary as it is that the Silver Prince is now our enemy—and it's extremely scary—that's not what's been weighing on me these past few days, not what's been keeping me up at night.

Taya. Nate.

Graylin is the one to turn to me now. "What you're saying makes sense, Maddie," he says. "And I think we all agree that we must end the soul trade and save the captive Solarians. But we can't do any of that if the Silver Prince takes over Havenfall."

I bite the inside of my cheek. He's right. They're all right. I know this. But that doesn't make it feel any less urgent. And I can't shake the deep-down feeling that it's all connected, the silver and the souls and the Silver Prince.

Without Havenfall, we won't be able to save anyone. Yet I hate the idea of just hunkering down here, constantly on the defensive, with no way to learn more or do anything except build walls around us. In two weeks the delegates will be gone, and with them any chance of finding out what they know. It makes me feel trapped, makes me feel like a little kid again, my knees pressed against the cupboard door while my mother and brother fight for their lives outside.

"We'll work on it, Maddie, I promise," Marcus says softly. "We won't let it go on forever. But first we need to deal with the Prince. We'll make sure Havenfall is safe, and then we'll take down the soul trade. Forever." He holds my gaze. "Deal?"

I nod. "Deal."

But I'm screaming inside, and it's an effort not to bounce in my seat with nerves. Whenever I have a free moment, I resolve to myself— whenever Marcus doesn't need me to strengthen our defenses against the Silver Prince—I'll research the soul trade and make a plan, so that when the Prince is dealt with, we can strike immediately against the traders.

But . . . I don't know where to start. I'm just one person. And even if I had all the resources of Havenfall at my disposal, even if the people here were willing to follow me like they do Marcus, I still couldn't search the whole world. The only place I know to be frequented by the soul traders is the antique shop outside Havenfall where the Heiress used to meet up with her contacts. But I blew her cover by following her there and getting captured, so she's out of commission as a double agent. And when Graylin, Willow, Sal, and the Heiress returned to the shop later to rescue Sura, the Solarian girl who was being held there, the traders were gone, the shop abandoned. They were just going to let her starve.

———

The next morning at breakfast, I fill a tray and bring it upstairs to Willow's room, where Sura has been sleeping on the couch. When I knock and go in, Willow is gone—off to attend to the duties of a day at the peace summit—but the little Solarian girl is sitting quietly at the big desk by the window, working on a coloring book.

After the Silver Prince's attack, we sent all the human staff home for their own safety. I worried that there was no one to watch Sura. Willow's been swamped trying to manage the inn with a skeleton crew, and there are no extra hands on deck to babysit the kid who's suddenly appeared in our midst. But she's as quiet and well behaved as anyone could ask for, spending most of her time holed up here with picture books and crayons. I've tried to gently talk with her about what happened before we rescued her—hoping for some lead on the traders—but whenever I've asked, she's clammed up, and I don't want to push her.

She looks up and waves shyly as I come in.

"Hi, Sura!" I bring the tray over to her and set it down—full of toast with butter and strawberry jelly, chocolate milk, a couple of hard-boiled eggs. "Can I hang out with you for a sec?"

She smiles and nods, and I sink into the armchair in front of the dark fireplace. Outside of checking in on Sura, it's just a relief to be up here in the quiet. Without the staff, I've been doing a lot more chores for Willow—grocery runs, coordinating delegates' schedules, helping out with dinner. I don't mind it at all, but the silence and stillness is nice too.

"What are you working on?" I ask her after I've had a few sips of my coffee.

She tilts up her coloring book and shows me. It's a scene from that Disney Rapunzel movie, I think. The page shows a little girl in a poofy dress, holding hands with her mother, a dark-haired woman, as they look out the window of their tower.

Mom. Her face fills my mind like a lightning strike. With everything that's been going on in the last few days, I've scarcely thought of her, painful as that is to admit. For ten years now, she's been sitting in prison, only a nominal part of my life—and now she's on death row, convicted of killing Nate. But she's innocent. I always knew she didn't kill him, but until a few days ago, I'd never known what actually happened or how mixed up she was in the soul trade. She was one of the safe houses for the enchanted artifacts Marcus smuggled out of Havenfall, away from the trade. She knew Nate was a Solarian, and she protected him. Until the day when she couldn't.

"Sura," Sura says, pointing to the figure of the girl that she's colored to look like herself, with light-gold-toned skin and brown hair. She points next to the woman's figure. "And Feya."

I don't know who Feya is, but I hope the coloring book doesn't include the twist that the mother in the movie is the villain. Thoughts of Mom keep swirling around my head. Ever since that horrible night, since she's been in jail, she's tried to convince me that the public narrative is true; that she *did* kill my brother. Why would she do that? To protect me from the people who took him? To stop me from going and looking for him? She must know something.

And slowly, a plan forms in my mind. Something I can actually do.

4

AT DINNER, I ASK MARCUS to let me go visit my dad in Sterling, and Marcus agrees more readily than I expected. But I guess I shouldn't be surprised. My excuse—that I didn't check in with Dad while I was occupied with the Silver Prince—is true. And since Mom's been in prison, Marcus has always been scrupulously careful to stay on Dad's good side. We both know Dad doesn't love the fact that I spend my summers at Havenfall rather than doing something normal or useful, like summer camp or a job in town. But even when I went to Havenfall this summer without clearing it with him first, he didn't get angry with me. He and Marcus have both been careful not to tear our family apart any more than it already has been, and I'm grateful for it.

Tonight it's a relief to skip the dancing. After we eat, I go up to my room to pack while the Elemental Orchestra's music filters up from below. My heart beats fast in anticipation of movement, of seeing Dad. Then Mom.

Of course I didn't tell Marcus the whole plan. I had already filled out the visitor form on my laptop in my room last night, hunched over the screen in the dark. Mom must have some information about the black market, and I need to tell her I finally know the truth about Nate. Maybe now she'll finally open up to me. Maybe now the life will come back into her eyes.

The next day, I wake up stupid early—so early it's still dark outside my bedroom window—and Marcus drives me to the bus. We don't talk much on the way there, and when we pull off on the road shoulder that serves as a bus stop, Marcus parks the car without speaking. Outside, the world is gray and misty, quiet except for a few lonely birds chirping, their songs muffled in the fog. We sit in silence for a few minutes—neither of us have had our coffee yet. But then Marcus surprises me by drawing in a big breath, like he's about to make a speech.

"I'm sorry we can't do more about the soul trade right now, Maddie," he says. "I know it's important to you. It's important to me too."

He falls silent, waiting for me to reply.

I want to say *it's okay. I understand*, but the words stick in my throat. I get that we have to stay alert and keep Havenfall safe. I get that it's not likely the Silver Prince has decided to just give up after we chased him back to Byrn, no matter how much we all might hope. But I still haven't wrapped my mind around the idea of just sitting and waiting for something bad to happen. Thinking about it makes my body fill with nervous energy. Suddenly every cell in my body wants to run, fight something, take action.

The bus to Denver appears over the ridge, trundling stolidly through the morning mist. Marcus turns in his seat to look at me. His face is tired, haggard, the stubble dusting his jaw matching the shadows under his eyes.

"Does your dad know you're on the way?" he asks.

I nod, and the silence stretches as the bus gets closer. I get the sense that Marcus is waiting for me to reply further, but I don't entirely trust myself to speak without saying something snarky or giving my plan away. I've never gone to visit Mom during the summer before. If Marcus finds out that's in the cards, he'll put two and two together and figure out that I'm trying to dig up more dirt on the traders.

"Be careful, Maddie," he says. "I'll see you soon."

The bus lurches to a stop at the shoulder, providing a welcome distraction from the bubble of emotion suddenly swelling in my throat. I lean over to give Marcus a quick hug and then hop out, my backpack with two days' worth of clothes and snacks feeling weirdly light on my shoulders. I usually don't come down off this mountain until summer is over. It feels kind of wrong to do so now, like I'm abandoning the inn. I look over my shoulder, hoping to see the shape of it above me on the mountainside, but Havenfall is shrouded in fog.

"Do you have pepper spray?" Marcus calls after me.

I have to swallow a laugh. Whatever dangers might be waiting out there for me, I doubt pepper spray will be much of a weapon against them. But I know Marcus is just trying to be helpful, so I call "Yep" over my shoulder and pat my hoodie pocket where my key chain is. I wave to him as the bus doors hiss open and I climb aboard.

The driver—I think it's the same old man who drove me to Haven a month ago, though it feels like several lifetimes—smiles at me as I hand him my printed ticket and look down the aisle of the near-empty bus. Only a middle-aged woman sits near the front, sleeping with her head against the window and a backpack full of what looks like camping gear next to her. I find a seat halfway down and wave at Marcus once more through the window as the driver executes a careful, lumbering Y-turn. Then we're off.

The ride passes in a dazed blur. I only got a couple of hours of sleep last night, so the steady rumble of the bus lulls me quickly into a doze, despite the uncomfortable seat. When I come awake again, the sun has risen and the road leveled out; we're in the plains again, nearly to Denver. I text Dad an update.

Then, from the bus station in Denver, I grab an Uber to the mobile home park. It's a splurge I usually wouldn't make—usually it's bus or bike or walking—but I feel antsy and anxious to be indoors, to be safe. I remember the sick, sinking feeling that hit me when I first realized the Silver Prince had tricked me, that he was an enemy and I was in danger. Now, knowing that he may have found a way to travel outside Havenfall, it's as if that feeling has leaked like radiation and poisoned the whole world. I'm acutely aware of an edgy, sharp fear, as if at any moment the Silver Prince might pop out from behind the scrubby bushes along the side of the highway and engulf the car in flames.

That, along with the typical pit in my stomach that I always get on the journey back from Havenfall—ten years of accumulated anxiety kicking in, telling me that soon I'm going to be back at school, back in the routine, the Murder Kid alone and lonely and judged.

Finally, we pull up in front of my dad's house. My stepmom, Marla, has coaxed the yard that was once just dry dirt and cinderblocks into a thriving vegetable garden. Dad makes decent enough money as a mechanic, but after Nate's death—what we thought was Nate's death—and Mom's arrest, the press came after Dad hard, even though they'd already been divorced for years at that point. It got so bad that he sold his house and traded it in for one he could put on a truck bed, so that whenever someone sniffed out his address, it was no problem to just up and go. But he hasn't moved for years now. Not since meeting Marla, not since settling down here and establishing a garden, a routine, a life.

The door opens, and there he is. Dad lights up as soon as he sees me, his weathered lips parting in a big grin. He pulls me into a hug, the familiar smell of home cooking and faint cigarette smoke wrapping around me.

"Maddie." He steps back and holds my shoulders at arm's length, like always when I get back from Havenfall, and his eyes widen as he takes me in. "You look . . ."

I blink, unsure what he's going to say. I know I haven't gotten taller since he last saw me. Haven't gotten a haircut or anything. But I do feel different. I feel like everything that's happened this summer—the Silver Prince, losing Brekken, the Solarian door opening, Marcus falling ill, becoming the interim Innkeeper, blood and violence at Havenfall, Taya, Nate—has changed me on a molecular level. I didn't realize the change showed on my face, but somehow I'm not really surprised either.

"I'm okay, Dad." I smile at him, feeling the weight of everything that's changed since I last saw him.

The realization hits me with a thud. I can't tell Dad that Nate might be alive. There's too much to the story he can't know, since he doesn't believe in magic or Havenfall or Realms. But it feels wrong to keep that hope from him. Nate was Dad's family too. His adopted son.

"How was your trip?" Dad pulls my backpack from me and leads me through the house into the kitchen. "Marla had a shift, but she sends her love. And she got pancakes started for us."

Sure enough, a mixing bowl and pan sit in the sink, and pancakes are piled on a plate on the counter. The kitchen is clean and flooded with sun, and two glasses of orange juice and mugs of coffee sit on the small, weathered table. A familiar haze, mixed nostalgia and loneliness, settles around me as I sit down at the place settings Dad has laid out.

"How's Marcus?" Dad asks as he busies himself getting pancakes for both of us. He knows Marcus has been sick, but not more than that. "I know I wouldn't want to come down with anything in that little town. Does Haven even have a doctor?"

"Unclear," I say with a laugh. "There is a guy that the people of Haven go to with aches and pains, but I'd be shocked if he actually has a degree. Luckily Graylin took good care of Marcus."

"And what about you?" From across the counter, Dad's eyes zero in on me, narrowing in good-natured suspicion. "Have you been studying for your SATs like I asked? Are you still dating that guy Brock?"

"Yes to studying. And his name's Brekken." I feel my cheeks redden, not knowing how to answer his other question. It's not like I could go on normal teenager dates with Brekken, being that he's a soldier from another world. And there's no way I'm telling my dad about the kissing. Anxious to change the subject, I ask Dad, "How's Marla?"

Marla is one of Dad's favorite subjects, so the question is enough to set him off on a long, adoring tangent about how Marla is up for a promotion at the hospital. And just like that, things feel normal again. Well, almost normal.

The thing with Dad is, I once tried to tell him about Havenfall's magic and the Adjacent Realms. It was when I was a little kid, and he nodded along with me, asked questions, seemed to take me seriously. But then I overheard him on the phone with Grandma Ellen later, laughing. *You should hear the stories she tells, Ma. The imagination on her, I can't believe it sometimes.*

He didn't really believe me. He was just pretending.

While I know Dad didn't mean anything bad by it, the wounded betrayal I felt at that moment is still burned into my mind. Yet even so, I still find myself wanting to tell him what's going on with me, or at least as close to the truth as I can. So I do, picking my words carefully and twisting the story a little: how Marcus came down with a horrible flu and I had to run the inn in his absence, how reports of a mountain lion on the grounds were freaking everyone out. How Brekken's soldier training—in my story, he's started basic training in Wyoming—kept him distant, but a new friend, Taya, helped distract me. And that she had to leave the inn early for a gap year.

Dad follows along with bright eyes, nodding and hmm-ing and asking questions that I then have to improvise answers to. I don't know why I don't just outright lie to him—that would be a lot easier—but the truth is, Dad is my best friend outside of Havenfall, lame as that may be. I want him to know what's going on with me, even if it's a simplified, watered-down version of the truth.

In turn he tells me of the drama among his neighbors in the home park (debate over the same leaf blower I can hear in the distance now), my grandma's insurance company (it's doing well), and Marla's problems at work (an overbearing new fellow nurse who's competing with her for the promotion). Normal, everyday problems, and hearing about them makes me feel more normal. It's not that they're simple or unimportant—just that no one will die if the other nurse rubs Marla the wrong way, no worlds will be closed off if someone's leaf blower is too loud. This is what life is supposed to be like, where not every moment is a balancing act on a tightrope, and not every moment can lead to catastrophe.

So why do I miss the inn so fiercely? Why, even as I speak, do my eyes stray out the westward-facing kitchen window, as if I might be able to make out the mountaintops beyond the orderly slopes of our neighbors' roofs?

Here, life—at least my life—is safe and predictable and lonely. No one expects anything of me except to stay out of trouble. Dad and Marla love me, but they spend most of their time at work, and I don't have any other friends to speak of (perks of being the Murder Girl). It's easy to let the days pass, but each one is more and more stifling, and I'm terrified that if I can't have Havenfall, this is all that my future will hold.

It's an uneasy reminder that Marcus has a point. As much as I want to drop everything to hunt down the soul traders and bring them to justice, if the Silver Prince takes Havenfall, I'll have nothing at all left.

"Got something for you," Dad says, breaking into my spiraling thoughts.

I look up at him, trying not to let my alarm show in my eyes, the darkness of my thoughts. "What's that?"

"Follow me." He pushes back from the table and leads me outside. I follow, trying not to let my sudden panic show.

We head around back, where Dad's usual handful of car projects shelter under a plastic roof. He stops by his old green Toyota Camry—the one he used to drive before the engine gave out a couple of years ago. It's a little rusty around the edges, but clean, the paint shining under the late morning sun. The car has been fitted with new tires.

He tosses something at me, and I catch it before realizing to my surprise that it's keys.

"What is this?" I ask dumbly.

Dad shrugs modestly, but he can't help but grin. "I fixed 'er up. I was planning to sell her, but . . . when I heard you were coming home, I figured you could use it more."

"Wow. This is amazing!"

I stare at the Camry in shock, wondering what made my dad give up on his long-held rule-slash-bribe that I could get a car when I went to college. What expectations will counterbalance the gift? But whatever they might be, I'm not going to turn down a car. I grin and give Dad a hug. "Thanks so much, Dad."

"My pleasure," he says, beaming. Then the smile dims a bit. "I figured you could use it tomorrow, so you don't have to take that early bus. You know how I hate you riding when it's still dark."

Dad knows that I'm planning to see Mom. I told him when I originally called from Havenfall to arrange the visit. Just like he doesn't like my going to Havenfall, I know he's not a fan of the fact that after all these years I'm still going to see Mom at Sterling Correctional Center. He doesn't understand why I'd even want to—after all, he thinks she's the one who killed Nate. But he's never tried to stop me or talk me out of it. He's respected my choice. And now . . .

Unexpectedly, a gust of emotion hits me and my eyes fill with tears. Dad doesn't know why it's more important than ever that I talk to Mom. He doesn't know about Solaria or the soul trade. And yet, somehow, whether through sheer luck or some kind of fatherly intuition, he still came through for me right when I needed it most. Overcome, I wrap my arms around him in another tight hug, one that he's not expecting judging by the *oof* he emits.

"Thank you, Dad," I whisper, letting myself feel hopeful for the first time since the meeting in Havenfall's kitchen. "Thank you so much."

5

STERLING WOMEN'S CORRECTIONAL FACILITY IS familiar in the worst way. I have been here so many times for so many years, and yet it never changes. The parking lot feels as flat and endless as purgatory. The guards at the gate all wear the same mirrored sunglasses that hide their faces and show you yours instead, small and warped and scared when you drive through the checkpoint. The barbed wire along the top of the fence curls high and even, stretching as far as I can see. Everything is gray—the ground, the walls, the uniforms—and rather than making the blue of the sky pop, all that gray seems to leach the color out of it, like the earth is infecting the heavens, or feeding off it. This place is enough to make you forget that magic exists. Enough to scrub all the individuality out of you. Here, I'm just another inmate's kid, scared and lost and desperate.

A dark thought pops into my head. If Mom's sentence is carried out, will they take her somewhere else or kill her here? I suppress a shiver. I haven't been checking my emails to see if there are any updates from Mom's public defender about her death sentence. The last few years have been a depressing parade of appeals and reprieves and all sorts of administrative hoops in the public defender's attempts to give my mom more time. But it's almost scarier not to know what will happen next; to have the ax hovering overhead, but not know when it will fall.

The motions to enter the prison are rote for me now. After all these years, I bet I could do them in my sleep. Go inside into a barren entryway where everything is concrete or metal. Stand there awkwardly while a bored-looking guard with chapped, bitten lips paws through my backpack, then calls over a female guard to do the same to my person. I stand still, try not to act tense or worried—though I'm very aware of my body, the tightness in my shoulders, how weird my hands feel hanging limp at my sides—and wait for it to be over, having learned long ago that any attempts at small talk would only result in an annoyed look and stony silence. The guards are efficient, but a place like this must burn any kindness out of you.

Eventually it's over and I'm escorted to the visiting area. Just a long, off-white counter bolted against a wall of scratched, clouded plexiglass, with plastic dividers separating each slot and metal stools similarly bolted to the floor.

I settle down on the uncomfortable seat. Mom's not here yet, so there's nothing to look at but the faint shape of my reflection in the plexiglass, like a ghost emerging from the bare cinderblock. I search my reflection for the difference that Dad saw in me earlier. So much has happened since the last time I came here. But I just look pallid and sickly and small, same as always, same as everyone here.

A few minutes later, Mom emerges from the back door that leads to the cell blocks, and for a moment our reflections line up and overlap in the glass. Beyond the limp braid and haggard stress lines, she looks like me. Has my sharp chin and round eyes. One brown, like mine, and one green. She's my mom. My heart jumps, and this, too, is familiar. The moment of hope when everything else falls away and for a moment I forget about the plexiglass, I forget where I am, because my mom is in front of me and that's all that matters. For a second, all I can think about is how much I've missed her.

Then the rest of it comes into focus, the jumpsuit and dead eyes, and the hope crashes down. But I force myself to hold my mom's gaze, to smile, because things are different this time. I'm not helpless. She doesn't have to protect me from the truth anymore. I lean forward as she slumps down on the chair on the other side.

"Maddie," she says. "It's good to see you. How's Havenfall? How's Marcus?"

She sounds exhausted, her voice scraping out of her throat. I tell myself that's a good sign. Better tired than totally affectless. "He's . . . fine," I say, and have to stifle a despairing laugh at how disconnected we've become, how much I'm not telling her. I hate lying to her, but when we only have a half hour before the guards turn off the intercom, there's no time to waste, not when there are things I need to say. "Mom, I have to tell you something."

She blinks. I guess that's all the acknowledgment I can expect, so I go on, lowering my voice. "I know Nate was taken . . . I know what really happened to him." It feels strange and shocking, even still, to say those words out loud.

Finally, a spark of life. Mom's eyes widen for just a second before snapping back to blankness. "What do you mean?" Her inflection is robotic, even more so than usual.

"I found out about the silver. The soul trade." It's hard to keep my voice down so the guards won't hear; I want to yell the words, let them spill out. "I know the truth about the Solarians. That they're not evil. That Nate was one. Is one."

Finally, Mom reacts, rocking back in her seat. Her eyes are round and alert. Her hands come down to grip the edge of her chair.

"He might be alive, Mom." Hope feels like a balloon inflating inside my chest, pressing against my ribs. It's almost painful. "I'm going to try to find him. And take down the soul trade. I know why you said you killed him, but you don't have to lie anymore." A bit of a laugh escapes me. "I know you wanted to protect me from the traders, but trust me, I made enemies of them all on my own." I take a deep breath, trying to cram all the complicated feelings I have into the short, simple words. "Take it all back. Tell everyone you're innocent. Please. I need you alive, Mom, not dying to protect me. I need you to help me find him."

The change that's come over her is complete. It's like she woke up, like I'm looking at a different person. Her eyes are big and bright, her back straight, her lips parted. But the expression on her face—I don't know what I expected, but I didn't expect guilt.

"I didn't kill him," she says. "But it is my fault."

The words are pins in the hope balloon. The painful pressure vanishes, replaced by an even more painful vacuum. "I don't understand," I say blankly.

"I failed," she whispers.

I think of her name on Marcus's list of "hosts," and my heart breaks a little. Of course. It was her responsibility to protect the Solarian boy she adopted; of course she blamed herself when he was kidnapped. I think of how guilty I've felt for all these years simply because I stayed frozen in the cupboard during the attack. How much worse must it be for Mom?

"It's okay," I say. "I'm going to make it right." Never mind that I have no idea how. "Do you know who kidnapped him? What are their names?"

She shakes her head. "Maddie, you can't take them on alone."

"I'm not alone," I promise her, and pray that that turns out to be true. "I have Marcus. I have Brekken, Graylin, Sal—"

"They're more powerful than that." Mom drops her head. Her eyes have a haunted look, like she's lost in memory. "There was a reason Marcus and I worked in the shadows. We didn't want anyone we loved to get hurt. But even that wasn't enough to keep you kids safe." She raises her head and fixes me with a look that feels almost like a glare. "I don't want you playing hero with the soul traders. They're dangerous."

"I *know* that," I say, trying hard to take even breaths and stay calm, not wanting to draw the guards' attention. But it's hard when frustration is mounting in me every second. "Mom, it's not like I'm going to barge in on them Rambo-style or anything. I just need a name. Just a place to start."

I didn't expect her to resist like this. I thought that I'd be bringing her hope, in the possibility that Nate is alive. It didn't even occur to me that we wouldn't be on the same page. Why doesn't the idea fire her up like it does me? My frustration overflows, and I snap, "Don't you want to find him?"

The stare Mom fixes on me isn't like her usual expression during these visits. It's not dead or empty—but even fully present, it's still bleak and cold, absent of hope. "We don't know that he's alive. The traders are cruel."

That hurts to hear, but I don't let it dissuade me. "But how can you stand not knowing? Don't you think it's at *least* worth looking into?"

"I don't want to lose two children."

That shuts me up. I stare at my mother, reeling, trying to figure out what to say next. But to my surprise, she goes on, slightly softer.

"We're not meant to love people from other worlds," she says in a low voice, the last word trailing off in a whisper. Like she's trying to be gentle but doesn't quite remember how. "We can't save them. We can't follow them. It's better to just keep our heads down."

How can she say that? I stare at her, stunned into silence. Coming to Sterling Correctional, the long boring drive, the invasive search—as depressing as it all is, I felt hope on the way here that I hadn't felt in years. Hope that my mother was finally going to come alive, and we'd save my brother together. But now I feel that hope slowly being snuffed out inside me. "Are you saying I was—I am—wrong to love Nate because he's a Solarian and I'm a human? He's my brother."

"No—just . . ."

Mom shifts in her seat, and I register a flicker of twisted satisfaction that I'm making her uncomfortable. For ten years she lied to me about what had happened to Nate, sat here in safe silence while I tore myself apart with grief and guilt.

"I'm not saying—" Mom seems flustered, a bit of color rising to her sun-starved cheeks. She shakes her head, her ragged braid swinging from side to side. "It's because of love that the traders found us."

I blink. "What do you mean?"

Mom bites her lip and turns her face away. But there's just a blank wall there, nowhere else for her to look except at me. And in a sick moment, I'm grateful for it. I want her to be forced to meet my eyes. I want to understand.

"Tell me," I insist, leaning forward about as close as I can to the plexiglass without pressing my nose against it. "Please, Mom. I promise I won't do anything stupid, I just want to know."

For a long moment she doesn't say anything, and I brace myself to sit here for twenty minutes of painful, loaded silence. But finally, when I've just about given up on hearing more, she lets out a heavy breath and speaks.

"I fell in love with a man of the Realms," she says, so quietly the mic barely picks her up. "I fell in love, and everything fell apart."

My heart is racing, even as I sit as still as a statue. Inside, I'm rifling through my memories for any mystery man in our childhood, but I can't picture a face, just a tall shadowy figure that might well be a manufacture of my imagination.

"Did he betray you?" I whisper.

She nods. "He would have never had knowledge of us or Nahteran if I had been wiser. But I trusted him. I was a fool."

"What was his name? The man you loved?" I ask.

The question falls from my lips breathlessly, thoughtlessly, like a little kid eager to hear the ending of a bedtime story. For a moment, I don't care that the name might be the key to cracking the soul trade, to finding Nate. I just want to know this one thing about my mom, who has always been so mysterious to me. I want to know the name of the man she loved.

She waves her hand dismissively. "It's not important."

"Please," I whisper. My hand is against the glass, and I don't remember putting it there. "Mom . . ." I don't know what makes me say it, but I hear myself say, "I'm in love with someone from the Realms too."

Her eyes narrow a little at that. "I'm sure you don't need me to tell you that it'll never work."

"Then tell me why not," I challenge. "Tell me what happened with you and . . ."

After a stretching moment, my mother sighs. "Magpie," she says. "That wasn't his name, but that's what I called him, what everyone called him." She closes her eyes for a long moment, and when she opens them again, they're burning. "His name, though, was Cadius."

ONCE I'M BACK AT HAVENFALL, I dream about birds. I don't usually get nightmares here, with the mountains surrounding us like massive, steady sentinels. But tonight I dream about birds filling the sky, birds diving and falling and screaming, birds with broken wings and accusing eyes. I dream of moonlight flashing, glittering, just like the key under the windowsill on my nightstand. It was the last thing I saw before I went to sleep. The key to my mom's long-untouched suite, borrowed from Willow, since I knew Marcus wouldn't give it to me.

The third time I wake, I sit bolt upright in bed, drenched in sweat. It finally sinks in that I'm not going back to sleep after the clamor of the dream-birds. Using the light of my cell phone to supplement the moonlight, I pull on the sweats that are closest at hand and pad out into the hallway, closing and locking my bedroom door quietly behind me.

Mom's old room is on the first floor, near Graylin and Marcus's suite. As I creep down the hall, I'm nervous about getting caught by my uncle, but everything is still and quiet. Not even a cleaning crew is about. Everything in the inn is silent, so much so that I can hear the rustle of the wind through the pines outside. It makes the scrape of the key in the lock to Mom's suite extra loud. The mechanism sticks, resists, and for a moment I think I'm not going to be able to get in. But then the tumblers give way, and the door swings open.

The hinges have been kept oiled, even after all this time, but it's clear as soon as the door closes behind me that the cleaners haven't been inside. The curtains are drawn, leaving the room in near-total dark. I use my phone light to pick my way across the room—the phone screen illuminating only a few feet of floor at a time—and pull back the curtains, releasing the moonlight as well as a cloud of dust. Pressing my sleeve over my mouth, I turn around to look at the room for the first time in a decade.

It's just as I remember it. Well, almost. Marcus seemingly hasn't touched Mom's stuff—whether out of sentimentality or the wild hope that somehow she might come back, I don't know. But everything is still here. There's the big fluffy bed that could hold the three of us: Mom, with me and Nate on either side. Her blanket was woven of Fiorden wool so thick it seemed to give off its own heat. There's the fireplace with its ledge of mountain granite, and the picture window with an alcove full of pillows and blankets, where I loved to curl up and pretend I was a princess in a castle. Even the ancient portable TV Mom had toted up here at some point, a gray cube with a bulbous screen and a slot for VHS tapes.

I have a vague memory of snuggling under the blankets with Nate, watching cartoons while Mom worked across the room at the big oak desk. I remember her bent head, the way she bit her lip when she concentrated. What was she doing back then that required such focus?

The moonlight is enough to see by, so I slide my phone into my pocket as I pad through the room. Dust has accumulated in the corners. It softens hard edges and swirls in the air as I pass, giving everything a surreal, dreamlike appearance. I feel separate from my body, like I'm floating somewhere above myself and looking down as I proceed through the deserted room. I'm aware of feelings—recognition, shock, sadness, grief, anger—but they're all muted, like my heart is wrapped in cotton gauze.

There are happy memories here. Mom reading to us in bed, patiently intervening when we'd fight over what book to read. I wanted *The Rainbow Fish* every night. Nate wanted *Bread and Jam for Frances*, even though he must have been a little old for it. I can almost hear the voices she did for each character and see the light in her eyes. But the cozy images are accompanied by too much pain to look at straight on.

If I were her, where would I have hidden something precious?

After a moment of pondering, I cross over to the closet and open the door. Whoever oiled the door to the suite neglected to do the same here. It squeaks loudly—but then the sight of her clothes hits me, and it's like a blow to the chest. Even in the moonlight all the colors are discernible—reds, blues, greens, yellows, pinks. I'd forgotten that about Mom, how much she loved bright colors.

Just as she had in her closet back at our old house, there's a box full of old shoes and belts and knickknacks on the floor beneath the hems of the dresses. I plop down on the carpet, feeling like I want to cry as another small dust cloud rises around me. But the tears don't come. Something else has taken over.

I reach into the box and extract a sweater I vaguely recognize, worn thin, its once wine-red color now caked gray with dust. I shake as much free as I can and press the cleanest part of the sweater to my face, breathing in, trying to find some smell of Mom or of home. But there's nothing there. Just mustiness.

I drop the sweater, feeling crushed and frantic, and reach back into the box. Maybe something buried deeper will have been kept safe from the dust. If I were Mom, and I had a secret—something I wanted no one else to find—this is where I would put it, buried among mundane things. And sure enough, the next thing my fingers touch is a square leather edge. A book cover.

I extricate it from the box, careful not to tear what I can tell by touch are age-worn pages. Tilting my phone so the light shines over the cover, I feel something snag in my chest. It's a photo book, the kind you buy at a craft store. The red leather cover and the page edges are gilded to lend an air of fanciness. There's a little plastic sleeve embedded on the front cover, one small spot to give a photo prime placement. And in it is a shot of me and Mom and Nate in Havenfall's gardens, her arms around our shoulders, flowers rioting all around us. She is wearing a yellow dress, and her hair is long and loose, held back only by a pair of sunglasses pushed to the top of her head. Next to her, Nate and I have big, hammy smiles. Havenfall's front door stands open in the background, ready to welcome us home.

In a daze, I bring the scrapbook over to the bed and sit down on the side, reaching for the lamp switch on the nightstand. The bulb sputters and flickers worryingly at first, but then holds, casting the room in dusty yellow light. I page through the pictures, feeling like I'm in a trance. Me and Mom and Nate on a hiking trail. Me and Mom and Nate at the doughnut shop in town. Me and Mom and Nate in the Havenfall kitchen, baking something.

Then the pictures start to change. They feature the same places, but instead of us, of Mom, they feature a man. I can tell that he's a Fiorden, tall and handsome with aristocratic features and fine clothes made of velvet and silk. He has short dark hair, bright brown eyes, and a slightly wicked smile. There are pictures of him and of my mom, but never of the two of them together. When I look closely at the crystal pin fastening his cloak at his shoulder, I see it's carved in the shape of a bird.

I can't stop staring at his face. It's less than an inch high in these pictures, faded after more than ten years. But my mother loved him, this Cadius. Who was he?

Suddenly, it's too much, his handsome smile and what it represents—this huge secret Mom kept from me. I go back to the box in the closet and keep digging. This time, my fingers close on silk, and I pull—but something heavy comes loose and clangs to the floor, making me jump almost out of my skin. Something that was wrapped in the fabric. I sit totally still, heart pounding, sure at any moment that Marcus is going to barge in on me. But the door of the room is thick. I remain alone in the silence and darkness and dust.

The lamp is on in the room, but the closet is still filled with shadows. I turn my cell phone on the pile, and metal glints beneath the light. It's so bright I almost pull back in surprise. I see gold, untouched by dust.

The closest word I can think of to describe the object before me is a *gauntlet.* The delicate tapered cylinder of gold flares at the end, shaped and sized for a wrist. It looks like finely wrought armor, opening on tiny hinges and closing with a delicate latch. Intricate scrollwork, vines, and gothic patterns cover its surface. I recognize some of them from Brekken's clothes. This gauntlet came from Fiordenkill. From Myr.

Tentatively, I pick it up and turn it over. It's beautiful, untouched by the rust and decay all around. I never knew Mom had anything like this. I would remember if she had showed it to me. Was it a gift from

Marcus, maybe, or one of the delegates? The Magpie, Cadius? It seems clear enough what happened—Mom fell in love, not knowing the Magpie was a soul trader. And he betrayed her to get his hands on Nate's soul. But I don't want to act rashly. I want proof before taking this to Marcus.

Something on the inside of the cuff catches my eye. I tilt the gauntlet up and angle my phone light inside to see. The interior is smooth except for two engravings: the letters *C. Winterkill* and a small bird symbol. Same as the one in the photo of the man in the cloak.

I take the gauntlet with me when I go, heavy in the pocket of my hoodie. The scrapbook too.

Halfway back to my room, I see light under the door of Brekken's room. I pause, then stop, feeling silly.

He's probably asleep, I tell myself. *Asleep and just forgot to turn the light off.*

But then I hear soft footfalls behind the door, like he's pacing. I don't know quite what makes me raise my hand and knock, only that I don't want to be alone right now. I want to tell someone what I found, what I know.

Brekken opens the door. He's wearing a soft-looking tunic and loose linen pants, and he's barefoot.

Is this what he sleeps in? It seems strange that I've never seen him like this before.

He blinks in surprise. "Maddie."

"Hi." My voice can't decide whether it wants to be a whisper or not. It's an effort to keep my eyes on his face—sleepy, open—rather than on his mussed hair or bare shoulders.

Focus, Maddie.

"What is it?" he asks, his low tone matching mine. Then his gaze sharpens. "Is everything okay?"

"Everything's fine." I nod. "Just, can I come in?"

"Of course." He stands back to let me pass.

The only light on, his bedside lamp, leaves everything shadowy and hazy. Brekken's room is smaller than mine. The bed takes up most of the space, with the nightstand and a small desk crammed in beside.

I stand next to the bed, suddenly self-conscious. Why did I come here? Hurriedly, I take the scrapbook and gauntlet out of my pockets, not wanting him to think—I don't know what I want him to think.

As Brekken closes the door and pads over to me, I quietly relay the story of going to see my mom at Sterling Correctional, leaving out the part where she told me we weren't meant to love people from other worlds. Then I show him the gauntlet.

"I found this in her room," I say, turning it over so he can see the design. "I think it might be—his. The man she was in love with. I think he was a Fiorden." My mom's words echo in my head. *The Magpie. Cadius. C. Winterkill.* It could all be a coincidence, but maybe . . .

Brekken takes the gauntlet and examines it, his face furrowing in focus.

I try not to stare. The already short distance between us seems shorter here in this small room, and I'm very aware of his recently vacated bed behind me, the covers turned down and rumpled.

Focus.

"Winterkill," Brekken muses.

My heart jumps. "Do you know that name?"

Brekken nods. "It's a castle in Fiordenkill, in south Myr. A wealthy lord's estate. Cadius Winterkill lives there. But . . ." He hesitates and sits down on the bed, still looking at the gauntlet. "He has an ill reputation. I wouldn't think your mother . . ."

"An ill reputation?" I echo. "What does that mean?"

After a moment of indecision, I join him on the bed, keeping an inch or so of space between us. I feel like I'm finally getting somewhere with this Winterkill stuff, and I don't want to be distracted . . . plus, it's not really clear to me where Brekken and I stand. Yeah, he kissed me under the influence of truth serum, but it's been a couple of days since then and we haven't discussed it. What if he doesn't want to take things further? What if he does?

"I don't know the details," Brekken says, a little evasively. "There always seems to be some lavish ball or other happening at his estate, even in frozen times when food supplies are low. And my parents have never gone. They say he's corrupt. And no one's quite sure how he made his fortune. His family raised birds"—he taps the icon on the gauntlet with one fingernail—"but there's no way it all comes from that."

My heart beats faster. A wicked lord, a misbegotten fortune? That lines up with what I know about the soul trade. "She had this too."

I pull out the photo book and flip to the section where the man starts appearing. I only looked at a handful of pictures back in Mom's room, but now, with Brekken, it feels easier to face. I hand it to him and let him turn the pages, leaning in close to look over his shoulder. He studies the same pictures I saw, looking intently. Then he turns the page, and I gasp.

It's my mom again. But—somehow—she's not in Havenfall. She stands on a snowy hill, bundled up in a thick peacoat, hat, scarf, gloves. Practically all you can see of her are her eyes, but those are enough to tell that she's beaming.

Yet that's not the astonishing thing about the picture. It's the backdrop. The trees surrounding her are so tall that the branches aren't even in the frame. The sky between the trees drips with aurora colors.

I've never seen this place, but I know immediately where she was. My mother was in Fiordenkill.

"How is that possible?" My voice is shaky as my hand reaches out, almost of its own accord, to trace the picture.

Out of the corner of my vision, I see Brekken shake his head. He doesn't know. But I can't tear my gaze from the image. My mom. In Fiordenkill. The colors surrounding her are ice blue and indigo and blinding white. And—gold, in the space between her coat cuff and mitten. Gold patterned with branches and leaves.

Brekken holds up the gauntlet. It's too small an image to tell for sure, but I know we're thinking the same thing.

"It's like the story," he says in a hushed, awed voice. "The knight traveler." He turns his body toward me, and there's almost a feverish light in his eyes. "Maddie, it's real."

7

THE GAUNTLET.

Stories about knight travelers and dead enchanters.

The Silver Prince possibly having other access points to Earth.

Cancarnette's scornful words about magpies, collectors of enchanted objects.

Mom being convinced that her involvement with Cadius Winter-kill led to Nate's kidnapping. The man she and everyone called the Magpie.

Mom wearing the gauntlet . . . in Fiordenkill.

I don't know what it all adds up to, but it must be something. It has to be.

I sit across from Marcus in his office off the tunnels beneath the inn, trying not to fidget as he reads over my list of—clues? ideas? leads?— the things I wrote down to stop them all from ricocheting around the inside of my head. I watch his eyes rove from side to side. Laid out like this, I'm hoping he sees that it's too much to be a coincidence. Mom brushed up against the soul trade when she had an affair with Cadius Winterkill, the Magpie. They were able to travel between the realms using the gauntlet—and now someone is traveling between realms to propagate the soul trade.

What are the chances that the Silver Prince has also found a way between the worlds? Could he be involved too?

Despite all of that, though, I can't help but be distracted by the dark circles beneath Marcus's eyes. Since the Innkeeper is tied to the inn, it hit him hard three weeks ago when the Silver Prince disrupted the natural balance between the Realms. Graylin and I didn't know what had rendered my uncle unconscious—or if he would ever wake up. We thought he'd been the victim of a Solarian attack, his soul eaten like in the stories. Graylin used Fiorden healing magic to keep him alive, and it worked. My uncle is back on his feet now, back running the inn.

But the magic changed him, making him not quite at home in this human world anymore, though none of us want much to acknowledge that fact. His health is still touch and go; some days he's had to stay in bed most of the time, sending me to oversee peace summit business in his place. Yet he looks all right today, except for the paleness of his face and the shadows under his eyes that have become the new normal.

"I haven't seen this before," he says finally, putting the gauntlet down on his desk in a nest of scattered letters, pens, and loose paper. "But I recognize that name. Winterkill."

"Brekken said it was a wealthy estate in Myr," I offer, leaving out the bits about lavish parties and magpies. I want Marcus to come to the same conclusion as me on his own. Then he'll be more likely to let me do something about it.

Marcus nods. "Yes. It used to be an honorable family, a noble one. Cadius Winterkill was a delegate at the summer summits for a while, about twenty years ago." Marcus traces a finger along the gauntlet's edgings, looking troubled. "But then something changed. There have been rumors Cadius is involved with the soul trade, buying and selling bound silver from his estate. I've never met him, but I've heard enough whispers to take them seriously."

Cold trickles down my spine. "Do you think Mom had something to do with that? Like maybe she went undercover with this guy?"

"I never knew her to do anything of the sort." Marcus chuckles, but it's a melancholy sound. "Your mother was almost as bad a liar as you are."

I can't help but notice how he uses the word *was*. Like she's already gone. "Well, it's another lead, then," I say, trying to sound chipper.

"There are other rumors too." Marcus opens a desk drawer, but he pauses before dropping the gauntlet in, turning it over in his hands instead. "Graylin told me there was talk that Cadius had an enchanted suit of armor . . ."

My eyes flit to the gauntlet and back to my uncle. "Enchanted to do what?"

He's already looked through the photo book, but I flip again to the photo of Mom in Fiordenkill and turn it around to face Marcus, to emphasize my point. "What if it allowed whoever wore it to travel between the worlds?"

I don't think I'm imagining the hint of wistfulness in Marcus's eyes as he looks at the picture. Is it for his sister, or for the other world?

"I just don't know how this could be," he says, and it sounds like he's talking half to himself. "If there really is a way, how have we never heard about it before?"

"There are whole worlds outside of here," I say, my heart beating fast at the thought of it. "There's probably tons of stuff we don't know. Just waiting to be found."

He looks up at me, expression sharp. "What are you plotting?"

"Plotting?" I blink, but I know Marcus won't let me get away with playing dumb. "Not plotting, just thinking." I reach out and take the gauntlet from where he's set it down on the desktop. Maybe it's just my imagination, but it feels slightly warm in my hands, like something alive. "We could use this to find some actual answers. They're not going to just come to us."

"You want to go to Fiordenkill," Marcus observes.

I swallow, my mouth suddenly dry. *Guilty.* "Haven't you ever been curious?"

"Of course I am," he replies, a little sharp. "But even if this *thing*"—he indicates the gauntlet—"will let you survive there for a while, we don't know how long the effects last. We don't know the intricacies of Myr politics. We don't have proof that Winterkill is connected to anything at all. Are you sure this isn't about Brekken?"

"Brekken?" I sit up straight, surprised and a little insulted. I mean, it's true that I've always dreamed of seeing Brekken's homeland. But that's not what's driving me now—it's that we have a solid lead and the means to follow it. Yes, I have feelings for Brekken. It would be silly to pretend otherwise. So I have a crush—that doesn't mean my common sense has evaporated. I'm tempted to remind my uncle who ran the inn while he was out of commission and Brekken was missing.

"Look." Marcus lifts the photo book, finger tapping on the open page. "We in this family have a bad habit of falling in love with Fiordens." The second half of his statement hangs in the air, unspoken: *Do you want to turn out like your mom?*

I know he's changing the topic, but I can't help taking the bait. "It worked out for you, didn't it?"

"I got lucky," Marcus says, exasperated. "You know that. I got some-one obsessed with stories, so life at a crossroads is perfect. Graylin's happy here, where he can read and write and talk to the delegates. Do you think Brekken will be happy sitting at Havenfall forever? Putting down the sword and spending his days listening?"

A bubble of hurt grows in my chest. "He's a good listener." I point at the gauntlet. "Plus, maybe it doesn't have to be like that. If this thing really works."

"So you're going to spend your life in Fiordenkill?"

"I didn't say that." My cheeks heat. The other side of the scale weighs heavy here too—even if it is somehow possible to live in another realm, that would mean giving up on being Innkeeper. But I don't want to think about that right now. I didn't come in here to decide how I was going to spend the rest of my life. *If Brekken even wants me.*

"I'm not talking about forever," I say, angry now. I stand up, and Marcus does too, but I keep talking, cutting off whatever he might want to say. "I just can't sit here while the soul trade goes on and Nate might still be alive. I can't do anything about the Silver Prince, so let me go to Fiordenkill and do *something.* And anyway, I think it's all connected—"

Marcus's next words come out in a yell. "I don't want you to roll the dice with your life!"

His raised voice startles us both, and silence falls. Then Marcus plops back into his chair, lifting his hands in a gesture of apology or surren-der, I'm not sure which. In the silence, a draft from the tunnels sneaks through the open door into Marcus's office, making me shiver. The faintest of breezes, tinged with the scents of ice and ash.

"I'm sorry," Marcus says after a long, tense moment. He drops his head and pinches the bridge of his nose. "But put yourself in my shoes for a second here, Maddie. What would I tell your dad if something happened to you?"

My heart twinges, and I slowly sink back into my seat. That hadn't occurred to me. I feel thoughtless, a little shamed. Still . . .

"Think about the look on his face if I can bring Nate home."

Marcus flinches. We stare at each other, like a standoff in an old Western movie.

"I know it'll be risky," I go on after a moment. "But the reward—even the possibility—don't you think that's worth it?"

After several more seconds that feel like several lifetimes, Marcus lets out a heavy sigh. He runs his fingers through his hair, after which the stress curls bounce higher.

"If you do this, there are going to be rules," he says.

My skin tenses with excitement. I want to let out a whoop of victory, but I hold it in and keep my face as neutral as possible, in case Marcus changes his mind.

"Of course," I say, trying to sound mature and confident and competent. "Lay them on me."

"Graylin goes with you."

That surprises me. I've hardly ever known Graylin to leave Havenfall, not even to go into town. Like Marcus said a minute ago, he's content here. But I can't deny that the idea of having Graylin beside me in Fiordenkill is a comfort. "Sure, if he wants to."

"And Brekken."

I raise one eyebrow. "No argument from me there."

But Marcus stares me down. "And I expect him to protect you with his life."

"Okay." I don't plan on putting my life or *anyone's* life in danger, so it's easy enough to agree to that. Assuming Brekken wants to come with.

"Before you leave, Graylin will do research on the gauntlet to make sure it's safe," Marcus says, reaching out and reclaiming the object from me. "And once you're in Fiordenkill, if it seems at all like it's not working, if you get so much as a runny nose, you turn around and come right back."

Once you're in Fiordenkill. I never thought I'd hear those words. Just the sound of them makes my pulse race. But Marcus isn't finished.

"And one more thing," he says, enunciating every word. "I need you to promise, Maddie. Whatever you find there at this Winterkill place, whatever you see, you will not interfere. No matter what."

He stops to let the words sink in.

It takes a second.

"Wait, but what if—"

"No," he cuts in. "No matter what."

"We're talking about the soul trade!" I burst out. "The Solarians are suffering!"

"So report back."

Marcus's voice is resolute, no wavering in it. "Come back and tell me what's going on, and we'll figure out what to do. But you can't take on all of it alone. None of us can."

I have to bite my tongue to keep from arguing further. Marcus is right. Logically, I know he's right. But that doesn't make it any easier when I eventually say, "Okay. I promise."

No easier to make a promise I'm not sure I can keep.

———

My heart is in my throat as I go to find Brekken. Marcus is going to run the plan by Graylin, but it's obviously on me to put the question to Brekken. No big deal, right? I just have to find out whether he wants to put his life and his future in Myr on the line by helping me sneak into his homeland and spy on a corrupt lord.

There was once a time when I'd have had no doubt Brekken would say yes. When we were kids and he was my partner in every adventure.

But things feel different now that he's a soldier. What if whatever it is we share doesn't work outside the bounds of Havenfall? What if he doesn't want to move against his own country for me?

No. I remind myself that when Brekken went missing a few weeks ago, he was working to gather information about the soul trade among his fellow Fiordens. He kept what he was doing a secret from everyone, even me, because he thought Marcus was on the traders' side. He hates the trade as much as I do. He'll understand why we have to do this.

I wish I could tell Taya, I realize as I walk through the dark halls. Wish it fiercely. I've tried my best to keep thoughts of her at bay these last few days, because I fear that if I allow myself to sink into that morass, I'll never get back out. Never get past the feeling that it's my fault she's gone. I don't even know if she chose to go through the Solarian door, or if all the magic and blood we—she—shed in our fight with the Silver Prince in the tunnels upset the volatile magic of the doors and sucked her in. She's in Solaria alone, and while she might be a Solarian, she knows nothing of that world. She hadn't even known about other Realms before coming to Havenfall this summer. If something happens to her there, how will I ever forgive myself? If I even ever find out?

Now that I've let my thoughts run rampant, I feel panic set in. My heart races and my palms sweat. This can't happen. I have work to do. Turning down the hallway toward Brekken's room, I take a deep breath and try to break off the thought loop. *How do you eat an elephant?* Dad's voice sounds in my head. *One bite at a time.*

There's nothing I can do to help Taya right now, with the door to Solaria being closed. Plus, she wouldn't want me to dwell on it at the expense of helping others. I wonder if she can come back. If she wants to.

There is something I can do. I can knock on Brekken's door. Brekken can help me move forward. Forward to Fiordenkill.

8

TWO DAYS LATER FINDS GRAYLIN and me heading upstairs to one of the meeting rooms. We've just come from the library and another crash course in the Fiorden language. The strange words Graylin taught me rattle around in my head. *Ranir losir a sephe? Where is the entrance?*

No matter how many words he crams into my head, no Fiorden who looks at me for more than three seconds will mistake me for one of them. It feels like a waste of time to learn the language. Then again, it's not like there's much else I can do. And if I just sit and wait, I think I'll explode or lose heart.

"I was thinking," Graylin says as we climb the stairs. "Once we get into Fiordenkill, I'd like an old friend to take a look at the gauntlet. She's a scholar of matter, specifically metal, at Myr's university. She may be able to tell us something."

"Sounds good," I reply on autopilot. Nerves fill my stomach as we climb the stairs in tense silence.

Brekken's project this morning was to tell Princess Enetta about our plan to investigate Cadius and ask her to help us locate the Winterkill fortress. Enetta is a good woman as far as I know, but it's a big ask, and potentially disastrous if she takes it the wrong way. We're asking her to betray one of her own people, an influential noble at that, to help Solarians.

Graylin and I exchange a nervous glance outside the meeting room's closed door, then I step forward and push the door open. Brekken, Marcus, and Enetta sit clustered at the center of the long oak table. Their low talk ceases, and all three look up as we come in. Skylights let the afternoon sunlight pour down into the room, illuminating the map of Myr that Brekken has spread over its surface. I half expect to see little carved chess pieces scattered on the aged paper.

"You have quite the undertaking ahead of you," Enetta says as we sit down.

Her tone is cool, neutral, and I stare into her eyes to try to figure out how she feels. Will she help us? Her eyes flicker over my wrist as I take my seat, and I know what she's looking for. But I'm not wearing the gauntlet. It's back in Marcus and Graylin's room, while Graylin runs a few last tests to make sure it's not dangerous and to see if he can decipher how it lets its wearer cross the boundaries between worlds.

Before us on the table, Myr sprawls out in blue ink: a dense cluster of hash marks to represent the capital city; wide, flattened upside-down Vs to represent mountains and narrow ones for trees, and small rectangles scattered over the expanse of the map, each labeled with text in a language I don't read.

"Cadius is one of the wealthiest lords in Myr," Enetta goes on. "He has gold mines on his property, and that is why he has a private army contracted and stationed on his estate. No wall surrounds it, because everyone knows the soldiers will dispatch any trespassers. That is, if his bears don't find you first."

I look at Brekken across the table, but his eyes are downcast. My shoulders slump in discouragement. "So there's no way in?"

I might be willing to risk my own life, but I don't want to gamble with Brekken's or Graylin's.

"No way that's not dangerous, no." Enetta's cool brown gaze holds mine. "But there may be another option." She taps her fingers on the map. "He holds feasts every moon, lavish parties to placate the governors and stop them from looking too closely at his business dealings. This is well known. But anyone with morals, myself included, will have nothing to do with his feasts. I didn't know the whole truth until this loyal soldier came to me." She looks approvingly at Brekken, whose eyes flicker.

"My loyalty is to what's right," he says simply, and my chest warms.

Things might have been weird between us. We might not agree on what the best course of action will be, but I don't doubt Brekken's intentions anymore. He's a lodestone, always pointing to his north star.

After the meeting, he catches up to me in the hall after the adults have dispersed. He lifts a hand to wave me down, and I see with surprise the glitter of gold, reaching up from his shirt cuff to wrap around his palm. He's wearing the gauntlet.

"Graylin gave it to me," he says in response to my confused look. "To see that it works. He suggested that we . . . go somewhere." He waves vaguely in the direction of the front door.

"Go where?" I echo, confused. Then it clicks. "You mean outside Havenfall?" I take a step back, mildly appalled. I figured Graylin had some sort of test he could run. The scientific method. Not just using Brekken as a guinea pig.

"But what if it doesn't work?"

Brekken shrugs. "Then better to find out here than in Fiordenkill, don't you think?" He beckons me toward the door.

He looks way too happy about this, and I can't help thinking of Marcus's words earlier. *Do you think Brekken will be happy sitting at Havenfall forever?*

"Um . . ." I stall, trying to think. The picture of Mom in Fiordenkill wearing the gauntlet seemed like plenty of proof that it worked, when it was just my butt on the line. But now that it's Brekken offering to try it out, the whole thing seems a lot flimsier.

An idea hits me. I read online that the Fourth of July celebrations last week had been postponed down in Loveland because of thunderstorms—thunderstorms that missed us in Havenfall, given the bubble of good weather that seems to hover over the mountaintop. They moved it to the next Friday instead—which is tonight.

So that's how Brekken and I end up driving half an hour east as the sun sinks down, down out of the mountains. In the passenger seat of the Toyota Camry Dad gave me, Brekken navigates and I follow his directions, almost vibrating with tension, afraid at any second that whatever magic is allowing this will give out, and Brekken will start shaking and sickening, too far into our world for his Fiorden blood.

But it doesn't happen. Instead, Brekken seems to perk up more and more as we go down the mountain, looking out the window with avid interest, to the point where I have to remind him to tell me the next turn. At the sweeping, immaculate green park where the show is happening, we don't venture into the picnicking crowd. I'm aware that Brekken is recognizably, if subtly, *not human*. Instead, we sit on the hood of the parked Camry, craning our necks to look up at the sky as the fireworks whistle and burst above.

They're beautiful, but I keep getting distracted by Brekken. While we've been in the town of Haven plenty of times before, for ice cream or hiking or sneaking drinks, we've never gone farther. It's strange to be with him like this, on the outside. To see him not amidst the glitz and glamor of the delegates, but juxtaposed against everyday human life, the disorderly crawl of cars trying to cram into a parking lot, the smell of barbecue and cigarette smoke and the gunpowder from the fireworks, overheard conversations about work and school and weather and traffic, hundreds of cell phones upturned to capture the fireworks and memorialize them.

Against it all, Brekken looks even more beautiful, more unearthly. I'm not sure that I like it. It's a reminder of just how different we are, he and I. But when he reaches out across the car hood and catches my hand in his, I don't pull away. Nor when he slides slowly against me until our sides are pressed together, both of us leaning on the other.

"Brekken," I murmur in the lull between two shrieking fireworks. "Are you sure you want to go to Fiordenkill with me?"

I weave our fingers together, sparks firing in my blood just like the ones raining down from the sky. I don't know why I'm afraid all of a sudden, but the fear is here now and I feel like I need to give voice to it.

"Maddie." He looks down at me, strange light playing across his cheekbones, tiny reflected fireworks scattering in his eyes. "Of course. You know I would never let you go alone."

"It's just . . ." I take a deep breath and shift my weight on the hood. "Something could go wrong. We could get caught."

"Then wouldn't you shelter me?" he asks. His voice is gently teasing, but there's an edge of something serious there too. "Keep me safe at Havenfall?"

"Of course." I look hastily back at the sky. "But I don't want you to risk your future on my account."

For all I disdained Mom's and Marcus's warnings, I can't seem to get their words out of my head now. They echo there, like buggy recordings.

I'm sure you don't need me to tell you that it'll never work.

We in this family have a bad habit of falling in love with Fiordens.

Do you think Brekken would be happy here at the crossroads?

In the moment of quiet between words, everything working against us crams into my head and I almost convince myself that all this, the fireworks, the kisses we've shared, his closeness now, are flukes and delusions. That he only cares for me as a friend, and everything else is spun sugar and wishes. But then he speaks.

"I'd risk everything."

All traces of jokiness are gone now, his voice dead serious.

I don't look at Brekken, scared that if I do my face will reveal too much. But I can feel his eyes on me like a laser beam. He waits for me to turn to him, and finally I do.

The world seems to have quieted around us. Like a dome has fallen over Brekken and me, a summer snow globe, the fireworks forgotten except for how they illuminate Brekken's eyes. He brings his other hand over, grasping my right hand with both of his.

"I know things have been . . ." He trails off, biting his lip.

I'm not sure what he's getting at. Busy? Crazy, scary, changed?

Part of me just wants to go back to being kids, the easy closeness we had. But another part of me is ignited by this strange tension, wants to lean into it. A moth to the fire.

"Things have been what?" I prompt.

He shakes his head. "I don't know." He is very still, I realize suddenly, almost unnaturally still. Like he's nervous. The only movement for a moment is the flutter of his pulse against my wrist, until the rest of his words spill out in a rush. "But I know I want to be with you, Maddie."

The sentence hits me as sharp and breathtaking as a frost wind. I open my mouth, close it, take a breath and try again. I don't need to think about it. It's just strangely hard to get the actual words out after shoving them down for years.

But I manage it.

"I want to be with you too."

For another few seconds, getting the words out is all I can do. I feel frozen, all the hesitation of years of not knowing how Brekken felt holding me still, pinning my limbs to my sides. But then something breaks open in me. He wants me. He just said it. He wants me, and I want him, and he's here and I'm here and I want him. Want to be with him. There's so much that could keep us apart, but right at this moment none of it matters. Tomorrow I can worry about it, but tonight Brekken's eyes are the only thing in the world.

So I lean in and kiss him.

Leaving all the fearful things for another day.

9

THE NEXT MORNING FINDS US assembled in the tunnels in front of the doorway to Fiordenkill. I can feel the cold breeze on my face. Marcus raided all the closets and found Fiorden clothes for us, fur coats and such.

We form a short line. Brekken, me, and Graylin. Two Fiordens and a human. Also here to see us off are Marcus, Willow, the Heiress, and Enetta. Despite all the help the princess of Myr's given us, she can't take the risk of coming with us and being caught. The ramifications of moving against Cadius Winterkill, for her, would be too high. So instead she's supplied us with maps and weapons. We're ready, or at least as ready as we can be.

There are still a million thoughts bouncing around my head, but it's like they've receded, their wasps' buzz fading to a muffled hum. There's fear there, yeah, but it's distant. Worry, too, but I push it away. The gauntlet that protected Mom in Fiordenkill is on my wrist now. We have a plan. We'll be all right.

As long as nothing goes wrong.

Marcus turns to me. "You ready?"

My heart pounds, but I feel calm. I can smell the ice on the wind. I feel determined. Brekken squeezes my hand once, his bare skin slipping against my woolen glove.

I hold my breath. And we step forward through the doorway.

I see Brekken disappear first, the pale blue light of Fiordenkill swallowing him up. Then it's Graylin's and my turn. We cross the threshold from darkness into light, from this world into the next, and the ground drops out from beneath my feet.

There's pressure and a howling cold wind. The sensation shocks me and takes my breath away, takes everything away. I can't feel Brekken's presence, or Graylin's. I open my mouth to call out for them, but the wind steals my words away too. I'm not sure I have a body anymore. I'm not sure I even exist. I'm scared suddenly, terrified, and it's Mom's name that flies to my lips. But then her face materializes in my head, cold and soulless as she told me never to love someone from another world.

Then as quickly as the crossover started, it's over. I hit the ground hard on all fours, feeling something cold and solid beneath my mittened hands. There is a howling in my ears, and the ground seems to be quaking beneath me, though I can't tell if that's just the aftereffects of passing through the doorway. I stay very still and focus on breathing. I can feel my lungs again, and I wait for my senses to come back to me. My heart is hammering.

The first thing I notice is the wind. What I always knew as a faint, tinny whisper emanating from the other side of the Fiorden doorway is now a high, unceasing fury, centered somewhere very far above my head, twisting and rising and falling like the keening of a living thing. It pulls at my clothes, sneaks up the small openings at my wrists and ankles. If I didn't have my face to the ground, pressed to my hands in a kind of downward dog position, I'm sure it would be blasting my face. The ground feels like packed snow—it's sunk in a little under my weight. For a moment, I can't hear anything but the wind, and panic fills me. Did something go wrong? Am I alone in Fiordenkill?

Then there's a heavy thump somewhere off to my right, and a familiar sound as Graylin curses when he hits the snow and rolls. Slowly, cautiously, I raise myself up into a kneeling position. I feel like I've just done the most intense workout of my life. All my muscles ache, my heart pounds, and my senses come back on high alert, adrenaline pumping through me.

I'm in Fiordenkill.

More specifically, I'm in what looks like a large, grand stone courtyard, walled off with massive slabs of shimmering white marble. Set into the one behind me is a doorway that mirrors the one on the Havenfall side, through which I can see the drab mountain gray of our tunnels. The walls contrast with the starry night sky, blending in with the carpet of pristine white snow covering the ground. Pristine, that is, except for the places where our company has broken through. Graylin is getting to his feet by the far wall, smoothing out his long green wool cloak and pulling up the hood. Brekken stands a few yards away, at the entrance to the courtyard, already standing guard. Beyond him, I can see a strip of glittering road, and my heart thrills at the sight.

It's so cold. Sitting up, I fumble in my jacket, scooting backward in the snow to be out of the danger zone. I pull my scarf out of my collar and take my hood off, quickly wrapping the scarf around twice and then pulling my hood back up. I thought I was prepared for the cold, but there's something different about this even from the brutal Colorado plains winters I'm used to. It feels like this cold is deeper somehow, entrenched, maybe since it never lets up.

Spring doesn't come to Myr. There are other countries in Fiorden-kill that are more temperate, but not by much. Graylin once told me that Fiordens weren't like humans, in that humans tended to view cold as something scary and bad, lonely, deadly. Fiordens don't see it that way, he said, maybe because they don't know anything else. Their berries and herbs grow just fine in the cold, and the animals they hunt and domesticate could only exist in the snow. I run through all the information I've learned from Graylin, from Brekken, from the library and the delegates as I stand up on shaky legs. Feeling like a moment that I've been waiting and preparing for my entire life is finally here.

I tip my head back, look at the sky, and gasp, the sound muffled by my layers of scarf. I had glanced up upon first coming through, but not really looked, not really seen until now. There are so many stars. Thousands, it seems like, and they're bigger than the stars on Earth, closer. Instead of a uniform cool blue, they appear in all colors, blue and purple and red and orange and gold. And that's not all. At the edge of the sky, a curtain of interwoven colors is appearing, creeping over the top of the marble wall. Shimmering strands of pale green and blue and pink, swaying gently between the stars like seaweed caught in a soft current. The aurora. It hovers at the fringes of the horizon now, but when it covers the whole sky, that's the Fiordens' signal to enter the doorway into Havenfall, for the summit to begin.

I cross over the snow to Brekken, my feet sliding awkwardly in the slightly-too-big boots I've borrowed. My body feels different in a way I can't put my finger on. Lighter. *Is it possible that there's less gravity in Fiordenkill?* I wonder giddily as I approach Brekken.

He looks different here in his home world, different enough for me to pause a few feet away, just so I can look at him a second longer before he notices me. The light here is strange. Although it's night, it's not dark by any means; the light from the stars and the aurora, reflected off the marble walls and the snow on the ground, casts everything in an ethereal pale light. It reshapes Brekken, deepens the contrast between his pale skin and copper hair and blue eyes and the deep green of his soldier's coat. It sharpens him, bringing out the fine angles of his face and the hollows in his cheeks and around his eyes. It makes him look less human.

It makes me remember what he is. While the delegates have never seemed not-foreign to me, strange in their habits and speech and manner; while even Graylin catches me off guard sometimes when his accent sneaks through or he catches a falling wineglass with supernatural reflexes; something had shifted over the years and allowed me to see Brekken as just like me. Maybe I was trying to convince myself there was some kind of future for us, that he could stay at Havenfall, stay on Earth and be happy. But looking at him now, it's so clear that this is his home. Maybe he would be happy elsewhere, but it would never be home, the way Graylin has made it so.

Brekken is looking intently out at the road, the wind tugging at his hair like a familiar friend. His eyes gleam with the reflected sky, and his posture is tall and proud, a soldier's. Beyond him, through a huge black wrought-iron gate, I can see a long straight road shimmering with ice, lined by great thick-trunked trees with graceful, downward-pointing boughs, like silvery pines.

He doesn't seem to notice me there until I take another step, the snow crunching beneath my feet, and he turns toward me, blinking, clearing some unnameable emotion out of his eyes. A soft smile curls his mouth.

"So what do you think?" he asks.

"It's beautiful," I whisper, looking at the reflections of the stars in his pupils. "But why is this area empty? I thought the doorway was always under guard."

"It usually is," Brekken replies. "But my mother pulled some favors and arranged for the guards to be elsewhere tonight."

"Thank goodness." I'm too embarrassed to admit that I hadn't even thought about guards on the Fiorden side until now. I was too focused on the next steps of the plan we made: learn as much as we can about the gauntlet, stop over at Brekken's grandparents' home to get ready and gather our strength, and then make our attack.

"Do you know the way to Winterkill?"

Brekken shakes his head no. "But they do," he says, lifting his finger to point.

I follow the line of his arm, down the stretch of ice road, and my heart jumps into my throat. Someone is coming—no, something—something huge. It's strangely silent except for a soft whooshing sound that gets louder and louder. Finally I understand what I'm seeing: a huge sleigh made of black polished wood, trimmed with silver and bone.

The sleigh is pulled by five ice wolves, each as big as a horse.

My jaw drops. They bound toward us, paws silent against the ice, blue and black eyes gleaming in the starlight. Teeth too. Their coats are black and brown and silver and white. The wolves are bound together and to the sleigh by leather harnesses. As they pull to a stop a few yards from the gate, I see that a woman with long copper hair is holding the reins. She dismounts and comes toward us, patting each of the wolves as she passes them. Steam rises from the animals' coats and from their open mouths, long red tongues lolling out between white teeth. I'm so transfixed by them that I don't realize at first that Brekken has opened the gate and gone out. Not until he strides up to the woman and envelops her in an embrace.

My gaze snaps to them. After a long hug, the woman pulls back, holding Brekken by the shoulders.

"My son," she says with a big grin on her face.

And as soon as she does, I can see the resemblance between them, the ivory cast of their skin, the mischievous grin.

Something goes hollow inside me. Of course I've heard plenty about Brekken's parents over the years. Both generals in Myr's army, they were delegates at Havenfall before I was born. They're highly decorated and Brekken looks up to them. I had never given them much thought before now, but seeing Brekken with his mother fills me with a sense of longing that feels like a gut punch.

What would Mom do if I hugged her like that? Our visits are no-contact, so I don't know for sure, but I can't imagine any other response but her just standing there, stone-still, her arms limp at her sides.

Still, when Brekken turns toward me with a smile, I do my best to return it. He beckons me forward, and I step out of the courtyard gate. Graylin is a few steps behind me.

Deeper into Fiordenkill.

Even though I only move a few feet, it seems to me that the cold gets more intense. And I start to feel the stirrings of pain deep in my bones, in my veins. My body tells me to go back to the doorway, back to safety. But I trust that the gauntlet on my arm will keep me safe. It has to. Just for a few days, I tell myself.

"Mother," Brekken says with a smile as I get close, looking between the copper-haired woman and me. "This is Maddie. The girl I told you about."

I can feel my eyes widen a little at those words. What has he told her about me? But I keep my cool as best I can, smiling and extending a hand. She ignores it and goes in for a hug, her slender arms wrapping around me tightly.

"Madeline," she says warmly, pulling back so she can look at me the same way she did with Brekken. "I am so pleased to finally meet you. I'm Ilya."

"I'm glad to meet you too," I say, blushing, hoping it doesn't show too much under the scarf.

Ilya's face is uncovered, of course. She's as unbothered as all Fiordens are by the cold. Sprays of fine lines fan out from the corners of her eyes and mouth, but otherwise she could be thirty.

"Brekken told me how well you held the inn together this summer while your uncle was ill."

Surprise and warmth fill my chest. Brekken thinks I did a good job? And he told his parents? Well, his mom, at least. I recall he once told me that his father traveled for months at a time, chasing rare elk on commission from the royal family.

Ilya lets me go, still smiling. "Well, we can catch up later," she says, her Fiorden accent making each word distinct and elegant. "Now, let's focus on getting you people somewhere safe." Ilya separates from me and goes to greet Graylin.

Brekken squeezes my hand briefly—I startle at the pressure of his fingers over my mittens—and draws me to the side of the sleigh.

I follow, intensely aware of the presence of the ice wolves. Instinct makes me keep my head down, not to let my gaze meet those dark, intelligent eyes. They seem happy enough, though, panting slightly and shifting their massive weight. Brekken pats their flanks as we pass, just like his mother. Part of me wants to touch them, too, but I don't dare.

At the sleigh, Brekken opens a door in the side, revealing a comfortably appointed interior with four front-facing carved seats heaped with furs and a sleek bone-colored railing to keep riders in.

"Stay awake during the ride if you can," he says. "I'd like you to see Fiordenkill."

My face tingles as I imagine sitting up there in the cold. But at the same time, something in my chest ignites at Brekken's words.

Brekken busies himself with our supplies, sliding the stuff we've brought—Fiorden bags and Earth duffel bags full of clothes, money, food, weapons—between the benches. Graylin and I thought we should travel as light as possible to avoid notice, but Marcus and Brekken share a Boy Scout's mentality of never ever getting caught unprepared.

Brekken's mom climbs into the driver's seat up front, and Graylin hops into the middle row, making it look as easy as climbing a single stair. The treads of the sleigh go up to my thighs; the railing is three feet above the top of my head. I catch my reflection in the polished black wood, looking around in vain for a ladder or steps.

"Uh . . ." I look pleadingly at Brekken.

He grins, steps forward, and grabs my waist, lifting me until Graylin can grasp my forearms. Graylin pulls me up, and I clamber awkwardly over the railing, claiming a seat in the back row. Brekken jumps up last and joins me in back.

Leaning down from the side of the sleigh, Ilya closes the gate to the doorway and locks it with a key pulled from within her long green wool coat. Then she snaps the reins, and just like that, we're off, the sound of the sleigh's treads slicing across the snow louder than the wolves' paws.

I wonder what time it is here, and then realize I don't even know what time system Fiordens use. I know their days are longer than ours, about thirty hours if I'm remembering Graylin's lessons rightly. But there's no moon by which to measure the night, and the aurora stays where it is, a quiet, bright presence at the edge of the sky. I know that over the course of the year it advances, until their warmest month— which still isn't warm enough to melt the permafrost. And then the aurora covers the whole sky for one bright day and night.

"It's beautiful," I whisper to Brekken.

I had always figured that the doorway between Haven and Fiorden-kill was located within Myr's capital city, but it doesn't seem like it; beyond the elegant row of trees lining the road, all I see are more trees, quickly growing wild and deep. Trees and ice gleam through the thin dusting of snow on the road. Maybe that's why we seem to be going so fast. The trees whip by us on either side. But the wind isn't as bad as I expected; the sleigh is cleverly designed to ward it off. I'm able to look at the sky, the trees, and at Brekken, who is watching not the landscape go by, but me. When our eyes meet, he smiles.

"What are you thinking?" he asks me.

I feel dizzy by the onslaught on my senses, too awed by the beauty of Fiordenkill to think much of anything at all. But I try to come up with something smart to say.

"I'm thinking how weird it is that after wanting to see your world my whole life and never thinking I'd be able to, now I'm here. And it's for such a dark reason. But I'm still happy to be here."

"I'm happy you're here too," Brekken says simply. The starlight plays over his face, disappearing into darkness occasionally when we pass under tree branches, then washing him with light again. "Is the gaunt-let working? Are you feeling any pain?"

I consider it. If I focus, I can feel a slight pain, an ache deep in my bones, a feeling of needles like when my foot falls asleep, but deeper. Yet it's faint, easily ignorable. It might even be my imagination. I smile. "Yeah, it seems to be working."

Here, tonight, with the landscape zooming by us, the stars burning in their sphere and the aurora flickering at the edge of the horizon, it's easy to ignore whatever small discomfort I feel. Brekken is holding my hand, and we're pressed together, from our shoulders down to our thighs. The sleigh protects us from the wind, and he looks so very lovely in the starlight.

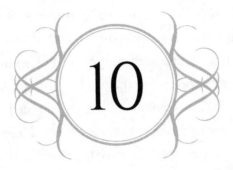

10

AT SOME POINT, I FALL asleep on Brekken's shoulder, warmed by his proximity. His skin always felt cool to me in Havenfall, but here it seems warm. He still has his arm around me when I wake up, blearily, to a silver sun rising ahead of us, lighting the ice road up in a blue blaze. I look ahead at Graylin, suddenly nervous. I haven't told anyone that Brekken and I are—whatever we are. Dating? Together? *Kissing*, my brain helpfully supplies, and I blush and shrug away from Brekken. No way am I telling anyone that Brekken and I are *kissing*. Especially Graylin or Marcus. But I'm kidding myself. They probably already know.

I shake away the embarrassing thoughts. *No one is worried about who you're kissing, idiot.* Not with the daunting task ahead of us.

We're most of the way to Winterkill, Ilya tells us, but we don't want to approach it by day. Lord Cadius is hosting one of his feasts tonight. We'll hide out today, rest up, go over our plan, and get our disguises in order. Tonight seems almost too soon—there's not time to stake out the place and consider our attack from all angles. But the longer we stick around Fiordenkill, the greater the chance of being caught. Not to mention that even though I'm wearing the gauntlet, I can feel the ache in my bones getting stronger, more insistent. It's still not painful if I don't think about it, but it's a reminder that we need to get in and out quickly.

The sleigh finally stops when the sun has just climbed over the horizon, at a complex of low stone buildings surrounded by a high wall of ice. There are a few cabin-like structures clustered in one area, with five long, low buildings spaced out in a circle around it. The snow here isn't pristine like in the doorway courtyard. It's trampled and gray, and there's a sharp, musky smell in the air of roasted meat and sweat.

As Graylin helps everyone out of the sleigh and into the cabins, I tug at Brekken's sleeve. "What is this place?"

Brekken grins. "My grandparents raise ice wolves for the army. They're touring the southlands right now for the warm season, and Mother is looking after the pups. It all worked out perfectly. Here, look."

He grabs my hand—casual, unassuming—and leads me across the snow toward one of the outer buildings. I glance back over my shoulder, looking at the wolves that pulled the sleigh as Ilya unharnesses them. They're beautiful, but I'm not sure I want to meet more. But Brekken is already unlatching the heavy wood door and swinging it open.

I gasp, and this time it's out of delight, not fear. Because—*puppies*. Half a dozen wolves tumble out of the barn door all at once and overtake Brekken in a storm of happy barking and whining. They jump on him, and he falls back on his ass into the snow, laughing as the wolves swarm him. They're massive, already the size of German shepherds, but visibly puppies. They're pudgy, and their paws are too big for their bodies. Their movements are clumsy and overenthusiastic.

I let out a laugh and fall on my knees next to Brekken, and the baby ice wolves notice me and fall on me with just as much joy. One gray wolf jumps at me and licks my face before I can lift my hands to block it. Six tails wag furiously, and the gray one grabs my mitten in its relatively small teeth and tugs it off. I laugh and grab out for it, but the pup bounces away and crouches, its butt wiggling high in the air, daring me to give chase.

"Thunder!" Brekken scolds. His hand darts out, quicker than mine, and snags my mitten from Thunder's teeth. "Be polite."

He hands it back to me with an apologetic look on his face. I take my other mitten off and tuck them inside my coat, holding my hand out to a smaller, black pup who is cautiously sniffing my leg. She bumps my hand with a warm, wet nose, and then lets me scratch her between the ears, leaning into the touch. Happiness fills me. I know we still have a great challenge ahead of us, but right now I don't want to be anywhere else in all the worlds than here in this land of ice, kneeling in dirty snow, with wolves all around us and Brekken at my side. For a moment I can almost forget that anything is wrong. Forget the task looming ahead of us and the lives that hang in the balance.

Inside the cabin feels similar to a cozy mountain home you might find back on Earth, but everything looks just slightly different, more organic somehow. The angles are softer, the edges of things rounded as if we were inside a giant hollow tree, like in a fairy tale. Every surface is covered either in books or intricate, naturalistic carvings of flowers and trees and animals. Dust motes float serenely in the wintery sun flooding through the windows.

Graylin is sitting at a carved table in the corner, along with a Fiorden woman I don't recognize. She's older, with very pale skin and black hair and eyes, and is dressed in a kind of robe or kaftan that's forest green and belted at the waist. She looks up when we come in, her eyes fixing immediately on the bit of the gauntlet that shows between my mitten and sleeve. I go still, Brekken bumping into my back. This must be the old scholar friend that Graylin mentioned back in Havenfall.

They both stand to greet us, dropping their conversation in Myr's language and switching to English.

"Kae, this is Maddie," Graylin says, looking from the woman to me. "Maddie is Marcus's niece, the one I told you about. Maddie, this is my very good friend Kae."

I shove down my nerves. After so many years, I've gotten used to Graylin and Brekken, and Ilya has such a warm presence. But now, meeting a new Fiorden, an automatic reaction goes off in my body, a tightening of my skin and speeding of my heart. Like a reminder that Kae's not human, or that I am very, very far from home.

"Nice to meet you," I say, and extend a hand.

Kae casts a curious glance, making me realize too late that they probably don't shake hands here. But she's reaching out, grasping my fingers briefly with her own icy cold ones.

"Likewise, Maddie Morrow," she says, her voice faintly accented and ethereal. "What a wonder to see a Haven-dweller here. I often wished to attend the summit at Havenfall, but my work has kept me here." Her fingers drift to my wrist, pushing up the hem of my sleeve. "Have you experienced any sickness or pain from being in our world?"

I shake my head. "Not that I've noticed." I can hear the nervousness in my own voice.

Will she ask me to take the gauntlet off?

But she doesn't, just dropping my hand and retreating to the table.

Graylin joins us while Brekken busies himself in the kitchen, and soon I'm drinking something steaming that tastes like a mix of tea and cider while Kae looks at the gauntlet, my arm stretched over the table, palm up.

She pries one tiny gold-carved leaf from the armor and holds it with iron tongs above a candle flame. She and Graylin converse in low Myr voices, while Brekken chats with his mother in the kitchen. Left out of the conversation, I can't help but feel antsy and impatient. Every second spent here is a second we're not at Winterkill. Not rooting out the traders.

Kae's black eyes stay fixed on the leaf as it starts to soften in the flame, the tong tips sinking into the metal, the curled shape drooping. The leaf's gold starts to change colors. But instead of turning a bright pinkish orange like I expect normal metal would, it darkens, changing from gold to rust to dark green and then black. Smoke lifts off it, getting thicker and thicker, and when Kae pulls the tongs away, the leaf has disappeared.

I stare. "What happened?"

From the doorway, I see Brekken is staring too, eyes wide.

"Phoenix flame," Graylin whispers.

"What is that?" I look from face to face. "What are you talking about?"

"Never have I seen anything like this," Kae says in a hushed tone. "I thought it only a myth."

Graylin glances at me, eyes uneasy. "We have a story here," he explains, "about a god who cried tears of metal. Metal that looked like this."

"Okay . . ." I look back at my arm, uneasy. "What else?"

"It's said to be magical," Graylin goes on. "But that was only ever a story . . ."

"I feel like we can start assuming all the stories have a grain of truth," I say wearily.

93

"Do you remember the story I told you?" Brekken says from across the room, his eyes meeting mine. "In the story, the gods cried for the knight and his lady, and he forged his armor out of their tears."

He paces over to us in the silent room—silent except for the soft hiss of the candle flame.

"Do you think . . . did he really exist? Him and his armor?" I'd waved the story away as wishful thinking, no more relevant to real life than the storybooks Mom used to read to me.

Another stretch of silence.

Then Graylin speaks. "Fiordenkill is different from your world in many ways. Our gods are closer to earth here."

"And our past is not so far from our present. We know that our stories are shaped around a heart of truth," Kae adds.

I glance at Brekken, confused. "What does that mean?"

Kae's eyes are fixed on the gauntlet, a mixture in her expression of wonder, of avarice, and of fear. "The armor was said to carry the knight to the world of the gods."

"A world," Graylin says, "that is now believed to be another Realm, like Haven and Byrn and Solaria. Now closed off, but another Realm. Which implies . . ."

I let my eyes fall to the gauntlet. What they're telling me—it *implies* that it's true what the pictures of Mom and the Fiorden lord seemed to suggest. That this gauntlet, and the suit of armor it's part of, could carry me—not just here to Fiordenkill—but wherever I wish.

"But there's something else," Kae says, an eerie and ominous quality in her voice. "The story says that where the knight went, harm followed."

My heart sinks. Isn't that always the way? Nothing good can exist, it seems, without some bad thing as a counterweight. "What do you mean?"

"Where he trod, the fabric of the world seemed to grow thin and weak." Kae's voice has taken on a lyrical cadence like a storyteller's, but the tone beneath is deadly serious. "A warm breeze came from nowhere. The smell of metal. Plants and animals began to die, and wanderers and hunters went missing."

I look at Graylin but can't tell anything from his face except that he's troubled.

"What does that mean?" I ask, my voice small. The gauntlet on my arm, which had started to feel like a source of comfort, suddenly feels heavy and cold.

"It's another story," he murmurs. "One that I always thought was just a story. It's called the Wound in the World."

The words themselves have a fairy-tale quality, and I can see the effect on all three Fiordens; he, Brekken, and Kae all stiffen. I look from Kae to Graylin to Brekken.

"Like another doorway?"

"Not a doorway," Graylin says. "Nothing so orderly. More like a wall in a house that, having been battered by the wind for many years, begins to show cracks."

"So . . ." I clear my throat, tracing over some of the dark whorls carved into fantastical shapes on the table. "What's the wind in this situation?"

Silence falls for a moment, until Brekken offers, "The knight?"

"Not the knight." Kae shakes her head. "His armor. More specifically, what it's made of."

"Phoenix flame," I say, echoing the strange word from earlier, turning my wrist back and forth so the gauntlet catches the light.

I think of the hole in the ozone layer back on Earth, an invisible tear in the sky that humans, out of ignorance or uncaring, ripped further just by going about our lives. A sense of foreboding fills me. "Is it . . . am I doing damage just being here?"

Is it just me, or does Kae's expression get cooler? "If our conjecturing here is correct, yes, the mere presence of phoenix flame does damage to the barrier."

"Not much," Graylin interjects quickly. "Clearly. We haven't seen any effects of it as we traveled."

Guilt seeps into me as I look between them. It's not like I can do anything, I can't take the gauntlet off, but I hate the idea that I'm doing damage to Fiordenkill just by being here.

"But if there was more of it . . . more of the phoenix flame . . . then the cracks will start to show?"

"For instance, a whole suit of armor?" Graylin adds in.

Kae nods wordlessly.

"So if Cadius Winterkill has the armor . . ." Brekken puts it together. "He has a way between the worlds. That's how he's running the soul trade."

"If we can get our hands on the armor, will the wound close?" I ask.

But before Kae can answer, Graylin cuts in.

"This trip is for reconnaissance only, remember?" He addresses me, dark eyes drilling into mine with serious intensity. "That's what we promised Marcus. We don't have the resources for a confrontation."

"I know that," I reply. "But just humor me for a second. Would it close?"

Kae holds my gaze. "Maybe," she says quietly. "I do not know for sure. But it is possible."

"I know we can't confront Cadius," I press on. "But if all it takes to stop him is stealing one suit of armor—"

"Winterkill won't make it that easy," Brekken says. His voice is thoughtful, distracted, fingers drumming against the pitted tabletop. "But if we see the opportunity . . ."

"We won't take any stupid chances," I promise Graylin. A renewed sense of urgency and hope gathers beneath my breastbone. "But if we get lucky, we don't have to wait for a chance to come back. We could bring the soul trade down tonight."

————

The rest of the day passes in a blur of preparations. It seems to me that time is moving faster, now that our goal is clearer. What awaits us at Winterkill is still murky, but now there's a focus point. The phoenix flame armor. A single object, corroding the barrier between the worlds like water seeping through floorboards. Water or, more appropriately, acid, creating a gap through which the traders can carry their silver and souls.

It turns out that in addition to being a scholar, Kae is also a gifted practitioner of healing magic. As evening falls across the stretch of snow outside, she and Graylin work together to alter my appearance to look more Fiorden. I sit as still as I can at the table, feeling awkward and antsy, like I always do when I get a haircut. But instead of scissors in my hair, it's hands on my face, a gentle magic playing over my skin, sinking beneath the surface.

There's no mirror and I keep my eyes closed, so I can't see what they're doing to me. It feels strange, but not unpleasant. My skin stretches slightly, heating and tingling. It's almost like feeling myself get sunburned, but somehow pleasant.

At last, Graylin steps back. "All right. I think that's about all we can do."

I open my eyes, blinking as the cabin comes back into focus. I'd kind of zoned out, and I didn't realize how much time must have passed. The world through the thick windows is dark, and starlight glitters off the snow. My heart speeds. It's almost time to go to Winterkill.

As Graylin and Kae step back, examining their work critically, Brekken appears in the periphery of my vision. He's holding something—a hand mirror, I realize, old-looking, the carved wood handle worn smooth and the surface mottled silver.

Brekken's blue eyes are wide as he looks at me, with a mix of wonder and trepidation. It makes a flush of self-consciousness rise to my cheeks. Caught up as I was in the danger of what we're about to attempt, I didn't really feel the wonder of it—my face, my features changed and manipulated by fairy-tale magic, all so I fit in better in this strange world of ice and starlight. Winterkill's world. Graylin's world. Brekken's world.

The whole cabin seems to go still as I reach for the mirror. Ilya, measuring fabric at a desk against the far wall, pauses in her work. Graylin tenses. Kae turns and sweeps from the cabin—maybe she needs fresh air, or maybe the sudden tension and pressure in the air is too much for her. And Brekken is still, his eyes on me.

My reflection slides over the small, aged mirror, and I swallow a gasp—of surprise, a little alarm, and wonder. It's my face, but not quite. The planes of my face have sharpened, my cheekbones look more blade-like, and the hollows at my cheeks and temples more shadowy. My skin is pale except for roses of color high in my cheeks, like I've only just come in from the cold. My ears seem a big longer, and my hair slightly more reddish. I look strange. I look beautiful.

Before I can examine my reflection too long, Ilya rushes in, wielding a wooden case filled with what seems to be Fiorden makeup—powders in bone-carved boxes, mysterious liquids in bottles of colored glass. While Brekken and Graylin head outside to prepare the sleigh, she goes to work, accentuating the changes magic has wrought.

Then she presents me with what she's been working on—a long green velvet dress, simple but elegant, and a cape of fine black fur with a silk-lined hood. She also hands over leather boots for underneath, with high heels to make me taller. Everything fits perfectly. I guess I know where Brekken got his meticulous nature, but between the heels and the voluminous skirt, I hope everything goes according to plan tonight. That I don't need to run.

"Well," Ilya says when I stand. She sounds pleased with herself, and takes up the mirror to angle it my way. She tilts it up and down to give me the full picture. "What say you, Maddie Morrow of Fiordenkill?"

She says it in a joking, teasing way, but it still sets a chill sweeping up my spine. I gaze at the girl in the mirror. Tallish, slender, elegant. Someone who would look at home in this perpetual winter. At home next to Brekken.

All in all, no one who looked closely would mistake me for a Fiorden, but hopefully no one will look twice.

"Thank you," I tell Ilya, my voice thick with a bit too much emotion. "Thank you so much."

Then I turn toward the door and turn my mind to the task ahead.

Infiltrate Winterkill.

Find the Solarians.

Free them.

Get the armor.

And through it all, one question gets louder and louder in my head.

How, exactly?

11

THAT NIGHT, WE RIDE THE short remaining distance to the Winterkill estate in tense silence. The scenery outside the sleigh is as beautiful as ever, the aurora casting a dappled, multicolored light over the ice road and the pristine snow. But it feels colder, darker, and I don't take the landscape in, instead letting it rush by my unfocused eyes. While I've been anxious to get on with everything—to get to Winterkill and take down the soul trade—now that it's right in front of me, the fear I probably should have been feeling all along is sinking in. Brekken was right earlier. None of this is going to be easy.

It'll be worth it, I remind myself, trying to breathe deep, slow my racing heart and the prickling of sweat on my palms. Worth it, if we can save even one captive Solarian. Is such a thing even possible?

Eventually, the great wolves' fast pace starts to change. It registers deep in my bones, causing me to look up ahead before I even quite realize we're slowing. What I see makes me draw in my breath. A towering silhouette looms in front of us. Wreathed in fog, it looks even darker against the night sky. It would hardly be visible at all, except for how it pierces the aurora and blocks out the stars. A massive maze of turrets and buttresses and walls and towers surrounds the grounds.

I keep my eyes on the estate as the wolves take us closer and it comes slowly into focus. As we approach, some of the fog seems to clear away and I realize the castle of stone and ice, rather than being dark, is actually blazing with light. It rises above a thicket of pine trees and pours light from its windows. Even at a distance, I can see other sleighs gathered up front, some pulled by wolves and some by great gray deer with white antlers. Then we plunge into the trees skirting the fortress, and the world goes dark.

It's startlingly scary. I can't see for crap, but I guess the wolves can, because we keep going at top speed, the sleigh turning with surety as the road twists and winds through the trees. I can feel them on either side of us, like conscious presences, and smell the sharp woodsy scent of sap and snow.

When we emerge from the trees, the world seems brighter than it did before, brighter than can be accounted for by my eyes adjusting. I realize with a jolt that we've emerged straight into a great, gardened courtyard, the windows of Winterkill spilling light all around us.

It's beautiful, like an otherworldly, wintery version of the gardens at Versailles. Great trees, sort of like weeping willows but bigger and paler, march in orderly rows in all directions, draping pearly white vines over gray cobblestone paths. Bushes with glossy black leaves and round red flowers hug the sides of the castle. Ice sculptures dot the gardens—rearing bears and birds in flight and knights standing triumphantly atop slain enemies—and seem to capture and refract the starlight from above, casting the gardens in a shifting, living light. All around us,

Fiordens in fine velvet gowns and fur cloaks are disembarking from sleighs.

Laughter and conversation floats through the air, both in English and the Myr language. As the partygoers filter inside through a set of open doors on the other side of the courtyard, footmen appear out of nowhere to attend to the sleighs and the animals. Great wolves shift their weight and eye the elk and reindeer that other parties have used to pull their sleighs.

Nervousness is a lump of ice lodged in my throat as Graylin swings down from our sleigh and speaks to us in a low voice.

"Remember the plan," he says. His posture is casual, one hand resting against the sleigh side, but his eyes dart around nervously. "Don't interact more than necessary. Don't attract attention. Keep in touch"—he pats the walkie-talkie on his belt, hidden under his cloak—"and don't get separated. I'll meet you back here in an hour."

I nod in response, patting the place where my walkie-talkie is hidden to show that I have it. I argued on the way here that we should all split up—we can cover more ground that way—but Graylin wouldn't hear of it, since I don't speak the Myr language and don't have much in the way of self-defense skills. I know he's right, but I hate feeling like deadweight.

We disembark and walk toward the castle, aiming for an inconspicuous side entrance rather than the propped-open doors admitting the crowd. The feel of a party is in the air, but my limbs are heavy with anxiety.

Graylin comes up next to me. Here, he seems different from the gentle, soft-spoken soul I've always known. Wariness is in his eyes, and there is a subtle tension in his movements.

"Promise me you'll be careful in there," he says under his breath. "We are only gathering information."

"I will," I whisper back, resisting the urge to remind him I've promised exactly that a dozen times already. "Always am."

"I don't know what I'd say to Marcus if I lost you."

That takes me aback. Graylin's never said anything like that to me. I don't know how to respond. But I don't get the chance to think of something, because Graylin veers off. His job, for now, is to chat up the crowd to see what he can discover; Brekken's and mine is to get the lay of the land.

Brekken and I continue forward, my hand on his arm, and suddenly the doors are in front of us and we're crossing the threshold. We're inside.

What greets us is an opulent hallway, narrow and oppressively dark despite the glass lamps spaced at intervals along the walls. Deep, velvety rugs line the floor and shimmering brocade tapestries cover the walls. They zig and zag without logic, broken by occasional alcoves holding stuffed beasts—bears, deer, wolves—or wild sculptures of wood or stone. The overall mood is claustrophobic, threatening.

A few people walk by us, Fiordens either in drab servants' uniforms or bright, extravagant finery, gaudier than what the delegates at Havenfall wear. They don't pay us any mind, and we don't speak, not wanting to draw attention to ourselves. I wish I had been better about studying the Myr language growing up, or that I was taller. I wish a lot of things, but I can't dwell on them here. We have a job to do.

Eventually, the hallway feeds into a wide, crowded foyer, and it's a simple matter from there to find the feast. People are streaming in and out of a set of tall double doors at the end of the room. There is light and noise and music. The atmosphere is festive, not so different from the nightly dances at Havenfall, just bigger, louder, more crowded, and fancier. But an air of menace hangs above it all, because I know the truth about this place. Everything—all this luxury and elegance—is funded by the soul trade.

Maybe that's why there are guards stationed every twenty yards or so along the fortress walls. Uniformed in forest green wool coats with gold buttons, they stand tall and still amidst the swirl of the party. The gleaming, jeweled swords at their hips could plausibly be just decoration, but I don't think they are. Although the other partygoers seem not to be bothered by the weapons, I can't help but notice them. They are a reminder that this is a dangerous place. A deadly place.

Without a word, we pass through into the ballroom. It's massive, all dull gold and gleaming stone. The floor is made of different kinds of wood, but as polished as if it's covered by melted diamonds. Its surface is smooth and soundless beneath my boots, and I have to be careful not to slip, though it doesn't seem to slow down the people dancing all around us. Skirts and capes and tailcoats whisk through the perfumed air. Rather than dance in consistent pairs as you'd expect on Earth, people here dance alone, sweeping and swirling, elegantly coming together with others, before separating, changing partners, and then separating once again. The overall effect is dizzying, and I'm glad for Brekken's strong presence beside me.

A head table dominates the front of the room, and my gaze is drawn as if by a magnet to the Fiorden man who sits in the middle of it. Is this Cadius? My mother's love? He's tall, broad, and imposing, with a patrician face and neat dark hair. There is a small smile on his lips as he looks out over the hall. On a small dais between the head table and the rest of the room, a band plays strange stringed instruments I haven't seen before.

Perhaps this is a normal enough celebration. But there's an edge in the air, some kind of tension, a cruelty in the savage tempo of the music and the high laughter ringing from all directions.

My instincts tell me to pause, hoping not to be noticed, but Brekken propels us forward, bending down as he does to whisper in my ear.

"Don't slow down," he whispers. "That'll make everyone look at you. Even if you don't know what you're doing, keep moving."

I nod my understanding. He's right, of course. The room is a blur of motion and bright color. As much as I want to squeeze myself into a corner and hope no one notices me, that's a surefire way to be noticed. So I keep pace with Brekken as we walk past the band and join the dance.

We fall into step easily, the muscle memory of however many summers in Havenfall's ballroom taking over, even though the music is different. Even with the task ahead of us, part of me just wants to appreciate this moment, my body pressed close to Brekken's as one of his hands twines through mine while the other cradles my waist. But I can't feel the romance. Something seems so wrong here.

And then I realize why the light in the room has such a strange quality. Silver is inlaid into the walls and ceiling, forming ornate shapes, such as flowering vines and snowflakes and the silhouettes of slender dancing figures. It's flush with the wall, as if the lines were carved into the wooden walls and then molten silver poured in. It reminds me of ancient pottery I've seen at the museum in Denver, where artists mended cracks in ceramic with liquid gold. But rather than beautiful, the effect here is sinister. There's an opalescent shimmer to the silver, like something alive moves under the smooth surface.

Something alive. Like a soul.

It's Haven silver, I realize with a shock. I'd been drifting toward the nearest wall, my hand reaching out almost touching the figure of a twirling woman engraved there, but I quickly snatch my hand back as if from a stove burner. I don't want to touch the metal created to hold Solarians' fragmented souls.

The evil of it makes me shudder. I keep my eyes open over Brekken's shoulder as we spin, and I see people looking up at the man at the head table, Cadius Winterkill, the lord of this castle. Lips part in leering smiles. And even though I don't understand the words people are calling out at him, I feel like I can make out their jeering, laughing tones.

Princess Enetta had said no one reputable went to these parties. How much does everyone here know about the soul trade?

"What are they saying?" I whisper to Brekken. I feel him tense at the little spot where his jaw rests against my temple.

"Nothing interesting," he says after a moment. "Jokes."

Anger shoots through me that these Fiordens—who must know what Cadius is up to—are joking. They are joking as the reflected light of the soul-silver plays off their beautiful clothes.

Automatically, my hand drops to pat the walkie-talkie strapped to my thigh, half checking to make sure it's still there, half hoping that I'll feel it chirp with a message. I don't want any part of this ball. I just want to find the Solarians who must be trapped here somewhere, get away from this place as fast as I can, and take everyone I love with me.

"Has anyone mentioned the Solarians?" I grab Brekken's waist tight, wanting to keep as close to him as I can, as much out of fear as of desire. "Or the armor?"

I feel him shake his head. "Not that I've noticed."

"Maybe we should talk to someone," I whisper, trying to think above the clamorous music, which seems to take pleasure in its own discordance. "Just casually to see if anyone knows anything."

"They'll want to know who you are, and then they'll notice you don't speak the language."

Again I curse myself for never learning the languages of the Realms when I was a kid, when it would have been easy, my brain malleable. Graylin would have taught me, but I was too busy chasing squirrels and playing hide-and-seek with Nate, and later with Brekken.

I see a serving table set up along one side of the room and nod at it, leading Brekken to follow my gaze.

"You talk to someone, then. I'll, uh, go get some food or something." The last thing I want to do is eat anything, but we can't just dance around until the feast is over.

Brekken doesn't let me go right away, though. "We're supposed to stay together."

"I won't go out of sight," I promise.

He pulls back enough to look into my face, and I see the familiar glint of stubbornness in his eyes. He knows it's a good idea, but he doesn't want to separate.

"Who should I talk to?" he asks.

"Cadius? Would he recognize you?"

Brekken hesitates and looks up at the head table. "I don't think so . . ."

"Then talk to him."

I spin out from under Brekken's hands, pausing to kiss his cheek. I want to distract him from how antsy I am. I don't know why I feel such a sense of dread, like an ax is suspended over my head. Maybe it's just the effect of spending time in another world. Maybe I'm getting sicker, despite the protective effect of the phoenix flame gauntlet. Which would not be great, but I'd rather it be sickness than intuition that something is going to go wrong.

Without giving Brekken any more space to argue—and draw attention to us by speaking English in a room full of Fiordens—I stride off toward the serving table and grab a small wooden bowl, as I see others doing. The table is piled high with mostly roasted meats, the shapes uncomfortably reminiscent of the animals they once were. The center-piece is a huge roasted boar with the tusks still attached, sharp and dripping with grease. My stomach turns, and I go for a fruit platter instead, grabbing a random handful of what looks like small sticky blue plums.

Then I realize I don't know how to eat them. They seem messy. I'm searching for silverware when a sound cuts through the room. It's the clear peal of cutlery clinking on glass, like people do at weddings. I guess some traditions occur across worlds. Or maybe they've permeated through the portals at Havenfall . . . Or elsewhere, if Kae is right, and other doorways to Realms are possible where phoenix flame is present.

The music fades out, and the chatter of the large room dies quickly. Everyone turns toward the head table as Cadius rises to his feet. I look for Brekken, my heart in my throat and my plate slippery in my now-sweaty hands. But I don't see him anywhere.

Cadius begins to speak, his voice deep and rolling. I can't understand any of it, except for a few random basic words like *home* and *thank you* and *friends*. After a few minutes of this, Cadius raises his arms, his voice rising to a finale. Around me, the celebrants laugh and cheer. The haunted silver glitters all around us, and I can almost feel the weight of the souls inside. Souls like Nahteran, captive and trapped. And maybe like Taya now.

Stolen.

I want to scream. I want to collapse. I want to throw a knife or put my fist through glass. I want to kill Cadius. But I can't move.

Then the horror hits all at once, a concentrated punch to my stomach. Even though I haven't touched anything at the feast, the meal I ate back at Brekken's grandparents' cabin suddenly threatens to storm back up my esophagus.

Instinct takes over. As laughter and jeers rise up all around me, I drop my bowl back onto the serving table. It cracks, and sticky plums roll everywhere, but I don't stop to see if anyone noticed. Instead, I run from the hall as fast as I can with my gut heaving and my fist pressed to my mouth.

I have tears in my eyes and can't really see where I'm going, but I hear people jump out of my way as I stagger to an alcove and throw up between a taxidermied wolf's front paws. Brittle moth-eaten fur crackles beneath my hand as I sling an arm around the wolf's neck for support and the stink of stomach acid burns my eyes.

Once I've finally emptied my stomach, I look up, wiping my mouth with the back of my hand. Scandalized stares surround me; though my vision is still too blurry to make out details, I feel the weight of judgment. I stare back, unblinking, too angry and disgusted to care about the attention. If I were in Havenfall, someone would materialize right about now with a damp washcloth, a glass of water, and a comforting hand, but I know better than to expect any kindness here. A nest of snakes is too kind a phrase. As my eyes clear, the remnants of tears trickling down my cheeks, I channel my judgment into my gaze, letting all these vultures know I find them as disgusting as they must find me.

I can't take this party much longer. I head back toward the ballroom, intending to find Brekken so we can get outside and I can breathe the fresh, cold air. But when I step inside and look around, I don't see him. Just so many fast-moving strangers, a whirl of unfamiliar, unfriendly cloth and flesh.

12

FEAR PLUMMETS THROUGH ME. WHERE is he? Panic speeds my heart as I look at face after unfamiliar face. And then—a glimpse of copper hair at the far side of the ballroom, near the north entrance. Relief fills me and I shoot toward Brekken, avoiding the veins of silver set into the walls, as he turns his head, his familiar sharp profile coming into view. But then I see who he's talking to.

Cadius Winterkill.

A stillness sets in. A feeling of calm, cold anticipation. *Play your cards right, Brekken*, I think, and skirt the room toward them, deliberately casual, keeping my head turned toward the orchestra as if that's my destination. Keeping Brekken and Cadius in my peripheral vision, I can see that the lord of Winterkill looks loose, drunk. He laughs uproariously at some undoubtedly hilarious joke, and Brekken laughs along with him, tipping his head back. Gradually, carefully, I edge close enough to hear their conversation. Which is in English, thank God. I wonder if Brekken steered them that way, or if Winterkill is putting on airs, using the language of the privileged, of the delegates.

"I'd love to learn how one conducts a business from a man such as yourself," Brekken says, leaning heavy on the charm. "Everyone says you're the best."

"I am," Cadius boasts, his voice wavery with drink.

His back is to me, but the arrogance is clear in the set of his shoulders and his swaggering walk. I can't help the thoughts that cloud my mind. How did my mother ever love him? How would she feel to know what he's become? Or was he this way all along, concealing his true self beneath the charming exterior, lying with every breath up to the moment he betrayed her?

It's enough to send a shiver of terror through me. If Mom could fall for a guy like this . . . how can I trust that anyone is who they seem?

I manage to catch Brekken's gaze over Cadius's shoulder. Brekken's eyes widen a little, then go soft with relief. All of it too subtle, hopefully, to be discerned by Winterkill or anyone else.

"Will you show me a token of your success?" Brekken presses, lowering his voice.

I have to strain to hear it. Even just watching the exchange, my heart speeds up. It's a bold move, bolder than I'd expect from careful Brekken. But if it works . . .

Cadius hesitates for a second, but then he nods and draws back toward the exit, beckoning. I can't see his expression, but I imagine it as fraternal, conspiratorial. I guess this is the same across all the worlds— that for evil men, the profit of corruption isn't always enough. They want to be seen, recognized, their genius acknowledged. Even when it's risky.

Catching Brekken's gaze again, I nod at him and mouth, *Go*. My pulse is racing. This wasn't part of the plan, but we'd be stupid not to take the chance dangling before us. Brekken nods back, minutely, and follows Cadius out the door. I wait a moment, and then follow too, at a distance. I grab a half-full goblet of wine from a side table as I go, in case I need to feign drunkenness at some point.

Early on, the halls are crowded with Fiordens, milling about, drinking, talking, and laughing. But they empty out quickly as Cadius leads Brekken along, speeding with drunken purpose. Soon, the estate seems deserted but for the three of us, and I fall farther back to escape notice, as far as I can without letting the two men out of sight. Down hallways, around bends, up staircases.

My nervousness grows the farther we go. We are clearly past the places meant for guests; the alcoves with their taxidermied animals have given way to simpler, though still ostentatious, decoration. Paintings and gaudy tapestries and vases of pale flowers adorn this part of the castle. If someone catches me this far from the ballroom, I'll have no plausible explanation for being here, goblet or no goblet.

I slow my pace again, listening for the sound of Cadius's heavy footsteps up ahead to guide my own since I can't hear Brekken's. Two things inexplicably fly through my head: *What would I tell Marcus if I lost you?* And *What would I tell your dad if something happened to you?*

So much fear. It governs every move in our family. We don't want to lose any more than we already have. But it feels like no one except me remembers that life isn't a series of losses. We could gain things too, if we're brave.

But then, up ahead, the footsteps slow and stop, and Cadius and Brekken's conversation starts up again, too low to hear. Carefully, putting each foot down slowly so my boots don't squeak against the polished stone, I move around the corner.

Up ahead, a partially open, heavy-looking oak door affords a view of an office. I see bookcases and a chair upholstered in sleek fur. Brekken and Cadius stand inside, talking, but the conversation has switched over into the Myr language. I can't make out any of it.

Frustrated, I draw back into the opening of an adjacent hallway, so I won't be seen when they leave. I followed them because I didn't want to be separated from Brekken, but maybe I should have stayed in the ballroom, since I'm little good to him as backup. We came here to observe, and I've seen a lot, but I can't think how we'd use any of it. What we *need* is to find the phoenix flame armor. Only then can we take this hub of the soul trade down. Maybe there's something in the office, a map, schematics?

My attention snaps to the sound of Cadius and Brekken leaving. The office door closes, and two pairs of footsteps walk down the hallway. Brekken's tread sounds heavier than normal, like he's doing it deliberately to warn me.

I shrink back against the wall, shuffling away from the opening to the main hallway, hoping the shadows are enough to cloak me. Brekken and Cadius pass, strolling casually back toward the ballroom, a delicate brass key dangling from Cadius's fingers. I want to signal to Brekken, to get his attention so we can escape and figure out our next steps, but there's no way to do so without Cadius noticing too.

I wait for their footsteps to fade, figuring I'll give them a head start before returning to the ballroom, as much as I don't want to. But as soon as I do, another idea seizes me.

The office door. It's only a few yards away to my left. I saw the key dangling from Cadius's fingers, but maybe . . . I sidle over and try the knob. It turns beneath my fingers. The door gives.

Shocked, I crack the door and slide inside before I can think too hard about it, shutting the door carefully behind me. My heart slams in my ears as it clicks closed. Brekken must have left it unlocked somehow.

Slowly, I turn to look around at Cadius's office, half in disbelief at my good luck and half wary that this is some sort of trap. It's a large, luxuriously appointed room, the decorations slightly less in-your-face than in the rest of the castle, but there if you look. Inlays of delicately carved bone scroll over the walls, climbing onto the bookshelves and sprouting into tiny sculptures of animals dancing along the molding. Paintings are set into the walls, fantastical landscapes rendered in oil and charcoal. There are woven tapestries lined in rich fur, shimmering with metallic thread. Bearskins—or something skins—cushion the floor, silencing my footsteps as I cross over to the desk.

In contrast to everything else in the room, the stretch of polished oak is bare, empty. I run my fingers along the glassy surface, my silk gloves hiding any fingerprints. Where to begin? Carefully, keeping alert for any noises that might tell me I'm not alone, I start opening the small doors set into the front of the desk, each leading to their own compartment. It contains the things you'd expect, quill pens and stacks of creamy paper, a wax stamp seal. Worry creeps in that this has all been for nothing. But then—a small compartment near the bottom of the desk yields a small, silvery key.

My breath catches, my fingers reaching for the key before I can decide if it's a good idea. I'm highly aware of how I don't have much time, how at any minute someone could barge in. Graylin would kill me if he knew what I was doing. If I was being cautious, if I was being safe, I would drop this and run back to the ballroom.

But that key.

I straighten up, looking around the office for anything with a lock. Immediately, my gaze falls on a cabinet on the other side of the room, near the window. A long, squat thing of black polished wood, with carved claw feet. Hurriedly, heart in my throat, I go over and slide the key into the small lock in the middle of the cabinet.

It takes me a couple of tries to get the key in the right way, but then something deep in the mechanism clicks. The whole front of the cabinet falls slightly open with the sigh of old wood.

I can feel the sweat pricking at my palms as I crouch and open the door wider. I don't know quite what to expect—soul-silver? Money? Weapons? But as my eyes adjust to the dimness, I realize it's papers, stacks of them, arranged into sheaves and tied with black silk ribbons. At first I feel childishly disappointed—that it's not something more dramatic. Then I shake my head to clear it. Glancing over my shoulder once more to make sure I'm still alone, I grab the nearest handful of papers and undo the ribbons, stripping off my gloves and stuffing them in my pocket to work more efficiently.

The writing before me is in English, which surprises me for a moment, until I make out a few more words. *Silver. Transfer. Soul.* Then it makes a cold kind of sense. English is what everyone uses to communicate with people from other Realms, since it's what we speak at Havenfall. Of course, then, it's also the de facto language of the soul trade.

I'm looking at a spreadsheet, strangely mundane despite the old-fashioned paper and ink. Someone has drawn a neat grid of lines—I imagine them using a straightedge—and filled the resulting rows and columns with objects, numbers, prices, and notes. Not too different from the papers I found snooping around Havenfall, back when I thought that the Heiress—and then Marcus—was complicit in the trade. Reading the record, a pang goes through my heart at the sudden, unwelcome memory of doing something similar with Taya. Of sitting with her in the twilight dimness of my room, puzzling over nonsensical phrases, trying to put the pieces together into a narrative that fit in with what we knew of the world.

But I shove that memory away. Now isn't the time to wallow in memories of Taya, wishing things could have turned out differently. That's never a helpful thing to do, but it especially isn't now, with a ticking clock and so much on the line. When any minute I could be caught and thrown out or jailed or worse. So I slam the door on my memories and return my attention to Winterkill's records.

There are two additional columns on this page, one that didn't appear on any of Marcus's or the Heiress's papers. It's filled with words I don't recognize, some of them repeated over and over again across several rows. It's alphabetized, but that's hardly helpful when I don't know what they mean to begin with. *Bairul. Banzon. Bhrima. Bulmont* . . . It reminds me of roll call at school when a substitute teacher comes in, stumbling over all but the blandest of names.

The end of the thought snags, makes my heart skip.

Names.

Could they be? I look again, hands trembling. The second column has more of what could be names, but they are not alphabetized and there are few repeats. Could these be given names, and the first column surnames? Of . . . of Solarians?

My hands are already reaching back into the cabinet, like they have a mind of their own. I turn up the edges of the pages to get a glimpse at the names, and then let the paper fall again. Searching until I see a column full of *N*'s. *Naasi. Naevan. Naimar. Naradeim. Narita. Natrath.*

No *Nahteran.*

Disappointment is bitter on my tongue as soured wine, but I don't let it stop me. I put that pile aside and reach back in, checking the names until I find the *T*'s. But that, too, is a dead end. No *Taya.*

I stare down at the paper, feeling utterly defeated and inadequate. There's a next step. There has to be, but I don't know what it is. I've caught so many lucky breaks. I'm in Winterkill's office, but I'm still completely helpless to find a single one of the captive Solarians. To save them.

But then something catches my eye. The *T*'s start halfway down the page in my hand. But before that, it's *S*'s. Specifically, a third of a page where the same two letters are repeated over and over again.

S.P.

My attention is caught, but I'm not sure why. I flip one page back. There it is again, except now the page is unbroken—a whole column filled just with *S.P. S.P. S.P.* The page below that is the same, and the one before that. The names in the second column are as scattered as ever. Was a whole family of Solarians victim to the soul trade? Confused, I look at the first-name column, trying to make sense of it. Then something makes my veins turn to ice.

Nahteran.

Suddenly, everything snaps into place. The first column isn't surnames at all. It doesn't refer to the Solarians whose souls are ripped from them and used for petty magic. It's *buyers.* Traders.

S.P. . . .

Footsteps from outside bring new terror rushing in, real-life horror to add to what's on the page. They're too close—can't be more than a few yards away from Cadius's office door. Setting the top page aside, I shove the records back into the cabinet—no time to reaffix the ribbon— and let the door fall shut. It clangs, making me flinch, and my hand darts out reflexively, but the noise is already made. All I can do is fold the sheet of paper with Nate's name on it and shove it into my bra. I take a quick sweep of the office to make sure everything appears just as it did before I came in, before tiptoeing to the door.

When I pause before it, everything is quiet. I wait, not even breathing, but I don't hear a sound. Maybe the person passed by. Or maybe I imagined the footsteps, all the fear I've been shoving down bubbling upward in the form of delusions. I'm not sure which I like less, but I wait a few moments before reaching out to open the door, in case I didn't imagine them—to let whoever I heard put some distance between them and me.

But when I do reach for the doorknob, it turns before I even touch it. I stare dumbly for a second, wondering if somehow Cadius's stolen magic has rubbed off on me—and then my brain catches up with reality and I throw myself backward, falling onto the bearskin in my scramble to hide.

But it's too late. The door opens, and a man's silhouette fills the threshold. I freeze, going entirely still as if that'll save me, as if Cadius will only see me if I move.

But then I realize—it isn't Cadius in the doorway.

My lips move, but nothing comes out.

Nate?

13

IT'S AS IF TIME HAS frozen around me, like my body and mind and the world has suddenly been encased in glass. I'm pretty sure my heart stopped beating. For a long, long, long moment, all I can do is stare at the boy in front of me, his name ringing in my head.

Nate.

Nate, the little boy in a red apron, singing along to the radio with Mom as he helped her make brownies.

Nate, who pushed me on the swing set and taught me how to make snow angels.

Nate, whose screams have haunted my nightmares for ten years. Nate who I thought for so long—so long—was dead.

He's not dead. He's standing in front of me. Grown up. With black hair now instead of blond, wearing Fiorden clothes, a leather breastplate, leggings, and a cloak. I'd recognize him anywhere, at any age, with any hair or clothes. Nate.

He steps inside and shuts the door behind him. His movements are quick and confident. He stares at me, head cocked. *"Losir a sedyn?"* he asks.

Through the haze, I remember the words from Graylin's lessons, and put it together. *Who are you?* But my voice doesn't work.

His accent is strange. It's Fiorden, but there's something else beneath it. A hint of the long flat vowels of our middle-America upbringing. And there's something else too, a musical, almost singsong quality to his words that's familiar from somewhere, but I can't place it.

Nate steps forward, glancing over his shoulder at the door before reaching down toward me. He asks something else in Myr's language. I think he asked me if I'm all right.

I open my mouth. Close it again. Open it, try to speak. Nothing comes out but air, a faint gasp. Nate looks concerned. His chin furrowing in the exact same way as when we were kids. It feels like a knife in my chest. He says something else, the strange words flowing out. Finally, I manage to push myself to my feet. I shake my head, my thoughts slowed to a sluggish crawl.

"You're not Fiorden," he says, switching seamlessly to English. "Solarian?"

I shake my head.

He cocks his. "Byrnisian?" His eyes flick along my face, checking for scales, maybe.

At last, I find my voice. "I'm human," I croak out. "Nate . . ."

My brother goes still. Still as me. For maybe fifteen seconds that seem to last a lifetime, we stand still and stare at each other.

Then Nate breaks the stillness to step back and pass a hand over his eyes, like he's making sure they still work. He blinks, his eyes welling up with tears. "Maddie?"

His tears call mine to the surface. I nod, trying to blink them back. "Yeah."

"Yeah?" It comes out almost like a soft laugh, incredulous. *It's been ten years, and this is what you say?*

"How is it you're here? What are you doing?"

I blink some more, trying to master the scattered storm of my thoughts. Forget Myr, all the words I know in English have flown out of my head. "I . . . I have phoenix flame."

Questions, things I want to say fight in my throat to be first out my lips. "You're a Solarian."

Nate blinks, taken aback. "Yes."

He looks down at himself, as if double-checking, and I look too. He's changed so much. He's way taller than me, and lanky; his skin is pallid, made paler by the startling contrast of his dark hair. Way different from me, with my compact build, sort-of-tan skin, and brown hair.

Duh. We're not related by blood. But the difference still startles me. More, he's transformed from the little boy I knew, with the quick smile and mischievous eyes. There are still hints of that, but I get the feeling that Nate has seen some shit this past decade. There are bags under his eyes, a hard set to his mouth that looks like it doesn't smile often.

Ever since Taya floated the possibility that he could be alive, the fear had snuck in the back of my mind that if he was alive, we'd find him crumpled in some trader's basement, chained up and stripped of his soul. But he's here. Now. He looks good. He looks strong, and most of all, he's alive.

"I . . ." Nate speaks, swallows, and presses the heels of his hands against his eyes. He starts again. "It's not safe here."

He looks around Cadius's office, and I wonder why he's here, but that's too complex a thought to put into words right now.

Nate moves to the door and puts a slender hand on the doorknob. Then he looks back at me, his eyes wide, like he can't believe this is real. "Come with me?"

Anywhere, I want to say, but my voice has flickered out again. He gives me one more short, disbelieving look before leading me out into the hallway.

The trip seems to take forever and no time at all. We pass people in the hall, Fiordens, but I don't really see them except as shapes, passing ghosts. I don't dare take my eyes off Nate's back as he walks in front of me; I have to remind myself to blink. Part of me is convinced that he's a dream, a hallucination, a wish, and as soon as I let him out of my sight he'll dissipate like a wisp of smoke. A dream or a delusion.

But he doesn't dissipate. He lets himself into a room in a quiet hallway, shutting the door behind us. I find myself in a bedroom, luxuriously appointed with Winterkill's same gaudy touches as on the first floor, but lacking any personal effects except for the mess.

Nate's bedroom is just as messy as I remember his childhood room being. Except now instead of Hot Wheels and Tinkertoys, Lincoln Logs and LEGOs, it's a tornado of clothes, a green leather satchel lying open on the bed after apparently having exploded all over the room. Nate mumbles some apology and sweeps an arm over a stuffed chair, catching the clothes piled onto it and flinging them into a corner.

Then he sits on the bed, not bothering to move the clothes. He just sits on top of them and props his elbows on his knees. My brother stares at me as I sit down, like he still isn't sure if I'm real. I know the feeling. There's so much to say—too much.

It's paralyzing; it stops me from saying anything at all except for "Nate . . ."

He clears his throat. "I, uh. I go by Nahteran now, mostly."

I fall quiet for a moment, considering this. "Nahteran."

I expect it to hurt, using this new name—no, his first name. But it actually doesn't. It suits him better, this older, haunted version of my brother.

"What are you doing here?" he asks me. "And *how* are you here?"

"It's a long story." I grin weakly. "But I'm here because of the soul trade. Uh, you know about the soul trade, right? Obviously."

Nate's—Nahteran's—face darkens. He nods, and my chest tightens. Suddenly I don't want to know what it is exactly that he knows, so I plow ahead.

"I came here to save the captured Solarians. And I'm not alone. Graylin is here, and my . . . friend Brekken."

Now that the words are finally coming, I can't shut them off.

Nate smiles slightly. "I remember Graylin. But Winterkill is a fortress, Maddie. You'll need more than a few reinforcements to get to the Solarians."

"How do you know?" I almost trip over my words. I look around the room, realizing for the first time the strangeness of it, how it looks like he's been here at least a few days. "What are you doing here anyway? You're not a captive anymore, are you?"

"No," Nahteran says, and it seems like the temperature in the room drops a few degrees. "Never again."

I wait, not sure what to say. I'm still so happy to see him, but nothing about him being here adds up. Something on this chair is poking me in the butt. I shift in my seat and pull a stray clothing item out from under me that Nate didn't catch earlier. I'm about to toss it on the pile with the others when I realize it's a Byrnisian jacket, similar to the one I love wearing to Havenfall's evening balls, only in a men's cut. The scales were poking me.

Looking around, I'm confused to see a mix of clothing from three out of four Adjacent Realms on my brother's furniture. I hadn't noticed before, but there are T-shirts and jeans lying around amidst the traditional Fiorden clothes. And even Byrnisian silk, robes, and jumpsuits in the bright colors they favor in that hot, volatile world. I turn the jacket idly over and freeze. There's something embroidered on the back. It's a spreading silver tree.

The Silver Prince's motif: S.P.

"What is this?" I whisper.

"Like I said, it's a long story," Nahteran says, meeting my eyes.

"But this . . ." I hold up the jacket with the insignia. "This is . . ."

I don't want to say the words, really. Don't want to give voice and weight to the truth taking shape in my head. But Nahteran doesn't say anything. Just waits in silence. So I have to say it.

"You work for the Silver Prince," I finish in a whisper.

Nahteran blinks.

I think about pulling out the folded piece of paper in my dress bearing his name—the trade log—but I decide not to. I don't want to push him toward things he might not want to talk about. My brother is here. He's alive, but I still haven't seen him smile and that makes it all feel not quite real.

At length, he pulls another armchair up close and flops down into it. Something about his movements seem so familiar. That quality of being unselfconscious, but still graceful somehow. Mom's little changeling.

"I want to tell you what happened," he says, sounding tired. "But I don't really know where to start."

I realize that he reminds me of Taya. *Taya, you were right.*

The thought of her is another knife in my chest. She had always held out hope that her brother was alive, when I had long given up mine for dead. She's Nate's biological sister. They were separated as toddlers, back before Nate was taken in by my mom and his name was Terran. Both names broken halves of what I guess must've been his first name, his birth name. Nahteran. Brekken told me that in Solarian, it meant *soldier*.

I bet his and Taya's Solarian parents never anticipated him turning out like this.

"Cadius took me and traded my soul to the Silver Prince," my brother says. His words are timid, like they're scouts sent venturing out onto dangerous land. "And then I was brought back."

So many questions live under the surface of those words. I still don't know how the unbinding happens, how the fragmented and trapped souls bound to their silver prisons can be returned to life and body.

Maybe Nate—Nahteran—can help, I think wildly. But I don't ask him, not yet. There are so many questions fighting to be asked, and through it all, something inside tells me I need to tread lightly.

"It was him," he says, his voice very soft and impossible to read. "The Silver Prince brought me back."

"And you've been in Byrn all this time?" I ask, trying to fit the time-line together. "But then how are you here . . ." I wave my hands around, vaguely indicating this room, this castle, this world.

Then something Mom used to say all the time floats into my head. *Use your words, Maddie.*

"I mean, I know Solarians can go anywhere," I rush to amend. "But why are you in Fiordenkill? Why didn't you tell me or Mom? She's in jail. Dad and Marla have been taking care of me since that night . . ."

Nahteran cracks a tired smile, throwing one leg over the arm of the chair, and my heart aches for the familiarity of it. For all these strange clothes and stranger surroundings, he's the same kid I remember on the couch in our old living room, biting his lip in concentration— just like Mom used to do when she was focusing on something—as he steered a video game go-cart around a sharp bend. But then the levity evaporates from his face, and his gaze goes distant.

"I remember someone breaking into our house that night," he says, eyes fixed somewhere beyond me.

I suppress a shiver, wondering if that horrible night is as cemented in his head as it is in mine. I hope not. It stained my life for the next ten years, a black shadow reaching its fingers into everything that came after, and I wasn't even the one screaming.

"But nothing after that," he goes on. "Not until I woke up, and I was in Oasis. So my soul must have been—trapped until Cadius traded the silver to the Prince. The Silver Prince was the one who told me what happened. He told me everything. I did the rest of my growing up there, I guess."

There's no animosity in his voice. There's nothing at all. The words are almost robotic, or like someone reading a story they remember from long ago, but don't feel any particular way about. It makes me uncomfortable. I've been carrying so much rage at the soul traders, at the Silver Prince, at everything. I want Nahteran to reflect it back to me. But he doesn't. I can't tell what he's feeling at all.

"Why did the Silver Prince bring you back to Fiordenkill?" I ask. More and more of the puzzle pieces are coming into view, but they don't make sense together. The edges aren't lining up. "I mean, from what I've seen of the soul trade, it's silver Cadius wants." I can't help but shudder, verbalizing it. "It's magic and power the Silver Prince wants."

Nahteran nods, and finally a bit of anger shows itself in the edge of his voice, kindles in his eyes. "That's true, most of the time," he says. He looks down at his hands. "I guess the Silver Prince saw more value in a ward who could shapeshift and travel across the worlds. I'm here on his behalf now."

My stomach clenches. "To do what?"

"To trade Byrn jewels for healing magic." Nate grins, though it doesn't reach his eyes. "At least, as far as Winterkill knows. So . . ." He sketches out a map with his right index finger on his left palm, a slight, idle smile curving his mouth. "Cadius thinks I'm Byrnisian. The other nobles think I'm Fiorden, and only the Silver Prince knows I'm Solarian."

Suddenly, his face changes right in front of me. His features elongate and sharpen into more Fiorden characteristics for a moment, before fading back to normal.

It's eerie, and I feel myself shiver. I'm glad to see him joking, but I can't get over the familiarity he seems to have with the Silver Prince. "The Prince tried to kill me. Several times."

"I know." Nahteran raises his eyes to meet mine. "I'm glad he failed. And I'm sorry I didn't tell you everything before. I couldn't." He takes a deep breath. "If the Silver Prince found out, it would have been dangerous for all of us. When he tried to take over Havenfall, he didn't tell me what he was doing until after you sent him back to Oasis with his tail between his legs."

Nahteran trails off into a harsh, bitter laugh, then goes on. "Information with the Silver Prince is dispensed on a need-to-know basis. And even if he had told me, I couldn't afford to let on that we're related. He would have used us against each other."

My brother's voice is even, calm, and that makes my feelings surge higher inside me, so tangled together I can't identify how I feel except *bad*. Wrong.

I don't know what I want him to say, but once I explained what the black market log meant, that his soul had traded hands to the Silver Prince like a pretty coin, I thought Nahteran would be angry. Furious. Anyone would. But he doesn't seem to be. I'm glad the Silver Prince brought Nahteran back—of course I am. But I can't help wishing he was just a little angrier.

Then I remember something important. "Oh." The sound escapes my lips unconsciously, as if my thoughts are overflowing my mind, spilling out. There are too many things to ask, too many things to tell. "Nahteran, I met . . . I met Taya. Your sister, Taya."

Nahteran goes very still at the sound of her name. Confusion and uncertainty steal their way across his face like shadows. "Taya."

I nod. "Do you remember her?"

His voice, when it comes, is quiet. "I do."

I've been avoiding thinking about Taya since the horror of her vanishing. It's too painful to remember everything that might have been, everything I did wrong. Too painful not knowing if she was okay, and worst of all, being utterly helpless to do anything about it, with the Solarian door sealed closed and no way to open it.

But I have to tell Nahteran about Taya. About all of it. Not telling him would be lying—worse than lying. I have to tell him, even if it's confusing and convoluted. Even if it hurts.

So I do. Everything from the moment we met—when she almost ran me over on the road up to Havenfall—to finding out she was a Solarian, our fight with the Silver Prince, and how she saved Havenfall by threatening to break the Solarian door open, disrupting the balance and letting the inn tumble down, turning the Prince's plans to rubble. How afterward, she vanished through the same door and how I don't know if she meant to or not. Everything except for the fact that I had a massive crush on her that hasn't quite gone away. That would just be too weird, on a lot of levels.

When the story is over, we sit in silence for a while. I don't want to cry in front of Nahteran, so I call on one of Dad's oldest lessons and try to focus on the positive. Taya could possibly be just fine in Solaria—that's her world, after all. And Nahteran is here. I found him. Nahteran is here, and he's whole. He's himself. He's sitting across from me just like old times. Probably more than a little traumatized, but not divided, not cast into an earring or an ashtray or . . . jacks.

My mouth goes dry and my hand shoots up, grasping at my throat for the necklace I've always worn. The silver jack on its silver chain. I unclasp it with unsteady fingers.

"Do you know what this is?" I ask, holding it out to him. It dances on its chain as my hands shake.

Nahteran's face goes very still and pale as he reaches out for it. As I drop it into his palm, I tear through my memories, trying to remember where I got this necklace. I've worn it ever since I could remember, as a memento of my brother. But who gave it to me? When?

Marcus. A memory swims to the surface, so soft and hazy I'm not sure if it's real. Marcus's jeep in the parking lot of Sterling Correctional. My uncle twisting to look at me in the back seat, his face racked with grief, tear tracks shining on his cheeks. Holding something small and shiny out to me.

Nahteran looks just as uncertain as me. "The Silver Prince always said . . ." My brother stops, clears his throat, and goes on. "The Silver Prince told me that he hadn't been able to find all the silver Cadius attached my soul to. That some pieces were missing."

"Marcus was looking for soul-silver," I whisper, feeling like I'm starting to fit this puzzle together. "For years. He pretended to work with the traders to bring the silver objects back to Havenfall. I wonder . . ."

My voice dries up, and I trail off. I don't want to finish that sentence, don't want to think about it. How broken Marcus must have felt if he found just one tiny piece of Nate's soul. Not enough to bring him back, but nothing he could ever let go of, not ever.

"How do you get it back?" I ask, gesturing at the jack with a still slightly unsteady hand. "The pieces of your soul, I mean . . ."

Nahteran looks far away. He is very still with the jack in his hand, still as a statue. "I don't know," he says. "But I think I'd need another Solarian to help." He holds the jack necklace back out to me.

"It's yours," I say.

He shakes his head. "I can't break the enchantment right now anyway. You hold on to it for now."

I blink, confused, but I don't want to argue with him about this. So I accept the necklace and fasten it around my throat. It feels familiar where it falls against my collarbone. Comforting.

"I'm sorry," I whisper, feeling suddenly unbearably sad. "Sorry for everything."

Nahteran shrugs. "It wasn't your fault."

I bite my lip. I've spent ten years struggling toward understanding just that, but it still feels wrong now. Like I should have done more.

"It hasn't been all bad," he continues. "The Silver Prince is a monster, but he took me under his wing, weirdly enough. And being under his wing—that helps me with my own goals. It's why Cadius lets me stay here, why I have access to anywhere at all. I'm the liaison to the Silver Prince in places where he can't go himself."

"And what are your goals?" I force my hands to be still, to stop fidgeting with the jacket. "You told me your official business. So what's your unofficial business? And what about the Prince?"

"My business is the same as yours, I bet." His smile kindles back to life. "To stop the soul trade."

"And the Prince's?" I press.

Nahteran hesitates for a second. "This is a place of trade," he says at length, glancing at the door, like he wants to check that we're still alone. "There are many things the Silver Prince wants. My job is to get them for him—"

That's the moment when my walkie-talkie crackles to life. My heart speeds up, and all my muscles snap to attention.

Nahteran looks down at the noise, looking confused as I dig the device out from under my cloak and press the button to listen. Graylin's voice, staticky and muffled, issues from the receiver.

"Maddie, come to the vault. We've found it."

14

"GRAYLIN?" I STAB AT THE walkie-talkie with my finger while Nahteran stands up, silent, with quizzical eyes. "Graylin, what vault? Where are you?"

But only another burst of static answers me. I wait, my heart in my throat, but there's nothing further. The device falls silent. For a long moment, Nahteran and I stand there in the silence. My body trembles, on alert.

We found it.

"What is it you're looking for?" Nahteran asks quietly.

"A suit of armor." The words spill from my mouth, as if expelled by the growing bubble of panic taking up residence in my chest. "A suit of armor made of phoenix flame. It's a metal that creates—creates tears, holes—"

I'm not explaining this well at all. I pull up my sleeve, showing the gauntlet, its gold pattern shimmering against my skin. "It lets people travel between the worlds, the Realms, but it damages the barrier. We think that's how Cadius has been getting souls in and out of Winter-kill. It's Mom's actually. She and Cadius have a past."

Nahteran's eyes widen as he looks at the gauntlet, seeming to process this new information. Then he raises his eyes to mine. "I know where the vault is."

My breath catches. "Really?"

"I think so. At least, I know the general direction."

Nahteran straightens his jacket and strides toward the door, suddenly all movement and purpose. I slip out after him, keeping pace with three steps for every two of his.

My head is spinning. Just a few minutes ago, I was holding the trade records in my hands, starting to put together who S.P. was. I was positive that my brother really was lost, that after everything, ten years of numbness and a few weeks of wild hope, I would never see him again. But now he's walking ahead of me, moving with a purpose and a certainty that I've scarcely seen, even in adults. For the first time I notice the slender, leather-sheathed sword hanging from his waist.

The party is raging on, everyone seeming louder and drunker and more awful than they did when we arrived. I'm not sure if it's because of the night wearing on or because my brain has overloaded its processing capacity. But even staggering, yelling, howling with laughter, the guests draw back to make way for Nahteran. He cuts through the crowd like a knife, and I follow, keeping one hand on the walkie-talkie.

Ever since I entered Cadius's office, I've scarcely spared a thought for Brekken or Graylin, even though we were supposed to stay together. Everything else flew out of my mind when I read my brother's name, and then saw the real him. I hope they're okay. I hope . . .

Nahteran leads us down to the lower levels of the estate, whereas earlier Brekken and Cadius had led me up. Here the ornamentation in the halls doesn't just get simpler, it disappears entirely. The light too. The oil lamps get fewer and farther between and then cease altogether. I move up beside Nahteran and pull out a flashlight, another of the useful things Marcus made us pack. It's too dark to see Nahteran's face, but he makes a surprised noise, almost a laugh.

"What is it?" I whisper, my frayed nerves making every stray sound and movement feel ten times more conspicuous than it probably is.

"I haven't seen one of those in so long," Nahteran says. "Can I hold it?"

The simple wonder at such a mundane object makes a quick shot of pain jolt through my heart. Wordlessly, I pass the flashlight over to him. I want to ask him so many things—what he missed most about our world, about us—but now isn't the time.

"Where is everyone?" I ask, making sure to keep my voice to a whisper, as the hall narrows on either side of us. "It seems like Winterkill should have guards everywhere."

"It does seem that way, doesn't it?" Nahteran laughs again, but this time it's a cold, sharp sound, empty of humor. "But no. It's been like this every time I've come here. Cadius is careless, but it says more about this world than about him, doesn't it?"

I look up toward my brother, wishing I could make out his expression. Fiorden eyes can see in the dark, probably, but all I can make out is the vague shape of Nahteran beside me, and the circle of dirty stone floor ahead of us illuminated with the flashlight.

"What do you mean? I'm not following."

"Cadius doesn't feel threatened," Nahteran says. "All these guests coming through the doors, the fact that almost anyone could get in—Cadius allows that because he doesn't feel there's a risk to his enterprise. And he's right, there isn't."

As the anger grows in Nahteran's voice, so too does his Oasis accent, I note with unease. The way he phrases things, the calm that prevails no matter what he's talking about—it's hard to put my finger on why, but it all reminds me of the Silver Prince.

"No one cares," Nahteran says, the end of the last word escaping in a hiss through his teeth. "No one will stop him. They all know about the soul trade, and they let it continue because of the profit it brings them."

My blood quickens to finally, finally feel my rage echoed in another. I know Marcus hates the soul trade, as does Graylin and the Heiress, and everyone I know working to stop it. Yet . . . maybe it's because they've been fighting the fight for so long, but sometimes it feels like their anger is blunted. Logically, I know it makes sense to take steps to protect Havenfall from the Silver Prince before going off to chase the traders. Isolated as we are on our mountaintop, we can't help anyone if the Silver Prince overruns us. But the thought of doing nothing while people are suffering still rankles. Especially once I knew one of them might be my brother. Nate. Nahteran.

"We'll finish it," I promise him. "You and I."

It's still dark, but I think I catch the flash of teeth as he smiles.

Soon, though, the quiet dissipates into a distant, muted clatter of shouts and clangs. It's the sound of a fight. My heart leaps into my throat, and I quicken my steps, breaking into a half run, Nahteran at my heels.

"*Left*," he hisses at a fork in the hallway, and I veer left.

The flashlight beam bobs and jerks erratically in Nahteran's hand, and I can hardly see. I think the hallway is narrowing, but I don't care. The faint noise gets louder and louder until I spot a rectangle of murky grayish-blue light, an open door, ahead.

I run faster, but just as I'm about to hurtle over the threshold, Nahteran grabs me across the waist, stopping me short. I wheeze, the wind knocked out of me, confused and indignant until my eyes adjust to the light and I see what's ahead of me. A thin wooden railing, just a couple of feet past the door, not sturdy and magnificent like everything else here, but spindly, studded with rough wood planks sharpened to points at the top.

Beyond that—a drop-off. A drop-off I surely would have gone over if Nahteran hadn't caught me.

He lets me go, and I fill my lungs and step forward, more cautious now. The light in here is strange, not gas lamps and torches like upstairs, but not natural either. It's pale and diffuse. I can't tell where it's coming from. But more important is what it reveals.

We've emerged into one of the middle levels of a great, cylindrical room. Unlike the tawdry opulence upstairs, the walls here are built of rough-hewn bricks of dark stone, fitted roughly together with some kind of concrete that swells from the cracks. It stretches far up above our heads, and down even farther. It's ringed with narrow, precariously constructed walkways of wooden planks, like the one Nahteran and I are standing on now, dividing the space into circular levels. And every floor is lined with openings, panopticon-style. Doorways. Some of which have doors—some which have nothing at all, just holes full of darkness—and some which have silver objects spilling out of them as from the mouth of a dragon's cave, magic hoards gleaming strangely in the unnatural light.

The noise is coming from the ground level, where maybe a dozen people—it's too dim and far away to make out more details—are fighting. They are crammed too close together to discern between the groups of foes, but I hear Graylin's voice floating up and Brekken's. My heart clenches. Before I can think, I'm running, circling the walkway until I find a rickety staircase. Nahteran behind me, I run as fast as I can without tumbling down.

Outnumbered, is all I can think. *They're outnumbered.*

On the ground floor, Brekken and Graylin are fighting with their backs to a strange stone pillar in the center of the room. Or rather—Brekken is fighting, his sword weaving a net of silver lightning that holds off the three Winterkill guards; while Graylin runs his hands frantically over the pillar, as if searching for something on its surface. It's maybe fifteen feet tall, with a pointed top, almost like an obelisk. It's carved of a darker stone than the floor around it, too dark to see anything that might be inscribed on its sides. What is Graylin doing?

I see Brekken notice me in the midst of his fight—notice both Nahteran and me. Brekken's eyes go wide, and his head jerks marginally toward us. But he doesn't stop fighting for a second. Not even as Nahteran steps in front of me, drawing his sword and dispatching one of the guards with one fluid motion. The Fiorden man in his green coat yelps sharply and hits the ground with limbs askew.

For a moment, I can't move. I scarcely even saw Nahteran draw his sword. And in the seconds that follow, the tables turned, Brekken's sword crosses the throat of the second guard. The third turns and runs, vanishing through one of the dark doorways that encircle the room. Nahteran takes a step after him, but then stops and pivots toward the pillar, toward Graylin.

I'm dizzy and torn between two thoughts: numb disbelief that two people are dead on the floor who were alive twenty seconds ago. And *damn, I need to learn how to fight.*

"Who are you?" Brekken calls out.

I look up, confused. It takes me a moment to understand he's talking to Nahteran. Brekken's sword is down at his side, but still held tight. His face confused. He looks between me and my brother. Graylin has turned around too. All eyes are on Nahteran.

I walk toward them, stepping carefully over the black puddles of blood on the ground, trying to figure out what to say, how to explain, but my brother beats me to it.

"My name is Nahteran." He steps forward to Brekken, his bloodied sword loose at his side, right hand extended.

Graylin's mouth drops open and Brekken's eyes widen.

It's clear Brekken remembers the name. He was the one who first figured out that Taya's Terran was my Nate. Brekken looks at me for confirmation, and I nod.

"Well." Brekken's voice is uncertain, but he steps forward and shakes Nahteran's hand. "I'm Brekken."

"A pleasure to meet you." Nahteran's voice is even, placid, like he didn't just run across a castle and take down a trained guard.

By contrast, standing in the shadows, I feel as though I can't get my heartbeat under control. Like it might bust out of my chest. I try to tell it that the danger has passed, but no dice.

Then Nahteran turns to Graylin, and I see the surprise and recognition spread over Nahteran's face again, same as when he saw me.

"Do you remember me?" Graylin asks softly.

Nahteran nods, lips parting like he's trying to think of something to say. He drifts toward Graylin. A smile breaks across Graylin's face, and his arms rise slightly, ready for the hug. But Nahteran doesn't go in for it. Instead, he produces something from inside his cloak. A small, flat golden object, strangely shaped, like a many-pointed star.

"This might help," he says, pointing at the pillar. "With that."

Graylin takes the star, and for a second he looks as confused as I feel. Then comprehension clicks in. He turns and paces around the pillar, stopping on the far side, and fits the star into what seems to be an indentation in the stone. I realize—it's an oddly shaped key.

I glance at him, confused. He didn't make it sound like he'd been to the vault before, just that he knew about where it was.

"What is that? Where did you get it?" I demand.

Nahteran seems not to hear me, but before I can repeat the question, a ponderous creak splits the room's silence. Then a deep, muffled crack. The stone pillar shudders and cleaves in two. I can see light through the middle of it. For a moment, the halves of the pillar stay upright . . . then they crash to the ground with a thud that makes my ears ring.

There in the nothingness where they stood, something shines.

At first, I think it's a body, or a skeleton. There are arms and legs and a torso, elegant gold lines I can't make sense of, like a rib cage dipped in gold. Then I realize with a shock.

Armor.

It's not a knight's full-coverage suit of armor, more like a series of curved golden ribs held together by gold chains. The corset is shaped like a person's torso, and there's one gauntlet that matches the one I'm wearing now. Suddenly, I realize something else. It *glows*. The light all around us seems to brighten. Somehow the armor had been lighting the room, even encased by stone; and now that it's been freed, the phoenix flame shines even brighter.

The armor sits on a wooden stand almost as high as the pillar. Almost too high to reach, but Graylin is able to unhook it with a sword. His eyes are wide. Everyone is silent.

It's clear that the armor holds power; I can feel it in the air. If we're right, this is how Cadius has been creating openings between the worlds.

I expect something to happen when he lifts it down. Like the sand cave in the movie *Aladdin*, collapsing around him as soon as he took the magic lamp. But nothing happens. The room is utterly still—just we four, the armor, and Winterkill's guards, who will never draw blades again.

Graylin uses his sword to set the armor down carefully, separating the pieces. He unzips one of the duffel bags we brought. I'd been so focused on finding the armor, I didn't think about how we'd get it out of the castle. Luckily, Graylin did.

Then I feel something beneath my feet. Something so subtle, I probably wouldn't have known had I not grown up at Havenfall, eager for every speck and thread of magic, attuned to anything out of the ordinary. I've felt this before, and I know I'm not imagining it. The floor is ever so slightly trembling.

I look down, instinctive fear making my mouth dry. We've already gone so far down below the main floor of the estate, I wouldn't have thought there could be anything else beneath us. But the tremor is growing, like something enormous far beneath us is clawing its way up. In the bright light from the armor, the floor is more visible. I can see the scratched and weathered flagstones, the Winterkill guards' blood collecting in the cracks.

Then the floor shimmers. Like water after a single stone is dropped in. I back to the wall, looking up to see that Graylin and Brekken have done the same. Only Nahteran has stayed where he is, gazing down at the armor.

"Nahteran!" I call.

His eyes snap over to meet mine, wide and a little wild. I point at the floor, which is now undeniably shifting and rippling. But he doesn't move.

"A doorway is opening," he says quietly. He looks at me and beckons. "Come here."

I follow his gaze to a pool of darkness spreading out from the armor like spilled ink. A yawning stretch of darkness. A darkness that doesn't make sense. The faint scary compulsion I always feel at the edge of cliffs, to step forward and see if I'll fly or fall.

I've always ignored that sensation. Obviously. But now it's like something has taken over my body. I step forward, feeling hypnotized, fully expecting the strange, transparent, shimmering ground to give way beneath my feet. I am unable to stop.

I flinch when I put my foot down. I don't fall, but it's like stepping onto the back of some great living thing. It gives slightly under my feet and shifts and trembles, making me stagger. But I manage to get to Nahteran's side.

"The gauntlet," he yells.

A deep, roaring rumble is rising up from below our feet. Brekken and Graylin are fighting their way forward, but the floor is heaving too much now for them to get close. The whole circle of the floor is pitching like a ship in a storm, with Nahteran, me, and the armor on an island of relative stillness in the center of it.

Nahteran reaches for my hand, his fingers moving toward the gauntlet's buckle over my wrist. He looks up at me, like he's asking for permission. Behind me Brekken shouts something, but I don't listen. He's my brother. I trust him. I look Nahteran in the eyes and nod.

He smiles faintly and unbuckles the gauntlet with brisk fingers, lifting it off my arm.

Dizziness descends right away, dizziness and lightheadedness and a deep, deep cold. I grab Nahteran's arm for support, trying to focus as he lays the gauntlet beside the rest of the armor, a shining pile of gold. But then Nahteran grabs my arm and pulls it out in front of me.

"Hold still," he says.

Utterly confused, I try to tug away, but he's too strong. There's the flash of a knife and a stinging, shallow pain across my arm. I yelp as Nahteran drops my arm and drops of blood—my blood—spatter the floor.

Everything intensifies. The floor's rolling turns into writhing. The rumble in the air turns to howling. A seam of golden fire rips open across the floor and then spiderwebs into a hundred glowing fractals, the edges peeling back like burned paper to reveal—

Upside-down mountains. The dead bodies of the Fiorden guards sink down into it, vanishing into the upside-down scene as if into quicksand.

Mountains swim into focus and the star-strewn sky beyond that, the moon swimming indistinct like a quarter at the bottom of a well.

The vault groans dangerously around us, like some giant living creature. The blackness of the floor shreds and burns away, then grows back again, like Fiordenkill itself is fighting to heal the wound in its surface. But it stays open around the suit of armor. I remember what Graylin called it. The wound in the world.

The sound of crackling flames intensifies; more of the black floor peels away to show more of the Colorado mountains. I catch the barest scent of mountain air—faint, but so familiar to me I would know it anywhere—and goose bumps erupt along my whole body.

Across from me, Nahteran has gathered the phoenix flame armor and the duffel bag. "Go," he shouts, jerking his chin down toward the inverted mountains. "Go!"

"What are you doing?" I step toward him, swaying on my feet.

The sight of the mountains beneath my feet is making me dizzier. It hurts to breathe. I reach out my arms for the armor. Adrenaline and dizziness clamor for my attention, screaming at me to run, but I cling to the mission we came here with. We're long past the time for secrecy, but the armor—that's the key—that's how we can stop the soul trade. I don't want to leave Winterkill, leave Fiordenkill, without it in my hands.

"Nate, please!" I yell, the nickname slipping out. "Mom left me that gauntlet!"

At that, for the first time since I found him, the expression of calm focus on Nahteran's face slips. Behind it is an anger that makes my heart freeze. He blinks, and when he opens his eyes, they're colder than all the ice and snow in Fiordenkill. Nahteran backs away from me. He's holding the armor, and the ground beneath his feet is still, while I am pulled down . . . down . . . down. I'm weightless, I'm trapped.

Brekken struggles through the softening stone and throws himself toward Nahteran, reaching for the armor. But Nahteran spins out of his grasp, easy and deliberate like a dancer.

My heart goes cold. I stare after Nahteran. Pure desperation pumps the blood through my veins and pushes the cry from my lips.

"Whatever you're doing, we can do it together," I yell, my voice scraping my throat. "You don't have to go back to the Silver Prince. We can help you!"

I don't want to lose you again, I think.

Nahteran turns and runs. Past Graylin and Brekken, who are trapped in the opening just like me, clawing toward me through empty space. Nahteran has the armor and he's running away. He's not coming with us. He's not coming home.

My waist slips through. My chest. I can feel a warm breeze on my legs.

I scream for my brother one more time before I'm sucked down into the stars.

15

THE FAMILIAR SMELL OF THE mountain and a warm summer breeze wrap around me, and for a moment that seems to last forever that's all there is. I can't see Brekken. I can't see anyone. There's nothing around me but air and stars.

Then I hit the ground hard onto rough, spiky grass and gravel. I roll to a stop on the hillside, pain shooting through my bones. I slowly push myself into a sitting position, head spinning and body aching. Looking around, I can tell we're in the mountains in Haven, on Earth, a landscape that feels familiar but which I don't immediately recognize. It's night and the moon is overhead among stars. We're high up, and the air is thin and cold, the kind you have to draw deep to get enough oxygen. And yet, I feel a sense of strength and wellness rising in me, from where my legs touch the ground on up. The air goes to my head like wine.

My vision is still a bit blurry, but I see someone lying a few yards away from me, facing away. I see a hand, stretched out against the damp grass, a wrist turned at a painful angle. My heart in my throat, I crawl over and reach out, touching a shoulder—but the person is cold beneath the green wool coat. And then it hits me—he's one of the Winterkill soldiers who Nahteran killed. I rear back, fighting down nausea.

Stumbling to my feet, I go as fast as I can—which isn't very fast—in the opposite direction. Looking around wildly, I see Brekken and Graylin uphill, and the relief that fills me is immense. The other guard's body is a little ways down the mountain. I avert my eyes.

Nahteran is nowhere to be seen. Of course he isn't. He didn't jump. He didn't come with us.

Not knowing what else to do, I climb up to where Graylin is brushing himself off. As I walk, I look around, the landscape starting to make sense and fit onto my mental map. I know these mountains. I look to the west and down the mountain, and there it is—Mirror Lake and Havenfall, tucked between the mountains and wreathed in trees. A few stray lights glitter faintly from its windows.

I exchange a glance with Graylin, hoping to see his regular self-assured smile, to be comforted that he has everything well in hand. That he knows what to do next.

Instead, I see only my own confusion and loss reflected in his face. And I know he's thinking the same thing as I am.

Nahteran betrayed us.

———

Back in my little attic room, back in my own bed, my body aches, and the room spins, no matter how still I lie. It feels like all the foreign-world sickness the gauntlet held at bay is crashing in on me now. I want to sleep for a month. But my mind won't let me rest. I can't get

Nahteran's face out of my head. My left arm stings under the bandage where he cut me. I can't shake the weight off my shoulders, the sensation that I've lost the most important thing of all. For a second I had a glimmer of hope that we could have him back. But now it's just Marcus and Graylin and me again, and our little family unit feels smaller and more fragmented than ever.

I hold the pain at a distance, because I have to. But I know it's there, lurking behind the curtain, ready to crash down on me at any minute. If I look directly at it, if I give the grief too much oxygen, it'll swamp me. It's like I've lost him all over again. Nahteran. Nate. He was happy to see me. He must have missed me. At least I thought so. But clearly not enough.

Even though Havenfall's corridors are quiet and flooded with pale morning sunlight and everyone's still in their rooms, the inn still feels crowded somehow. There's a heavy, unsettling buzz in the air. Once, when I was a kid, Nate explained to me how gas stovetops worked. For a while after that, every time Mom turned on the burner, I was terrified, fearing that she was filling the house up with gas that would explode any minute. That at any given moment we were breathing it in, turning the air, the walls, our bodies into kindling. That's what I feel like now. Like the whole inn is filled with something dangerous and flammable, ready at any second to ignite.

Still, the smell of coffee and pastries is a comfort as I open the unlocked door to Marcus and Graylin's front room. When I go in, Marcus is sitting on the couch, scribbling and crossing things out in a notebook held open on his lap. I know Graylin will have caught him up on what happened at Winterkill, but now we need to figure out what to do next. We hardly flew under the radar like we'd meant to. We lost the armor. We lost Nate. Assuming, that is, that we ever had him to begin with.

Brekken paces by the window. He glances at me with a small smile when I come in, but his eyes slide past mine without really meeting.

My stomach lurches uneasily as I pass him, sensing a cool distance between us. Brekken hardly spoke to me on the walk back to the inn last night. Once we'd both assured each other we were okay, he strode down the mountain toward Havenfall in silence. I chalked it up to him being stunned and exhausted, just like Graylin and I were. But now, I can't seem to catch his eye. What's his deal?

Graylin is at the little table by the kitchenette. Sura sits next to him with a book open between them. Before we went to Fiordenkill, he read aloud to her every morning, hoping to draw her out of her shell. I catch a glimpse of the illustrations—*Bread and Jam for Frances*.

My heart twists a little as I wave hello to them and go over to sit with my uncle. There must be a stash of picture books somewhere in the inn left over from when Nahteran and I were kids.

"Graylin told me what happened at Winterkill," Marcus says as he pours me a cup of coffee. "He told me you saw . . . That boy. Was he really . . ."

Marcus's voice trails off as I sit next to him on the couch. The mixture of suppressed hope and forced casualness in his face is a look I recognize well. I take a deep breath. I don't feel ready to talk about my brother, or even think about him, but I'm not the only one who loved him. I can't keep what I know from Marcus. He's Nahteran's family too.

So I shut off my emotions as best I can and tell him about how I ran into Nahteran in the halls of Winterkill. How he told me about some mysterious agenda the details of which he couldn't share. How after he was kidnapped from Mom's house, the Silver Prince traded Cadius for him and the Silver Prince took him in. How he's the Prince's officer now. And of course how he took the armor and ran.

In the gloom, I tell them all what I've scarcely admitted even to myself. That I'm afraid Nahteran brought the phoenix flame armor to the Silver Prince.

I don't want to believe it's possible. But I can't forget the sharp, sudden anger that kindled in his eyes when I said Mom's name. It makes a terrible kind of sense. After all, I always blamed myself for what happened to my brother. Blamed myself and blamed Mom, if I'm being honest. Why wouldn't he as well?

When I'm done speaking, Marcus looks haggard and haunted. He casts a look over at Graylin, but his husband and Sura are still engrossed in their lesson. I should comfort him, give him a hug or something, but right now it doesn't feel like it would help. Because I have no peace, no comfort to give.

"Nahteran must have a high status in Byrn," Marcus says, sounding troubled. "To be doing this kind of thing for the Silver Prince. Even if it's just a cover story, he must have the Prince's blessing to be in Fiordenkill, otherwise it would get back to Oasis."

I press my nails into my palms. The same thing had occurred to me, and even if Nahteran has a secret life of his own, the thought of him being that beholden to the man who tried to kill me hurts.

"You're sure it was him?" Marcus asks me.

I nod. "I wish I wasn't."

A knock on the door makes us all jump. Marcus gets up, his movements stiff, and cautiously opens the door. Willow stands in the hall. Her face is pale.

"Marcus, Maddie," she says, her gaze shifting from my uncle to me. "I . . . something's happened." She shifts on her feet. "Something you should see."

She crosses the room to Marcus and bends to whisper in his ear.

My heart sinks down into my stomach as I watch the color drain from his face. *We can't catch a break*, I think numbly. What will the next blow be? Where will the mallet fall? Have the delegates found out what we're doing and rioted? Did Cadius find some way to follow us out of Fiordenkill? Has Nahteran already deposited the armor in the hands of the Silver Prince? Are the two of them tearing open a new rift between Oasis and Colorado as we sit here?

Willow finishes whatever it is she's telling Marcus and steps away. For a moment, Marcus is very still; then he reaches to the side table and grabs his laptop. I glance at Willow, confused, but her face gives nothing away. We all drift in closer by mutual agreement, fearful silence thick in the air. Brekken ends up next to me, his arm pressed against mine. I can feel the tension in him.

Marcus pulls a news site up on his laptop and then props it open on the coffee table; we all squeeze onto the couch to watch as the opening music of *Good Morning Colorado* plays. Then an image of Sterling Correctional appears.

SCF. The building I've walked into so many times I could do it in my sleep.

It fills the TV screen, huge against a light gray sky. There's a ragged hole in the brick wall on one side, and smoke pours from it, obscuring the building and making it only an outline, then revealing it again. Dark smoke, thick and strange, moving slower than it seems like smoke is supposed to move.

A headline scrolls at the bottom of the screen in screaming capital letters: EXPLOSION AND BREAKOUT AT STERLING CORRECTIONAL FACILITY.

The shot changes to a young woman reporter standing in the familiar parking lot in front of the building. Behind her, I can see that they've roped off the prison with yellow crime-scene tape, and policemen move around the perimeter. In this wider shot, I can see that the smoke doesn't look normal. It rises into the sky in a slender, dark plume, not dissipating as quickly as it should. The smoke is gray with a greenish tint.

"Good morning, Colorado," the reporter says. "Ella Martinez here at Sterling Correctional Facility, where in the wee hours of the morning an explosion was reported which could be heard for several miles around. Three guards have been taken to the hospital with non-life-threatening injuries, and one prisoner is missing."

Without warning, the scene changes, and my stomach drops and my skin contracts. Mom's face fills the screen. It's a picture they took of her in court a couple of years ago. Her skin is sallow above the tan jumpsuit collar, her hair long and limp, and her strange eyes lightless. She stares out of the TV at us, not afraid, not defiant, not anything, just empty.

Then her picture shrinks to one corner of the screen, and facts pop up on a blue background. Ella Martinez's voice floats brightly over it all.

"Inmate Sylvia Morrow was discovered to be missing soon after the explosion, which took out a chunk of the wall of her cell. She has been an inmate here for ten years following the murder of her young son, Nathan, in 2009."

My eyes burn, and I take a sip of coffee, trying to chase the feeling away. I know, I know that's not true. Obviously Mom didn't kill Nahteran. But it still hurts to hear someone say it, especially in such a dispassionate voice. Especially after what happened in Winterkill, the sudden fury in Nahteran's eyes when I invoked our family.

"Recently, she was put on death row and was scheduled to move to a more secure facility next month," Ella Martinez goes on.

My stomach somehow sinks even further—I didn't know that she was changing prisons, even though I saw her a few days ago. She didn't tell me.

"She is considered a danger to the public, and anyone with information on her whereabouts is asked to call this number . . ."

A phone number pops up on the screen in large red digits, while my mom's face hovers in the corner of the screen. I take a long swallow of coffee, realizing Brekken's eyes are suddenly, for some reason, on me. But now it's my turn to avoid his gaze, feeling the burn of suppressed tears all down my throat, trying to blink away the water brewing behind my eyes.

The camera follows the column of smoke rising from the prison, trailing it up into the gray sky. The smoke doesn't look like anything else on Earth. It looks like magic.

———

Eventually, everyone drifts from the room except for me and my uncle. We stay glued to the news for a while, hanging on the anchor's every word, but no more information seems to be forthcoming. Ten minutes in, my phone starts blowing up with texts and calls from Dad that I don't answer. I silence the phone instead. But the messages glare up at me from the screen.

> Have u seen news?
> U ok????
> Plz call me.

I send a quick text back, not wanting to talk to him or anyone right now with the awful churning in my stomach.

> I saw. I'm okay. Call you in a few?

> Ok. Talk soon!

"The authorities are probably going to want to question us," Marcus says quietly. He looks pale and shell-shocked, his stress curls rising high. He turns to me. "Maybe you and I should go camp out at the condo for a few days, just in case they come looking."

The condo is an empty apartment in a boring one-story complex on the edge of town. It's Marcus's legal address, meant to keep the inn off all official paperwork. It's where he gets his mail and meets up with any visitors he doesn't fully trust. But I've never spent a night there.

"Why?" I hear myself ask. "We don't know anything."

"Just in case . . ."

The unspoken end of the sentence hangs in the air between us. Just in case what? Mom shows up here at Havenfall?

I should be happy. She was sitting on death row for a crime she didn't commit, and now she's out. I should be cheering that she's made a clean break, wherever she is. How or why shouldn't matter. But the image of the smoke on the TV screen sticks in my head. The destruction, the hole in the prison wall. Something isn't adding up. The Mom I know isn't capable of that kind of destruction. She isn't even interested in being free.

"I'm going to go make some calls," Marcus says, and turns to go.

"Marcus," I start, reaching out to snag my uncle's arm.

He turns back with a question on his face.

"You don't know anything about this, do you?" I ask.

I don't know what I want the answer to be. If it's *yes*, it means he's kept more secrets from me, when I thought we were done with secrets. But it also means that at least someone is in charge here. Someone has answers.

"Trust me," he whispers, his eyes drooping. "I wish I did." He doesn't flinch or look hurt. He just looks at me and shakes his head. "No,

Maddie," he says, and his voice is soft but strong. "I won't lie to you again. I promise."

———

Later, I call Dad.

"So," he says, none of the usual warmth in his voice. He just sounds wrung out. "Your mother."

"My mother," I echo because I don't know what else to say. I fidget with my comforter, tracing over the edges of the diamonds cut from Byrnisian silk and Fiorden velvet.

"You were the last person to visit her, the other day," Dad said, sounding wary. "Did she seem any different? Did she say anything strange?"

I shake my head. This, at least, I don't have to fake—I'm as at a loss as he is.

"No, she was . . . the same as ever. You know." I swallow. "Passive. Quiet."

At least when she wasn't lecturing me about my feelings for Brekken, or dropping mysterious hints about Winterkill and the gauntlet.

"What about your uncle? Does he have any ideas?"

"Nope," I say, distracted. "Not in the slightest."

Dad lets out a breath. I can imagine him putting his head in his hands. "Part of me is happy," he says, distant, like he's talking more to himself than to me.

For the first time, it sinks in for me how much turmoil he must be in. He thinks Mom killed Nate—always has. Even though I think Dad never stopped caring about her, it was the only explanation that made sense if you didn't know about monsters from other worlds or black market agents stealing children's souls. When Mom admitted to killing Nate herself—insisted it was the truth—what was Dad supposed to think?

"I didn't want her to die," Dad goes on.

I chew my lip, not sure what he wants me to say, or if I should say anything at all.

"But this doesn't feel right. She was in federal prison. Maximum security. Who was she mixed up with who could have broken her out?"

I swallow and shrug, though he can't see it. "I don't know."

It's not a lie. I might have some ideas. But I'm hoping I'm wrong. I twist the corners of the blanket around my fingers, wishing it could still give me comfort like it did when I was a kid.

"There's nothing either of us can do except wait," Dad says eventually. "So let's just wait. She's got to turn up eventually."

I don't know if I want that to be true. But the pain in Dad's voice gnaws at me. The worry. He doesn't know about the soul trade or the Silver Prince or any of it. For all he knows—for all I know, for that matter—Mom just caught a lucky break somehow. Maybe she's already on her way to Canada or Mexico or somewhere where she can be safe.

But I know Dad doesn't think that's the case. Neither does Marcus. Neither do I.

We can all feel it. Something is very wrong.

16

WITHIN A COUPLE OF HOURS, just as he predicted, Marcus gets a call from the Sterling Police Department, asking to interview both of us. We drive down to the condo to meet them, spending a hasty hour arranging stuff around the apartment to try to make it look lived-in before they arrive.

The interview with the two cops goes about as well as can be expected. Kindly Officer Oh and brusque Officer Sanders treat me like a kid. They don't expect me to know anything. I keep my eyes down and play the part of traumatized kid with a dead brother and murderer mom. It's not hard, as familiar with the role as I am. They only question me for about twenty minutes, but it still leaves me feeling drained and empty. When the front door closes behind them, their last question still echoes around in my head.

Did she have any enemies? they'd asked us, expressions serious. *Does anyone in your family?*

In the ensuing silence, Marcus clears his throat. "Sorry about that."

"It's not your fault."

Sitting in the austere, personality-free living room—decorated more like a hotel room than a gathering place for family—I take a gulp of the coffee he made for the cops. It's lukewarm now. I'm distracted, thinking, as I have been for the past few hours, of Mom's face the last time I saw her. Her expression gave no indication this would happen.

If she was planning an escape, why didn't she let me know, or at least drop some hint so that I didn't lose hope? The more I think about it, the more uneasy I feel. She was a woman ready to die, and she was friendless except for Marcus and me.

Did she have any enemies? Does anyone in your family?

There's the Silver Prince. The soul traders, the Byrnisian man who found me in the basement of Haven's antique shop, who ordered the black market buyer Whit to kill me. And of course there's whoever broke into our house all those years ago to kidnap Nahteran. Mom was a host, a rescuer of captive Solarians, and so she must have made herself a target.

Yes, we have enemies, Mom and Marcus and me.

———

Later, in my room, I get out my laptop and run what feels like a million web searches for Sylvia Morrow, setting a search filter for results from the last three days. Different phrases, tweaks on the same questions. *Sylvia Morrow prisoner. Sterling correctional Colorado jailbreak. Sylvia Morrow associates.*

The hunt for my mom has intensified since the jailbreak. There are articles now from national sites, not just Colorado ones. There are social media posts that I can't bear to look at. I can't deal with the vitriol poured out on Mom. But there are no sightings. No updates. Nothing new.

I want to go out to look for her, maybe tomorrow once the sun rises. I get as far as laying out the supplies on my bedspread: my backpack, my wallet, a dagger Sal gave me to protect myself. But then I realize I don't know where to go.

It's late. I need to get to bed. I still haven't totally recovered from the journey into Fiordenkill, which took a toll on my body. I have no appetite, and I keep thinking I see motion out of the corners of my eyes, when nothing's there. I can't stop the internet search. I know nothing's going to come up that I don't already know. But it's like a compulsion. I can't stop myself from looking anyway, turning over every digital stone. I can't let go of the faint possibility that I could be missing something, that if I just search the right words, refresh the news site one more time, I'll find the key . . .

A knock sounds at my door. One, two, three raps in short succession.

My head shoots up, a jolt of startled adrenaline shooting through my veins. *Mom*, I think immediately. She made it here. She found me.

I sit stock-still for a second, frozen in indecision. What do I do? Do I let her in?

I'm being stupid, I realize. What are the chances Mom has crossed the more than two hundred miles separating Sterling from Haven, waltzed into Havenfall—getting around the law enforcement that must be keeping an eye on the town—and is now knocking at my door?

Shaking my head, I get up and go to the door. But in the instant between turning the knob and opening it, I can't help but take a deep breath. One full of mingled hope and fear.

It isn't my mom on the other side. Of course it isn't.

It's Brekken, looking serious.

A wave of feeling rocks me back on my heels—disappointment that Mom hasn't magicked her way here after all, relief and gladness to see Brekken, and worry about the grave expression on his face. He's wearing jeans and a sweater, which is unusual for him, but his posture is all soldier. I don't think he could slouch if he tried.

"This is new," I say, gesturing to his outfit, trying for lightness.

He flashes a smile at me, but there's a hard look in his eyes. "Can I come in?"

"Of course." I step back.

In the quiet moment that follows, I realize I'm kind of annoyed with him. He knows how complicated and thorny my feelings toward my mom are, but he hasn't offered a word of comfort since we found out about her escape. Nor since Nahteran's betrayal at Winterkill. He said he wants to be with me, but that's two huge blows in less than twenty-four hours, and he hasn't been there for me. Does he think being together is only about making out and fireworks and barn lofts and sweet nothings?

For a moment, I have a flicker of hope that that's what he's here to do now, but the door falls closed behind us and he doesn't make a move toward me. His posture doesn't soften.

I turn around and lean against the door with my arms crossed. "What's up?"

Brekken sweeps my room with a glance, and his eye fastens on the stuff on the bed, zeroing in on the dagger. "What are you planning to do with *that*?" he asks.

"I . . ." I don't know, to be honest. All I know is that it feels awful to be sitting here doing nothing, when Mom is on the run, or worse. "I figured I'd go look around Haven. Check the antique shop maybe. If she was mixed up with the Silver Prince or the soul traders—"

"Do you really think that's a good idea?" Brekken's voice is brittle, and I notice for the first time that he's tense. He doesn't sit or move toward me, just stands by my bed, facing me with his arms at his sides. A military, disciplined pose, not a friend's and definitely not a boyfriend's.

I find myself wishing fiercely that he would just give me a hug. I mean, clearly I need one. That easiness we once had around each other—where did it go?

"She's my mom," I say, making my voice brusque to hide my distress. I scoot past Brekken to pile up the stuff on my bed and set it aside, my back to him.

The thought of his mom, Ilya, floats through my mind. I remember how welcoming she was to us when we went into Fiordenkill . Gorgeous, warm, competent, perfect. Bitterness spikes in me. I don't like it, but I can't suppress it. I know he's not the one I should be angry at. It's just fear making me ready to lash out. Making it worse is the fact that I don't even know why I'm afraid. Wherever Mom is, she's not behind bars, waiting to die. I should be happy.

"Listen, I think her disappearance might be a message," he says, slowly and carefully. "Meant for Marcus, or for you. Think about it. Your mother was off the chessboard. She has no magic and no power. Who would risk exposing themselves to humans to help her escape?"

Brekken's tone gentles a little. He steps toward me. "You and Marcus have the most at stake, and you told me she was a lost cause years ago."

Tears prickle at my eyes. "What are you saying?"

"That maybe someone took her and wants the Innkeepers of Havenfall to know it."

"Someone, like who?"

Brekken pauses, then squares his shoulders. "Like the Silver Prince, for one."

I knew what he was going to say, and yet—my chest tightens at the thought of the Silver Prince, with his cold eyes and vast, calculating mind, getting his hands on my mom. I rock back, and Brekken reaches out and touches my arm lightly, guiding us both down to sit on the edge of the bed.

But— "That's not possible," I say brusquely. "The Silver Prince wouldn't be able to survive in Haven, nor Mom in Oasis."

"There are ways," Brekken snaps. "If your brother hasn't managed to supply him with the armor or more phoenix flame, he could have human lackeys doing his bidding. Or some combination thereof."

I have my mouth open to make a retort, but as Brekken falls silent, I realize I don't have one. I remember in the antique shop where I found Sura, Whit—the human trader who would go on to try to drown me in Mirror Lake—was taking orders from a Byrnisian man I didn't recognize. Even if he's not on Earth himself, the Silver Prince clearly has some way to communicate with his men here. If I were him, I would task the humans with breaking Mom out of Sterling Correctional, and then bring her to the town of Haven. Not to the inn itself, but into the sphere of safety for Realmspeople it provides, so that Byrnisians could take her from there.

Maybe that's why I felt so driven to look for her in town, I realize with a slow, dawning horror. Maybe Brekken is right—the Silver Prince has Mom—and my subconscious was just the first part of me to realize it.

"Clearly I only know as much as you do," Brekken goes on. "I'm just saying it's a possibility. And if someone does have her in Haven, I don't think you should be running around town alone, on a whim."

I take a deep breath. "What am I supposed to do, then? Just sit here and do nothing?"

"It's not nothing." Brekken's voice drops; he leans ever so slightly closer to me. "Marcus still isn't well, Maddie, you know that. You have a duty to the inn."

The words feel like a precious necklace and a heavy chain, all at once. "Do you really believe that?" I ask. "Or are you just trying to protect me?"

"Why not both?" His hand slips across the space between us and wraps around mine. "You have a duty to keep yourself safe. For Havenfall. Are you really not at all concerned that the ruler of an entire world wants you dead?"

"Of course I'm worried about it." I glare at him. "But I can't just hide out in some bunker somewhere and wait for the Silver Prince to forget about me."

Brekken raises his hands in surrender. "You're right. I'm sorry. Of course you have to go. But can I come with you into town?" He gets up, paces, and grins ruefully at me. "You know how I hate feeling useless. Just . . . I'm scared for you."

"Sure, come with."

The thought of spending time with him doesn't make me as happy as it normally would. I look away from him so he won't see the truth in my eyes.

I'm scared for me too.

The next morning, I shoot Marcus a text, letting him know I'm going out for some air and Brekken will be with me. Then we head downstairs and out onto the sweeping front lawn.

It's a gorgeous day, at odds with the gray storm of worry and resentment churning inside me. The sky is an almost shocking August blue, and underneath it the mountains gleam like carved emeralds. A slight cool breeze stirs the pines, and the gardens spill over with exuberant bushes and flowers and trees, the last hurrah of summer before fall sets in. Delegates, in between meetings, stroll through the gardens, chatting and laughing. But then, I hear something odd. I hear the sound of an engine and tires crunching over gravel.

I look up. An old tan Toyota Corolla is trundling up the drive, slow and cautious around the bends. I freeze. We aren't expecting any guests. No one should be coming this way.

Brekken is tense beside me, his hand hovering near his waist. Together, we watch the car get closer and closer. When it's close enough to see the faces of the two people inside, shock jolts through me, tearing a gasp from my lips.

It's Taya.

And in the passenger seat . . . Nahteran.

———

My body goes on autopilot, carrying me down the slope toward them. The small part of my brain that isn't frozen by shock knows our new arrivals shouldn't be seen by the delegates in the garden. I walk down the middle of the road toward Mirror Lake. I don't know where Brekken went. Maybe to get Marcus, or distract the delegates. I know he said something to me before I started down this hill, but I can't remember what. My ears are ringing.

Taya sees me and stops. We're still, frozen halfway between Mirror Lake and Havenfall. Through the dirty windshield, I can see that her eyes are wide, her hands rigid on the wheel. She puts the car in park, right there in the middle of the road, and gets out, leaving the door open behind her.

She's cut her hair. It falls loose around her shoulders now, not long and braided the way she always wore it before. She's wearing a strange top, made out of one looping piece of cream-colored fabric, like something out of *Star Wars*, and skinny jeans and the same Docs she always had. She looks good, healthy. Her eyes are bright and the color is high in her cheeks. I take in all these details at once, trying to wrap my mind around how this can be possible. How she can be here. Here at Havenfall. Here on Earth.

She runs toward me and throws her arms around me.

I can't move. I can't make myself move. But I *feel*. I feel everything, a library of sensations compressed into a single instant. I feel her weight against me and the warmth of her, her hair brushing my cheek. Her smell is a mix of both the lavender shampoo that I remember and something else, something other, a spicy, flowery scent that I can't place but I think maybe I've caught before in the tunnels around the doorways. I've spent so long shoving away every thought of her, every memory, every wish, and in the space of thirty seconds she's cracked it all open.

Taya.

But the sound of the car door opening and shutting again makes my spine stiffen. We're not alone out here. I extricate myself from Taya and step back, looking at her open face and huge eyes once more before turning to the sound. To Nahteran, walking toward us.

In contrast to Taya, he looks nervous, uncertain. He wears jeans and a long-sleeved T-shirt, and his steps toward me are slow, measured. It's so quiet that even though he's yards away, I hear it when he takes a deep breath.

"Maddie—"

"Stop."

The command issues from behind me, up the slope toward the inn. It's cold and deadly; Brekken's voice.

I turn around. My heart is pounding so hard it hurts, like a tetherball being slammed around by so many different emotions: joy, fear, fury. I squint against the late morning sun. Brekken is standing a few yards up, his sword out and gleaming.

Behind him, Marcus and Sal have somehow already caught wind of what's happening and come out onto the drive. They rush down the hill to catch up.

I finally manage to find my voice again. "What are you doing here?" I croak. I'm not sure who I'm talking to—maybe everyone—but Taya is the only one close enough to hear me, only an arm's length away still.

She stares at me, blinking. "Terran—Nahteran—he . . ."

"I'm sorry." Nahteran's voice takes over when Taya's fades out. He half turns so he's facing me and Brekken and Marcus and Sal, and pitches his voice to carry. "I'm sorry. For showing up here unannounced, and for the rest of it."

"You betrayed us," Brekken says.

I've never heard his voice like this, colder than ice and sharper than an arctic wind. I've never seen him like this, absolutely still and coiled like a snake set to strike. It's scarier than watching him fight the Silver Prince's guards and the guards in Winterkill. It's one thing to know someone is a soldier and another to see that side take over. In this moment, Brekken seems like a stranger, the gentle boy I love so much gone and someone else stepped into his skin.

"You used us to get to the phoenix flame armor, and you stole it."

Nahteran doesn't argue. "I did."

Silence covers us all, deep and dense despite the normal summer sounds, the chirping of birds and the buzzing of insects in the trees. Those sounds feel muffled, distant. Someone might have dropped a globe over the six of us.

Then Taya pivots and quietly heads back toward the car. My heart plummets, and I want to run after her, but I don't dare move when there are weapons drawn. I don't want Nahteran to get hurt, regardless of what he's done or not done, yet we feel balanced on a knife's edge.

But Taya doesn't leave. Instead she opens the door to the back seat and leans in to retrieve something. When she comes out, the silence seems to deepen even further. She has the chest piece of the phoenix flame armor in one hand, a backpack in the other, inside which I can see the two gauntlets glittering.

He didn't give it to the Silver Prince.

"Nahteran found me," Taya says, and though everyone is looking at us, her eyes are on me. She's speaking to me alone. "Maddie, he used the armor to come find me in Solaria."

He found Taya. A profound relief fills me as her words sink in. Nahteran didn't betray us. He stole the armor, but not out of malice. Not to give it to the Silver Prince. He stole it to do what I couldn't find a way to do. He found Taya. He brought her back.

But . . .

Taya's expression isn't right. Her eyes are fixed downward on the armor—careful not to let the pieces touch. Her shoulders tense, and her mouth is pressed in a flat line. She looks like she's dreading something. And even though I wish Brekken would put his damn sword away, I know there's something I'm missing. With a jolt of queasy unease, I remember those last moments in Winterkill's fortress. How when Nahteran took Mom's gauntlet from me and joined it with the rest of the armor, that's when he was able to open the door using my blood.

"What else?" I blurt out.

Everyone looks at me in confusion. I go over to Taya. The gravel crunching under my feet feels ten times heavier than normal, like her dread is contagious. As I approach, she holds the armor out for me to take, but I don't want that. I want to tilt her face up to the light, to look into her eyes and understand.

"What is it? What's wrong?"

Taya doesn't speak. She just looks over at Nahteran, and he's the one who answers.

"I just got a message from the Silver Prince," he says, slowly and quietly, like each word is painful to get out. "Maddie . . . he has Mom."

17

EVERYTHING BECOMES KIND OF A blur for a while. Later, I'll remember standing out on the road, all of us frozen with horror while Mirror Lake glitters serenely in the background. I'll remember sitting with Nahteran and Taya and Marcus and Graylin in Marcus's office, listening to Nahteran explain, while Brekken and Sal guard the door.

But I'll recall nothing of the in-between, except for Brekken pulling me aside for a second before we all went downstairs. Whispering to me.

Maddie, don't trust him.

Now, we've all pulled up chairs around Marcus's big oak desk. My brother—can I still call him that?—insisted on a private place to show us the Silver Prince's message.

It stings. All of it. Nahteran came back, didn't he? But why didn't he tell us what he was going to do? Why make us think he betrayed us? And why do I want to trust him now, even after what's happened?

While all of this is running through my head, another drama is silently unfolding at the table. Taya and Marcus seem to be subtly sizing each other up. Taya and Marcus have history. When she and Nahteran were little kids and their Solarian parents were killed, Marcus and my mom intervened to keep them from the soul trade. They split up the twins to avoid attention. Nahteran came to us, and Taya went into foster care.

I wonder if Taya ever resented Mom and Marcus for separating her from her Terran, making her anonymous and alone. She probably ended up better off, seeing as how Nahteran spent his youth in service to the Silver Prince. But still. I know better than anyone that when it comes to family, logic doesn't always guide your feelings.

Nahteran interrupts my thoughts by taking something out of his bag. He unwraps a dark cloth from around it. It's a small, round silver mirror in an onyx casing.

Graylin gasps. "A scrying mirror." He glances at Marcus. "That's Turalian magic."

I notice Brekken's eyes dart from where he stands at the door to Nahteran, full of hostility.

"Yes." Nahteran nods, his mouth twisted with distaste as he places the mirror face up on the table. "The soul in here has been trapped for a very long time."

I chew my lip, remembering that Tural is the same Realm where the Heiress's truth serum came from, a Realm to which the door was closed mysteriously sometime in the eighteenth century. *Two hundred years ago.* So this mirror must have been created at least that long ago. I had no idea the black market ran back that far. Every time I think I've learned the full horror of the soul-silver trade, I learn something that carves deeper. It reminds me that even though we got the armor away from Winterkill, we have a long road ahead of us tracking down the enchanted objects as far as we can reach, and saving the souls inside where we can.

"The Silver Prince has the counterpart to this," Nahteran says, gesturing to the mirror. "When he chooses to, he can show me what he's seeing at that moment." Nahteran's gaze flickers from Marcus to me. "And this morning . . . it showed me her."

I notice he doesn't call her *Mom* this time.

"Is Sylvia all right?" Marcus asks quietly. "How is it that she is in Oasis?"

Nahteran looks down. He looks ashamed. "The Silver Prince has phoenix flame," he says. "Phoenix flame that I brought him from Fiordenkill. Not enough to create a stable doorway, like the armor can, but enough for one person to slip through from time to time." He swallows. "Think of phoenix flame as a sharp edge, something that can cut through the veil separating the worlds. The armor—think of that as a knife. It's concentrated phoenix flame, strong enough to cut a hole in the cloth. But if you only have a little, you can use it like a needle. In and out again."

This information fills me with horror, but if Marcus has a similar reaction, he doesn't show it. His Innkeeper poker face is in full effect.

"But Sylvia is all right?" he asks again.

"She seemed to be." Nahteran swallowed. "But then . . . he showed me something else in the mirror. A note. I wrote it down."

He pulls a tattered, folded piece of notebook paper from his pocket and flattens it next to the mirror. On the top half is a paragraph of writing in an unfamiliar, hieroglyphic-like language. Below that, though, Nahteran's translated:

Your adoptive mother Sylvia Morrow is in my possession. Bring me the phoenix flame armor at once, or her life is forfeit. You have three days to make your way to Oasis and present the armor to me.

The Silver Prince's demand makes my blood feel cold and sluggish in my veins. It's Tuesday. That gives us until Friday—to do what, I don't know.

"How did you unlock the armor?" I ask. "That key you used, the one shaped like a star . . ."

"I stole the key from Cadius long enough to replicate it," he says. "The Silver Prince was fine with Winterkill holding on to the armor for now and being the face of the soul trade. But if it ever looked like the operation was at risk—for instance, if someone tried to steal it—I was supposed to steal the armor and bring it to him."

"Why didn't you tell me you were going to get Taya?" I ask him. I'm aware these probably aren't the most important questions we need to be asking, but I need to know, for me. "I wouldn't have fought you then."

And I wouldn't have thought you betrayed us.

Nahteran takes a deep, shaky breath. "I don't think I knew right away. Going to Solaria was kind of a snap decision."

I feel cold inside, but . . . *He didn't give the armor to the Prince*, I remind myself. He rescued Taya, then brought it here instead. Yet it sounds like it was a tough choice. Whose side is he really on?

Taya is looking hard at Nahteran, though he won't meet her eyes. "How did the Prince know you had the armor?" Taya adds on. "If these guys"—she gestures across the desk at us—"were the only way to travel between the worlds except the portals at Havenfall, how did he find out? Unless . . . you told him?"

I look at her, surprised that she's following all of this and that she'd challenge Nahteran. She meets my gaze with eyes that are steady, bordering on flinty. She's changed a lot from the carefree girl I met at the start of the summer.

No, I internally correct myself. She was never carefree. But still, she's changed. And I don't know how to feel about it. Not that I should be worrying about Taya at all right now.

Nahteran glances between us. "The worlds only touch each other at certain places," he says, looking to Taya to answer her question. "I had to travel a couple of miles to get to a spot where I could open a doorway to Solaria. Someone might have seen me on the way."

To Marcus's questioning look, he shrugs. "It's complicated. I can show you the maps, once we figure out what to do about Sylvia. Plus," he adds darkly, "this isn't the only mirror pairing the Silver Prince has. He has eyes everywhere. I'm sure there were plenty of people at Winterkill to fill him in."

My stomach sinks. The Silver Prince is even more dangerous than we thought. It makes me uneasy, too, how knowledgeable Nahteran is about these subjects. He's clearly not new to traveling between the worlds. Even if the Silver Prince forbade him from coming back to Earth, how come he never even sent a message to Havenfall? Just to let Marcus and me know he was alive? I suddenly don't buy my brother's explanation that contact would put us in danger. A question bubbles out of my lips before I fully think it through.

"Why now?" I ask Nahteran. "Why turn against the Silver Prince now?"

Everyone goes dead silent. Nahteran just stares at me blankly at first, like it's a dumb question. But then . . .

"Because of you," he says at length, quietly. "Because I saw you and realized . . . that there was still hope, I guess." The sentence ends sheepishly, with him looking down at his hands.

That's not enough, a small voice in my head says. If he really missed me, missed us, so much, why didn't he try to come back sooner?

I push away the nagging thought. That, too, is another problem for another day. The Silver Prince gave Nahteran three days to bring the armor to him in Oasis. So we have less than three days to figure out what to do.

If you'd asked me a week ago, I'd have gladly traded Mom's life for any object in all the worlds, no matter how magical or precious. But we struck a blow to the soul trade by stealing the armor; now Cadius and his ilk can't smuggle Solarian souls between worlds without going through Havenfall. We haven't stopped it entirely. There are still Solarians being held captive in Fiordenkill. The enchanted objects clearly remain scattered around all the realms. And Havenfall isn't a perfect fortress; my heart aches to think of all the soul fragments that have probably passed through here without us knowing. Still, we're in a stronger position than we were.

And of course, acquiescing to the Silver Prince's demand would basically be giving him a free pass to come in and cause whatever chaos he wants here on Earth. He wouldn't be limited to Havenfall; the armor would protect him from sickness, like it protected me in Fiordenkill.

Knowing the Silver Prince is trapped in Oasis has been the only thing allowing me to sleep at night these past few weeks. I still have half-healed scars from fighting him. The idea that with the armor he could be anywhere, come at us from any direction, is terrifying to consider.

Suddenly, I'm not so sure if I can trade the armor for Mom. And the thought breaks my heart.

And yet . . . how can I leave Mom in his clutches?

Eventually, we break for the night, having talked in circles for hours without solving anything other than where to store the phoenix flame armor.

After hearing what happened at Winterkill, Marcus decided the armor is too powerful to keep in one place. We can't afford for it to burn a hole in Haven like it did when I reunited Mom's gauntlet with the rest of the suit. So he and Sal divided the armor into three pieces and hid them in three safes across Havenfall. The chest piece is in Marcus's safe, beneath his office desk; the right gauntlet is locked in Marcus and Graylin's suite; and the left is hidden in my quarters, locked into a safe in the closet.

Marcus and Graylin head up to bed, both looking wrung out; Sal's going to sleep in Marcus's office to guard the armor. That leaves me, Taya, Nahteran, and Brekken lingering in the narrow hallway, the only sounds being the distant wind from below, out of the Fiorden and Byrnisian doorways.

My head is still spinning, my mind trying to find new angles from which to attack the problem of Mom and the Silver Prince. But I'm starting to fear that there is none. No way out . . . except for through. We just have to choose.

It'll seem better in the morning, after some sleep, I tell myself, not believing it in the slightest.

I'm about to suggest we all go up and get some late dinner when Brekken walks off. He strides away toward the main staircase and goes upstairs without looking back.

"Nice to meet you too," Nahteran mutters.

Taya laughs, but I can't join her, remembering the helpless fury on Brekken's face in Winterkill's vault as he watched Nahteran take the armor and run. I don't think Brekken considers retrieving Taya from Solaria a worthy cause. I think he still believes that Nahteran betrayed us.

Part of me wants to run after Brekken, but the greater part wants to stay where I am. Taya and I have some serious catching up to do. And for Nahteran, ten years' worth. Yet I still find myself staring at the place where Brekken stood.

I get that, for him, the mission always comes first, and Nahteran messed ours up in a major way and put all of us in danger. But if I can hear Nahteran out and potentially forgive him, why can't Brekken?

Taya's stomach growls audibly, loud enough to startle me into a smile. I turn to look at them, and to my surprise, I feel the smile get bigger. I let a breath out and consciously unclench my shoulders. Brekken and I will clear the air. In the meantime . . .

"Let's go get something to eat," I tell Taya and my brother.

Upstairs, the delegate ball is happening, the Elemental Orchestra's music wafting through the halls. I give the ballroom a wide berth, leading Nahteran and Taya the long way around to the kitchen. New treaty or no new treaty, the delegates are still touchy on the subject of Solarians. I don't *think* any of them would do harm to Nahteran or Taya, but I don't want to take the risk. Soon I'll introduce them to everyone and explain what happened, but first we need to figure out what to do about Mom.

The kitchen has always been one of my favorite places at Havenfall, and it brings me a weird kind of pride to see Nahteran's wide eyes and cautious smile when we go in. It's been cleaned and closed up for the night, but I flick on the light switch and warm yellow beams flood the high-ceilinged brick room, bringing it back to life. It's large but cozy. Bundles of drying herbs from the gardens hang from the ceiling, and dishes and pots and pans sparkle on racks all around.

I take them to the pantry, where Willow keeps a stash of cereal, granola bars, fruit, and sandwich stuff. Plus some weird Byrnisian tea—sachets filled with dried and crushed blue leaves—which no one but Willow ever drinks, but which Nahteran immediately goes for.

We each scrounge up a meal and bring it to the rough-hewn work-table in the corner. I have Cheerios and tea. Taya has a sandwich and black coffee. Nate has turkey and cheese slices rolled up into cigar shapes with tortillas, which makes me smile—that was his favorite food as a kid.

"Sorry," I say as they sit down, trying to keep it light. "This isn't the grand Havenfall welcome guests usually get."

Taya has rounded the table to sit on the bench next to me, which I'm trying not to read too much into. She elbows me. Casual. Easy.

"I remember. But this is a lot better than getting dosed with forgetting-wine."

I laugh. I can't help it. "Sorry, rules are rules. But you're a friend of the family now."

I look at Nahteran. "Do you remember this place?"

I immediately regret the question for how it punctures the light mood. Taya's giggle dies away and Nahteran looks contemplative, considering the kitchen around us.

"Did Sylvia take us here a lot?" he asks.

I swallow painfully. I shouldn't expect him to still share my child-hood memories, after going through so much in the intervening years. But it still hurts that he doesn't remember. As does his calling Mom *Sylvia*. He didn't back at Winterkill, so why here?

"Yeah. Yeah, she did."

Taya looks between us, her brow furrowed. Then, she hesitates a moment. "You know," she says gently, turning to Nahteran, "you can just call her your mom. I don't even remember our . . . our bio-parents anyway. Sylvia adopted you."

I smile at her, feeling grateful, and then surprised as her fingers graze my arm under the table. I think it's supposed to be a comforting touch, but it sends an electric shiver up my wrist.

Nahteran's eyes are downcast. "It just doesn't feel right," he murmurs. "It's been so long. And then when we're sitting around discussing her fate like this . . ."

His eyes meet mine for just half a second, and I think I understand. He doesn't want to let himself get close again, when everything still hangs in the balance. When it could all fall apart.

I turn to Taya instead. "I still haven't heard a thing about Solaria," I say.

My tone is deliberately light, teasing, but inside I'm a knot of anxiety. What if Solaria was horrible? And it was my fault she was there. Well, not entirely, but if I hadn't become friends with her—dragged her into things—maybe she would have just had a relaxing summer tending to the gardens and then gone back to her nice, normal life.

Maybe not, though. Taya is still a shapeshifter, and that would have been hard to hide no matter what.

A palette of subtle expressions plays across Taya's face. Her eyes grow distant, and the corners of her mouth turn up. But there's a solemnity there too, a wistfulness.

"I'll tell you about it," she says, voice dreamy. She glances at Nahteran. "I'll tell you both. I promise. But not right now. It's a long story, and a good one if I do say so myself. I want to tell it when there's not an ax hanging over all our heads." She catches my eye and smiles.

I smile back. It's weird—it makes my chest ache a little, but not in a bad way. I know how it feels to have things you don't want to talk about. Sometimes because it hurts too much, but other times because you just don't have the words. For her, I hope it's the latter.

"Fair enough."

Nahteran picks at his food, shoulders hunched. Something occurs to me. Back in Marcus's office, he didn't really say much after relaying the Silver Prince's message. But surely he has an opinion.

"Do you think we should take the deal, Nahteran?" I ask quietly. "Trade the armor in for Mom?"

He blinks, the only indication that he's heard me. He's scarcely touched his food, except for disassembling all the rolls, tearing the tortillas and meat and cheese into pieces, and piling them on opposite sides of his plate.

"Nahteran," I press. I know he's been through a lot. I know he doesn't want to talk about it, but we only have two days left before the Silver Prince kills Mom. "You know the Prince better than any of us."

He takes a long sip of the blue Byrnisian tea before finally answering.

"The Silver Prince is obsessed with finding a way between the worlds," my brother says, his voice gone quiet and flat like it was at Winterkill, when he was telling me what happened to him. "The Silver Prince always has been, even before he tried to take over Havenfall, because he knew that might not work. But after you guys beat him back, he became even more obsessed with phoenix flame. He didn't want to blow up the soul trade by stealing Cadius's armor—he needs the trade to exist—but he wanted to make a suit of his own. He thinks if he just has a way through, he'll be able to take over and rule all the Realms." Nahteran's eyes rove around us. "But since the trade hub at Winterkill is shot to hell now, I guess he thinks he might as well steal the armor after all."

I exchange a glance with Taya, then look back at Nahteran. "Well, that's . . . a lot," I say, my mouth dry. "So you're saying we shouldn't give it to him?"

Nahteran shakes his head once, hard. "I'm saying it doesn't matter. If we don't, he'll find another way. The armor can't be the only phoenix flame in Winterkill, and he has people out searching for more. There are legends that Byrn once had a place like Havenfall, with multiple doorways, and he's looking for that too. If that doesn't work, he'll find something else." Nahteran takes a deep breath. "One way or another, he'll do it someday. He'll get through."

"Is he angry with you?" I ask softly.

After a moment, Nahteran jerks his head in a nod. I think I see a shudder rip through him.

We're all silent while that sinks in. Sometime in the last few minutes, the distant music from the ballroom has stopped, the dancing wrapping up. Somehow, the silence makes the inn feel darker too. And colder.

My Cheerios taste like cardboard all of a sudden. I push them away and pull my tea to me instead. "So you were looking for the armor too, when I found you at Winterkill."

Nahteran inclines his head by a fraction of an inch. The slightest of nods.

"And you were going to give it to him."

The skin around his eyes tightens. "I didn't exactly have a choice."

There's always a choice, I think, but don't say. *I wish you had sent us a message. We could have helped you. I missed you.*

"I just figured . . ." But I trail off. I don't know how to put my thoughts into words. I don't know what I'd figured.

"Besides," Nate says. "Would it really be so bad if there were more doorways?"

"What do you mean?" I feel cold. I stick my hands in my lap so Nahteran won't see them tremble. "Aren't you worried about what could happen if the Silver Prince could travel wherever he wanted? Anyone could."

"That's exactly what he wants to do," Nahteran says slowly, like it should be obvious. "Our people need to spread out, Maddie . . . Oasis is getting more crowded every day. The storms outside its walls are getting worse. People are suffering."

He looks down, real feeling coloring his voice. "I mean, the Silver Prince doesn't care. Of course he doesn't. But everyone is looking for a back door. Even the Prince won't be able to keep Oasis safe and comfortable forever. He needs to find new territory. Someplace for everyone to go."

"And he thinks Earth could be that place?"

I hear the anger leaking into my voice, not rising yet, but roiling under the surface. Nahteran hears it too and drops his gaze, a pink tint appearing in his cheeks.

"Do you think that too? That we should just roll over and give the Silver Prince whatever he wants?"

Anger has leached into my tone, but Nahteran's reply has none.

"You don't know him," he says, and again I hear that hollowness, the echoing of years of history I both do and don't want to know about. "He'll get what he wants, Maddie. He always does. Better to just stay on his good side and try to protect the ones you love."

18

THAT NIGHT, I CAN'T SLEEP. So I do what I sometimes used to do as a kid and sneak up to the east balcony. I can always count on the fresh air and the scatter of stars to calm my nerves.

But not tonight. Because someone is already here. Nahteran.

He turns to me and smiles, seeming unsurprised to see me. Did we come here together as kids, ever? I can't remember.

I'm shaken to see him, still disturbed about the stuff he said in the kitchen. That the Silver Prince plans to infiltrate Earth, and how inevitable Nahteran seemed to think it was—so inevitable that my brother was planning to help him. But I still can't bring myself to fully hold a grudge against Nahteran. I pad over to him.

He is standing with his hands on the stone railing, looking out at the mountains and the reflection of Havenfall in Mirror Lake. He looks tired. There are dark circles beneath his eyes. I wonder how much he's slept since we parted ways in Winterkill. Probably even less than me. He traveled to another Realm to find Taya. I wonder how he found her— one person he hadn't seen in fourteen years, among a whole world of Solarians.

Being in Solaria clearly meant something to her. I wonder if it did for Nahteran as well. If he had ever managed to get there before, or if it was his first time. If it felt like home when he stepped foot on Solarian shores.

Nahteran slides over to make room, and I cautiously take up a spot beside him. It still feels like we're out of step, though.

"This was your spot," I remind him, gesturing widely to show that I mean not just the balcony, but the whole inn, the grounds. The mountains. The stars. "We had a lot of good times here."

"Yes, I remember. Well, I sort of remember." My brother—if I can still call him that—flashes a contained, enigmatic smile. "I still know my way around. And there are . . . flashes of memories, if that makes sense." He traces one finger along the railing, as if expecting it to vanish under his touch. "I remember I was happy here. We were happy here."

He looks to me as if for confirmation. *Were we really here? Were we really happy?* And my wariness dissolves into sorrow, for how far apart we've grown, for everything taken from us.

Against my better judgment, I ask, "Was it horrible, your time with the Silver Prince?"

"Horrible?" Nahteran hesitates, clearly taken aback, and I feel bad for asking.

But on the other hand, it feels like something I need to know, to start sorting out where his loyalties lie now.

"Yeah," he says eventually. "On the one hand it was pretty awful. But I got used to it. You can get used to pretty much anything if it's all you know."

My heart twists. "But it wasn't all you knew," I say weakly. "You had memories. A family. Me and Mom."

"I know," he replies. He looks at me, eyes serious. "And believe me, Maddie, that's the only reason there's anything of me left."

"Mom told everyone she killed you," I tell him, speaking around a lump growing in my throat. She's been in jail for it ever since . . ." I don't want to say *since they took you*, so I just say, "Ever since that night. They were going to execute her for it before the Silver Prince kidnapped her."

Nahteran blinks. "I'm sorry to hear that. She doesn't deserve that."

"I don't know," I mumble. "She said she did. I think by the end, she was really starting to believe it."

When Nahteran looks sharply at me, brows raised waiting for an explanation, I reluctantly explain about how she had given up on the world. On life. On everything. But to my surprise, Nate doesn't look shocked or upset at the story.

"I don't know if this will make you feel better or worse," he says when I'm finished, "but it's possible the person I saw in the mirror wasn't her."

My breath catches. "What do you mean?"

"The Silver Prince has some Solarians in his employ," he says slowly. "Gifted shapeshifters."

It sounds like this is a painful memory for Nahteran to recount, judging by the roughness of his voice, but he gathers himself and goes on.

"He likes using them to control the people under them, including me. So for instance, he'd get one of them to shapeshift to look like Marcus, or Mom, or you."

I'm stunned silent, frozen. Finally, I find my voice to say, "So you don't think that was her? You don't think he has her?"

But before I even get to the end of that sentence, Nahteran is already shaking his head.

"I do think he has her," he says in a whisper. "The Silver Prince doesn't make empty threats. I don't know why I brought that up." His voice cracks. "I've never talked about any of this before."

"It's—it's okay," I stammer. "You can tell me about it if you want. Or you don't have to if you don't want to."

Nahteran smiles weakly. "It's just, it's hard to remember what's real and what's not sometimes."

I swallow. "Here is what's real," I say. To my surprise, my voice comes out strong; I don't know where that strength comes from, but I'm glad for it. "We liked baking brownies together—at least, you and Mom would bake brownies while I distracted you and tried to steal a bite of the batter. What's true is we made snow angels together in the winter and made cardboard boxes into forts. What's real is you sat next to me on the bus the first day of kindergarten, even though the other boys made fun of you. What's real is that every dog in the neighborhood was your best friend."

I'm tearing up now and have to stop and catch my breath before going on. I didn't even really remember all of this, but it rushes back as I speak, a waterfall of images.

"What's real is that you always picked flowers for Mom, and she couldn't be mad at you even though you wrecked her garden. You always let me choose the TV show, and you'd sit with me and watch whatever dumb little-kid shit I chose. What's real is that we loved you so much and it's honestly been freaking awful growing up without you."

One silent moment passes between us. Then, wordlessly, Nahteran leans over and wraps me in a hug. I hug him back, the tears escaping and rolling down my cheeks. Even though he's a foot taller than me now—which seems unfair—he feels like home.

"Please stay at Havenfall," I mumble into his shirt. "Whatever happens with the Silver Prince and Mom, stay here with us."

Nahteran lets me go and turns to look out over the mountains again, but keeps one arm slung over my shoulder. "I want to," he says kindly. "But we can't hide out forever, no matter how great this place is. Someone has to take our answer to the Silver Prince."

"Not necessarily," I whisper. "What if we choose not to make the trade?"

His arm around me goes tense. "Then I don't want her to die alone, in a world where no one cares about her."

"Then, what, you'll just go on working for him?" I ask. I don't mean to be combative, but my voice rises anyway, bitterness and fear mixing together inside me. "Or will he kill you? Because I can't imagine he'll just let you walk out again."

"I know that." Nahteran sounds contrite but resolute. "But it's like I said earlier. The Silver Prince will achieve what he wants in the end. If I'm at his side, maybe I can reduce some of the collateral damage."

"He's not unbeatable," I point out. "We beat him before. I beat him, and God knows I'm pretty useless most of the time."

A small, sad smile plays around Nahteran's mouth. "I disagree."

"Don't try to distract me with flattery." I elbow him lightly in the ribs. "Look. I know he's terrifying. I'm scared of him too. But if you just admit defeat in advance and go along with what he's doing, you're allowing it to happen. Trust me. I know I was bragging a minute ago, but I was *this* close"—I hold up my thumb and pointer finger half an inch apart—"to letting him manipulate me into giving up Havenfall while Marcus was out cold."

"If I fought him outright, I'd have been dead or brainwashed like Bram years ago," Nahteran says, wooden. "I figure it's better to be a pawn and retain my free will. Maybe save a few people along the way. Besides, Maddie . . ."

He hesitates, like he knows I won't like what he's about to say.

"Would it be the worst thing in the worlds if what the Silver Prince wants comes to pass?" he asks. "Whether it's in two years or a hundred, at some point, Oasis will fall and everyone inside will die. The Byrnisians aren't responsible for what the Silver Prince does. Don't they deserve a chance to live?"

I don't have an answer to that, at least not a simple one. So instead I bounce back another question. "What's his plan, then? What is the Silver Prince imagining?"

"I don't know exactly," Nahteran says without meeting my eyes. "But I can tell you what I'm imagining. Just peaceful coexistence, that's all. If I can figure out how to replicate the armor I can create safe zones where Byrnisians outside the wall can live here in peace. And not just Byrnisians. Solarians, though obviously they don't need the phoenix flame. Fiordens, whoever else."

Nahteran looks sidelong at me. "I heard some gossip about you and that Fiorden soldier, Brekken. Can't say I like the guy so far, but just think, wouldn't it be nice to at least have the option of being together with someone like that?"

My face heats up, and I fight the childish instinct to tell Nahteran to keep his nose out of my beeswax.

Because the thought of Brekken hurts. I know he's still angry with me for what happened at Winterkill, and I'm angry with him for being angry. For not trying to fix us.

But unlike my mom, Brekken and I have time. I choose my words carefully, aiming for diplomacy. For lots of reasons, I'm not trying to start a fight with Nahteran.

"I really don't think that giving the Silver Prince free rein over this planet is going to lead to anyone peacefully coexisting."

"True enough." Nahteran chuckles darkly. "But even the Silver Prince is not going to live forever."

My brother takes his arm from my shoulders and grips the railing tight, like it's the edge of a flying carpet. "Just imagine what could be if the Silver Prince weren't in the picture, Maddie. All the realms, open. You and me and Taya in that new world, together."

I glance over to see the hopeful, almost feverish light in Nahteran's eyes. It's kind of intoxicating. I'm almost ready to follow him into the wide unknown.

At the same time, though, I'm not so optimistic. "But the Silver Prince is in the picture. And he's more powerful than all of us put together. The only reason he's not steamrolling us right now is that he's trapped in Oasis; we can't just let him in and hope that it will all work out."

I circle back to the most immediate question facing us. "Besides, Mom wouldn't want us to give him the armor even if it meant saving her."

I'm not sure of many things—like if what Mom wants should matter, or which option I want to go with—but I'm sure of that.

But as Nahteran looks at me and smiles, the expression so familiar and simultaneously so alien, I'm not sure if my brother feels the same way.

"Maybe," he says. "But to me, a world without family isn't much of a world at all."

———

I wake up early the next morning, even after sleeping poorly. I had a hard time falling asleep and staying asleep even after staying up late talking to Nate. Like my body wants to stay on high alert for whatever else might go wrong in the night.

But the morning sky is bright and warm outside my window, and the birds are chirping in the pines. I open my window, and the sun and the sound lift my spirits. Maybe it'll be okay. Nahteran, Marcus, Brekken, and Taya are all here, all the people I love who I once thought were lost to me. If we can get Mom back from the Silver Prince, I think out to whatever god might be listening, I won't want for anything ever again.

I text Taya while I get dressed. I've not had a moment alone with her since she came back from Solaria, and I want to ask her more about that world, the place she found there.

And . . . While I really do want to know everything, I have another reason too. I need to ask her to intervene with Nahteran. To see if their bond—forged before I was even born—can get him to see reason, to stay with us. There has to be another way to get the armor to the Silver Prince, if that's what we decide to do. But I don't think I could bear to lose him a third time.

Nahteran's words from last night replay in my mind, over and over again. *Would it be the worst thing in the worlds if what the Silver Prince wants comes to pass? The Byrnisians aren't responsible for what the Silver Prince does. Don't they deserve a chance to live?*

It feels like a paradox. If Oasis is really dying like Nahteran says, of course the residents deserve to live. Everyone does.

But the answer can't be letting the Silver Prince blow holes in the barrier between the worlds. I still have nightmares from the fight with him in the tunnels. I can still see the cruelty in his eyes as he called wind and fire to his command, ready to end my life so he could take over Havenfall. I don't think peaceful coexistence is his endgame. Even when I thought him my ally at the beginning of the summer, he was always a more "the ends justify the means" kind of guy. Not to mention he's a lot of the muscle behind the soul trade. It almost makes it worse that he doesn't care about the suffering of the Solarians. They're just vectors to him, just tools to weaken the boundaries between Byrn and everything else.

It's not even 8:00 a.m., and I don't expect Taya to text back anytime soon, as I stand at the window, thinking over the paradox. Brekken's unbending morality, or Nahteran's farsighted acquiescence? Mom or the armor?

My phone buzzes, thankfully snapping me out of a thought spiral that can't go anywhere good.

Great minds! Just thinking about you. Walk on the grounds before breakfast?

Just thinking about you. My eyes fix on those words a little too long, my cheeks heating. Thinking about me? In what kind of way?

I push the flustered feelings away. Taya's spent the last few weeks learning how she fits in a whole other world. I'm probably the last thing on her mind. Or whatever fragile thing—friendship? something else?—was growing between us before everything happened. Before I discovered the soul trade, before she saved me from the Silver Prince, and before she got sucked into Solaria.

I feel guilty thinking about Taya, since Brekken and I have discussed being *together*. But it's not like I'm just going to never talk with Taya. She's my friend too. She saved my life, and I thought I would never see her again. But even as I'm trying to justify what's running around my head, I know I'm not being fair to Brekken. Still . . .

Just thinking about you.

I meet her in the front hall, where she's waiting with two mugs of travel coffee in hand. She's wearing a new pair of skinny jeans and her signature bomber jacket. After she went through the Solarian door, I made sure Willow kept her room just as it was in case she came back. Even when it was a long shot. And now she's here; she's back.

Morning light streams through the windows and lands softly on her. I take the coffee, and we walk outside in silence, the sky a Creamsicle orange and mist still clinging to the grass.

Her presence feels like a comfort, a contrast to all the moments I've spent with Nahteran so far—which have been joyful, but also difficult and fraught. It's easier to be with Taya. She challenges me—but we're in agreement about the important things. Yet . . . I don't ask her what she'd vote to do about Mom. I think I need to figure that out for myself.

By some unspoken mutual agreement, we start meandering toward the gardens. This early, the grounds are empty of delegates. We could be all alone in the world, just us and the mountains and the flowers, their bright colors muted by the mist.

"Nahteran has to come around eventually, right?" I tug my sleeves down over my hands. There's the slightest hint of fall in the air. It's not really that cold, but I shiver thinking of the haunted look in Nahteran's eyes last night, the history he hinted at of his growing up in Byrn. "He knows better than anyone that the Silver Prince is evil."

Taya looks at me with sadness in her eyes. "That's not the whole story, though," she says softly. "How many of us stay in a bad place because it's all we know?"

My heart twists. "Let's talk about something else," I say, not wanting to think about my brother anymore, how he might have suffered and how he might never be the same. "I still haven't heard much about Solaria. What was it like there? Were you happy?"

The last question slips out without my quite meaning it to. I wanted to keep it light, surface. But I should have remembered, it's never like that with Taya. It's as if her very presence scrapes the protective filter from me, pulls out the deepest questions swimming in my soul.

Taya takes her time answering. We're in the midst of the flower beds now, in a section full of riotous, star-shaped green flowers. I don't know which world these come from, but I know that every year, they bloom only when someone strokes their petals. A few bumblebees drift lazily from bloom to bloom, their hum underlying the smattering of birdsong coming from the trees.

Taya kneels down, facing the side of the path, and I stop walking.

I watch curiously as she scoops up a handful of earth in her hands and straightens back up, holding the dirt carefully in her cupped fingers.

"What am I looking at?" I ask.

Taya flattens her hands so that the dirt spreads out over her skin, her eyes fixed on it. Following her gaze, I see, to my surprise, that there are myriad colors hidden in the dark of the earth. Red, blue, green, gold, white, purple grains mixed in with the black. She carefully picks out one pebble that looks like it could be unpolished sapphire and brushes off the dirt before plunking it into the palm of my hand.

"I noticed this when I was working in the gardens," she says. "In Solaria, there are miles of blue stone beaches. All blue, under a gold sky."

The picture takes shape in my mind. "It sounds beautiful," I say in a hushed voice.

"I think delegates from all the Realms have brought their own soil to these gardens," Taya says. There's a current of feeling in her voice that I can't identify. She sticks her hands in her pockets and gives me that lopsided smile. "But Solaria, yeah. Yeah, I was happy there."

My heart twists in a weird happy-sad dance. Of course, duh, I want her to be happy. But there's a not so small spiteful part of me that wants her to be happy on Earth. With me.

"I have a history there," Taya says. "An extended family, even. That's something I never had on Earth. I was scared at first to not know anything about the world. The people were kind to me, but I still felt out of place. And I missed you."

That makes my breath catch. I'm trying to think of a reply when a snapped twig sound behind us makes me jump. I spin around to see Brekken striding down the path toward us.

My stomach drops, but not in the good way that it usually does when I see him. He looks like he's here on business.

"Maddie," he says when he's within earshot, his voice clipped. "Taya."

"What's wrong?" I ask, foreboding gathering heavy inside my chest. *What now?*

"Maddie," he says, his voice strangely clipped. "Can I talk to you alone?"

19

TAYA LEAVES US WITHOUT ARGUMENT. She can tell when something's wrong just as well as I can.

Once she's gone, I don't know if Brekken means to keep on walking
or not, but the sudden silence and stillness that descends is awful. So I
turn to the path again, beckoning for Brekken to come along.

We continue through the gardens. Brekken clearly has something
to say, and I can tell from his manner that it's not good. I've been so
wrapped up in Taya and Nahteran that I've scarcely spoken to Brekken,
and it's just now occurring to me how much that must hurt. I know it
would have hurt me, if the roles were reversed. Guilt and sadness sneak
through me even before he speaks.

"I'm sorry," he says. "About how I acted about Nahteran. How I told
you not to trust him."

I don't know what I expected to hear, but it wasn't that. Brekken hasn't been *acting* sorry. He's been cold and distant to Nahteran this whole time, and to Taya and me too, by association. I cock my head, confused.

"Why do you say that? Do you trust him now?"

Brekken smiles, but it has a wooden quality to it. His fists are clenched. "Not entirely, no, I'll admit. Something about all this—the Silver Prince and the armor and your mom—it doesn't feel right to me."

"Then why say anything?" I challenge. "Why apologize if you're just going to do the same thing?"

Brekken looks out over the mountains, his jaw working slightly. "I never wanted to hurt you, Maddie. And it's clear that I have. I want to make you happy."

"Well, I gotta tell you I'm not happy," I snap. "Don't you get that Nahteran has more reason to hate the Silver Prince than any of us? We only had to deal with him for a month. Nahteran has been with him for ten *years*."

"That's exactly what I'm afraid of!" Brekken's voice is layered with anger and distress. He stops walking and turns to face me square on. I stop too.

"Loyalties can change, Maddie," he continues. "Remember Bram? He was a Solarian working for the Silver Prince too."

I flinch at the memory of Bram—the man posing as the Silver Prince's manservant at Havenfall, who was secretly a Solarian. Whom the Silver Prince murdered, slaughtering him in his animal form so that with his spilled blood, the Prince could open the door to Solaria and trigger chaos at Havenfall. And to top it all off, it looked like a monster had killed him, stirring up the hatred of Solarians in the rest of us.

"Nate is nothing like Bram."

"*Nate*," Brekken echoes, the word dripping with skepticism and even contempt. "Still the nickname, even after all this?"

That sets me off. I step back from him. "You don't understand," I hiss. "You've always had a family. You've never been alone."

"Maddie." Brekken's voice is soft, like he's trying to comfort me, but it's not working. "I understand you've been lonely. But you've got to see what's right in front of your eyes—"

"My eyes are open," I retort. "What I see, what I think, is that every step of the way this summer, we've found out that the rabbit hole goes deeper than we realize."

I take a deep breath. I'm angry, and I don't want to cry. I can't believe that my best friend, the boy I love, thinks the worst of my brother. I can't let Brekken talk me into believing it too. I've lost faith in so much that I used to hold sacred. If I lose hope for Nahteran, I think I might crumble into dust.

Something shifts in Brekken's face, and I see sympathy creeping in. He comes close, wraps his arms around me, and pulls me into his chest. I stand still, not moving to embrace him in return. I feel emptied out.

"Nothing that happens now will change your memories," he says softly. "You'll always have those. He can't touch them."

"I know," I murmur. But it's more of an auto-response than anything else. Because I don't care about the memories, not really. Those are behind me, already tarnished by years of lies and silence. What I want now is to have my brother back, whatever that will look like. A small voice inside reminds me that my brother doesn't exactly want to stay.

"I didn't even come here to talk about Nahteran," Brekken says. "It's not about him at all. It's about you. I might not trust him, but he's your brother and I shouldn't have asked you to turn away from him. So, I'm sorry."

"Okay . . ." I bite the inside of my cheek. "Apology accepted, I guess."

"Thank you." He steps away from me, but I can tell he's still holding something back.

We're still in the gardens, on the outskirts now, and the air is heavy with the scent of late summer flowers. But the color and life seems to have faded from my surroundings, replaced by a sense of menace.

"I wanted to talk to you for another reason," he says. "We've received a message from Fiordenkill." He closes his eyes for a second as if he really doesn't want to say what he's about to say. But then he opens them again and goes on.

"Back in Winterkill, when we used the armor to create a doorway back to Haven . . . Apparently it continued to grow and swallowed half of Cadius's castle before Nahteran took the armor out of range and it closed up again."

"Good," I say. "I wish it swallowed the whole thing."

Even though that's kind of scary to hear, seeing as that same armor is currently sitting inside Havenfall.

Brekken doesn't smile. "Cadius is bringing charges against us for the destruction of his castle and the theft of the armor. Myr ordered that someone in our company return to stand trial for it."

I almost laugh out of relief. Out of all the consequences we could have faced for our excursion into Winterkill—Cadius being mad at us is one I'm completely okay with.

"Is that all? Too bad, then. It's not like they can come into Havenfall and drag us back."

"No," Brekken replies. His face and voice are somber. "But it will disrupt the peace with Fiordenkill if we don't."

"Can't Princess Enetta help us?" I point out. "She helped us get into Fiordenkill. She's on our side."

"Graylin is talking to her now," he says. "But I doubt it. She's only one royal out of the whole family. The rest, as I understand it, are sympathetic to Winterkill. Besides . . ."

Brekken's soldier posture breaks down a little, his head hanging down. He looks . . . defeated.

"People died, Maddie," he says heavily. "Guests at the party. Servants. And much of the soul-silver was lost."

That steals the breath out of my lungs. I don't care much about the guests, to be honest. They knew what Cadius was doing and decided to party with him anyway. But the servants had no choice in being there. They were trapped. Just like the Solarian souls bound up in the hoard of silver.

"Someone should be accountable for that," Brekken says.

I struggle to catch my breath. I don't know that I disagree, but I don't know what to say. Except . . . "What should we do?"

Brekken looks down. "I'm going to go back. I'm going to stand trial."

My heart plummets into my feet. I can't help taking a step back, like someone's hit me. "You can't."

"*You* can't," Brekken corrects me, his words toneless. "I can. Me or Graylin, and would you rather it be him?"

"No!" I yell, loud enough for the mountains to swallow my voice and toss it back toward us as an echo. "I don't want either of you to go! What happens if you lose? If they convict you?"

I don't know much about Myr's criminal justice system, but I know enough about ours to be very, very afraid.

"Cadius wants the death penalty, obviously," Brekken says. "But I'll have a chance to speak. I'll tell them about the soul trade, what we saw at the castle. It's not a done deal."

His stoic, almost casual tone tears at my insides. "It's too risky. Just stay here, hide out, Brekken. Please." I draw a shuddery breath. "Stay safe. If someone comes after you, I'll tell them you left, I'll think of something—"

"The other things I said still stand."

He rubs one hand over his eyes. His uniform is rumpled, and there's a faint layer of copper stubble on his jaw. On the Brekken breakdown scale, that's practically the equivalent of anyone else running naked and raving through the streets. I can't believe I hadn't noticed how close he was to falling apart.

"The peace with Fiordenkill is still at stake," he says. "And all that work you did to bring Solaria back into the fold. I'd hate to see Havenfall lose access to another Realm just because we were hasty and careless," he adds with a small smile.

He's trying to make light, I think, but I don't want any of it.

"Then I should go," I say, trying to sound braver than I feel. "The whole thing was my idea."

"You can't," he shoots back. "It will all have been for nothing if we send the armor right back into Winterkill's hands. And you won't get far without it. You'll drop dead after an hour in Fiordenkill, and Cadius won't get his trial, and then Graylin or I will have to go in anyway."

He lifts one hand, tentatively, and cups my cheek gently. "It makes sense for me to go, Maddie. You know it does."

Deep down, some part of me knows he's right. But I won't admit it, can't admit it. The words physically won't come out. I put my hand over his, pressing it to my skin, trying to quell the panic speeding my heart.

"There's no way you'll get a fair trial." I think with a surge of fear of the luxury at Cadius's castle, how he seemed to have the Fiorden nobles in his pocket.

"I do think so, actually," Brekken says. "A lot of Fiordens don't like Winterkill and are against the soul trade. They'll hear me out."

But that doesn't seem like enough. "I just . . ." My voice cracks, forcing me to drop it into a whisper. "I don't want to lose you."

"You might not," he says, almost cheerfully. "I'll argue my case. They might even decide to execute Cadius instead."

I laugh in spite of myself, but it comes out tinged with a sob. "'*You might not.*' That's not really a comfort, you know."

Brekken shrugs. "After everything with the Heiress, I promised myself I'd never lie to you again."

"When do you have to go?" I ask. My chest hurts, like Cadius of Winterkill has reached out across the realms separating us and has closed cold fingers around my heart, tugging, tugging.

"Three days," Brekken says.

He grabs my hand and starts walking down the sunny path again. It's weird how much his touch makes me instinctively relax, despite how horribly wrong everything still is. The tension in my shoulders unwinds, my heart starting to beat at a normalish pace again.

"So I'll have time to help out with the Silver Prince," he adds. "Whatever we decide to do."

It's an unwelcome reminder of that terrible problem that we're no closer to solving. More than twenty-four hours have passed since Nahteran first got the Silver Prince's message. One of our three days, gone without anything to show for it.

My phone vibrates in my pocket. I tense, already going to pull it out. Anytime my phone's buzzed in the last couple of days, my instinct is always that it's news about Mom. On the lock screen is a text from Marcus.

Come to my rooms please. Need to talk to you.

I show it to Brekken, who nods in understanding and turns back toward the inn. "I'll walk you there."

"We're not done talking about this," I say, catching up. "I want to make sure you have the very best testimony in the history of Myr. We'll get Graylin to write a speech for you. You can practice it before you leave."

Brekken's lips twitch in a smile—a genuine one, for the first time since he found me on the path. "Sounds good." He takes my hand and squeezes it tight. "I want to come back to you."

And with that, my heart flip-flops for the umpteenth time.

When I get to Marcus's living room, he's not alone. Nahteran is sitting on the couch with a mug of that weird tea he likes, looking tired and anxious. He's wearing a black sweater clearly borrowed from Marcus, judging by its bagginess and how the sleeve rides up his wrist when he waves to me.

By the counter, Marcus turns to me. He has a mug of coffee ready for me, too, and his face is grave as he hands it to me. "Maddie, thanks for coming."

"Of course." I take it and sit down next to Nahteran, an ominous weight settling onto my chest.

Marcus sits on the edge of the armchair across from us, his hands on his knees. No drink for him. His hair is messy as if he's been running his hands nervously through it all night.

"I don't want to beat around the bush," he says. His voice is hoarse. He used to be a smoker, back before I was born, and sometimes the gravelly edge still comes out. "I've been up all night thinking about Sylvia. About your mom. About what she would do if she were in my shoes."

I feel my muscles tense up. Suddenly, I know what he's going to say and dread fills me. *Please don't say it. Please don't—*

"She wouldn't want us to put the whole world at risk just for her sake," Marcus says. "We're not going to give the armor to the Silver Prince."

I go numb. The world around me fills with a buzzing, gray static. The only thing I'm aware of is Nahteran going rigid next to me. Meaning this is news to him too.

"But—"

The word falls from my lips without my deciding to say it, a wild exclamation. Yet it dies off, goes nowhere. I don't know why I feel so horrified and repulsed. It's not like I had decided where I stood; I hadn't been set on trading the armor. If anything, after my talk with Nahteran last night on the balcony, I was leaning the same way as Marcus. So why is my chest burning with a trapped scream of protest?

"Look." Marcus swipes the back of his hand across his face, catching a couple of tears before they can slide down his cheeks. "I'm not happy about this. Obviously. But I know your mom. And we can't—we can't throw everyone on Earth under the bus just to save her." He looks from me to Nahteran and back. "So we sit tight. We protect the armor and keep guarding the doorway to Oasis. As long as the Silver Prince is trapped there, we're safe. Havenfall is safe." His voice trembles. "Earth is safe."

I stare back at him, feeling like I'm floating above my body. I had been stuck on the knife's edge before, too trapped to step off in either direction, to make a choice, even in my own mind. But somehow, Marcus articulating his decision in such stark terms has broken my paralysis and I suddenly know what I think.

That this can't happen.

I won't let it happen.

I won't let Mom die.

I half expect to start crying as soon as I close the door to Marcus's suite behind me, but I don't. Instead, my whole body feels electrified, fired with energy and purpose. I start walking in a random direction, feeling like I'll explode if I don't burn it off. Nahteran falls into step next to me.

"There has to be another way," I say in a low voice, not looking at him, but trusting that he hears me. "There just has to."

"Sure, there is," he says. "Giving the Silver Prince the armor. But how can we do that without Marcus finding out? And do you really want to?"

"No," I hiss. Fury—not at Nahteran or Marcus, but at our circumstances, at the Silver Prince—throbs beneath my skin. "There's something else. There has to be."

My feet are taking us up, up, up. I scarcely notice the inn passing by around me. The first floor, the dormitories, meandering delegates, the staff quarters. All the way up to the top floor, the glass-walled room where a lifetime ago I had a heart-to-heart with the Silver Prince.

The problems I faced then—Marcus unconscious, knowing the delegates thought I was out of my depth as a substitute, what I thought was a monster on the grounds—felt so overwhelming then. So simple now. But somehow I feel like it'll be easier to think if I'm high up. If I can see everything around me.

Nahteran follows me wordlessly, and I'm grateful. It's nice to be trusted by someone, even if I don't entirely trust myself.

A few moments after we reach the glass room and close the door behind us, it opens again. I whip around to see Taya in the doorway. She looks from Nahteran to me, her brow creased in concern.

"Sorry," she says. "I just saw you guys across the hall downstairs. You looked upset, so I thought . . ." She trails off, her eyes wide as she looks around.

I suppose that the view must be breathtaking. I can't really see it, can't focus on the real world. My mind's eye is filled up with a memory of the Silver Prince, his handsome face and metallic eyes, the machinations that were always churning behind them.

"Come in, then," Nahteran says.

Distantly, I hear him relay to Taya the conversation in Marcus's office, the decision our uncle made on everyone's behalf. I hear that he's angry.

"You know the Silver Prince best, Nahteran," I say when he's finished, turning to them. The adrenaline sparking through my body has faded a bit, replaced by cold, consuming determination. "What are his weak spots?"

But it's Taya who answers first. "Pride," she says after a long silence. She looks at me. At Nahteran. At me again. "Right?"

Nahteran nods wordlessly.

"So we lean on his pride," I say, testing the words out. "We let him think he's won . . . How?"

"Fake armor," Taya suggests, as easily as if she's had the answer all along. "We make fake armor and trade it to him for your mom."

Nahteran and I both stare at her. My blood is racing.

There has to be a way we can get Mom back without handing over the phoenix flame armor. And maybe, just maybe, Taya's hit on it.

20

THE PLAN COMES TOGETHER QUICKLY, all three of us fired up by
the possibility of actually doing something. I know, and I think Nahteran
and Taya do too, that this is a hell of a long shot. But at least we have a
chance.

We pause at the top of the stairs. We each have separate jobs to do,
but I don't want to part ways just yet. Being with Taya and Nahteran like
this gives me hope for what seems like the first time in forever. Maybe
everything will be okay.

But we don't have time to waste. We head downstairs silently.
Nahteran peels off first, on the fourth floor that serves as the staff quarters. While Willow and Marcus and everyone else is at dinner, he's going
to steal the original phoenix flame armor from the three safes. We'll
need it to create the reproduction. And then to open a doorway between
here and Oasis.

Taya heads off to the kitchen. In one of her jacket pockets is my key ring, the Innkeeper's keys that will get her into the locked closet in the kitchen, where Willow keeps the gold plates and cutlery we use to celebrate the start of the summit. We need gold—not enough to recreate the entire suit of phoenix flame armor, but enough to gild its surface so that when we hand it over to the Silver Prince, it'll look close enough to the real thing.

I continue downstairs and walk past the dining room on the first floor where the delegates are having dinner, quick and silent, hoping no one notices me. Past Marcus and Graylin's door, even more quickly.

As far as my uncle knows, I agreed to his plan of saying no to the Silver Prince and dealing with the consequences for my mom, whatever they may be. Nahteran and I both did. But now that I've got a plan of my own, I don't know that I could keep the pretense up if I faced Marcus again. So I continue on to the armory, and unlock it with the one key I slipped off the Innkeeper's key ring before I gave it to Taya.

There's one high, narrow window on the far side of the armory. It doesn't let in much light, but the multitude of silver objects in the room catch it and refract it, amplifying it and turning it strange. The quiet seems thicker too. The door closing behind me shuts out the noise from the dining hall entirely, leaving me in silence and silver light. Haven light.

Overwhelming dread and guilt descends on me now. That I'm not doing enough, that I haven't saved anyone. But I can't let that slow me down right now. I need to find just the right objects with just the right magic in order to create the armor replica. I find that if I concentrate, if I empty my mind, I can get a glimpse—a whisper—of the magic trapped in each silver piece. It's less than an image, barely a feeling. But it's there, somehow. *Wind. Ice. Fire.*

Nahteran was the one who suggested we use soul-silver to deepen the deception. As soon as the Silver Prince put on our fake armor, he would sense the mundaneness of it. He'd know we tricked him, and make us pay for it. But if we used soul-silver, which emanated its own power . . .

We could defeat him by making the false armor into a weapon.

I start to gather objects from the shelves, trying to feel out the magic as I go. When my fingers brush the burnished sides of a silver tea kettle, it sings of flames and heat waves. I wrap it carefully in one of the T-shirts from my bag and tuck it inside, reaching up for more. It feels wrong. It *is* wrong. But it's the way forward, for now.

An hour later, I meet Nahteran and Taya in the abandoned tunnel to the Turalian door. Marcus had it boarded up years ago, but it's a simple matter to pry a couple of boards off, stack them to the side, and step through into the dusty blackness. The others follow behind me, each carrying their contributions to the project.

Nahteran's backpack contains the phoenix flame armor, its pieces separated only by layers of fabric. Taya's tote bag is filled up a third of the way with Willow's special-occasion kitchenware—a glittering heap of gold and copper—gardening gloves, and a camping lantern that throws off enough bright white light to see by, but makes us all look like ghosts and intensifies the shadows at the edges of the light's reach, making them shift and stretch like living things.

Nahteran lays the armor out on the ground—making sure to place each piece several feet apart from the others—and studies them intently. The Silver Prince has never actually seen the armor, so our reproduction doesn't have to be perfect. But it should be close. Meanwhile, Taya watches me lay out the soul-silver in the shape of the phoenix flame armor, looking as conflicted as I feel.

"How do you know what each object does?" she asks in a soft voice.

"By touch." I beckon her over, and when she kneels down beside me, I bring her hand to a simple silver bowl. I'm not sure if she'll be able to feel the magic too. But I can tell from the widening of her eyes that she does.

"That's wild," Taya says. She steps back from the bowl and gives the tunnel a skeptical look. "Hey, are you sure this doorway's sealed? Because the last time we were down here together with the Silver Prince, Havenfall was almost destroyed and I ended up on a one-way trip to Solaria. Now that I'm back, I'd kind of like to stay."

"Sealed shut with magic so powerful, Marcus says we'll never be able to open it again even if we wanted to," I reply.

She wants to stay.

"Okay," Nahteran calls out. "If you two are done reminiscing, I think we're ready to start."

Nahteran comes to stand beside us and looks down at my work. I've used ingots for the ribs of the breastplate, and arranged silverware in the shape of two gauntlets. I've also separated three small piles of silver objects off to the side.

"Fire, wind, and ice magic," I tell them, pointing to the three piles. My voice is on the edge of trembling.

Nahteran and Taya are both silent for a long moment. Then she asks me, "How do you use them? How do we get the power out of the silver?"

"I'm not totally sure," I admit.

I pick up a spoon—like the one Sura gave me, back when we were both prisoners of the soul traders in Haven's antique shop—and turn it over in my hands, feeling the wind magic inside raising goose bumps, as if the faintest of breezes already emanates from the silver surface.

"Before, I just kind of . . . willed it to happen. The magic is already in there, it just needs to be let out."

"Okay, good to know." Taya's voice is small, though, as she looks down at the silver.

"Let's split up the magic," I say. "I'll melt the silver until it's pliable with fire magic. Nahteran will use wind magic to shape it into the fake phoenix flame armor, and Taya will cool it with ice magic. Then we'll put it together. I'm sure I can scrounge up some tools around the inn."

We all agree not to do any test runs with the magic, knowing that once the magic is spent from an object, the bound soul seems to vanish from it as well. Even if using soul-silver is the only way to pull off this deceit, none of us want to use any more than necessary. We can't mess this up.

Here goes . . . everything.

It only has to look good enough, I remind myself, anxiety brewing in the pit of my stomach, before passing the spoon to Nahteran and taking the bowl from Taya. I close my eyes and take a deep breath and call forth the fire.

It responds as if the Byrnisian magic bound to the bowl has been straining at its bonds, roiling just under the surface. A flame springs into existence between my hands, startling me so much I almost drop the bowl. It's shaped like a candle flame, but larger and brighter, feeding on nothing, dancing in midair. I can feel the flow of magic, from the bowl to my fingers to the warmth of the flame, and it makes me dizzy and guilty and exhilarated all at once.

Setting the bowl in my lap so I keep contact with it, I lift up my hands, concentrating hard. Yet the flame seems like something alive, eager to do my will. It rises with my hands, and when I turn my hands downward toward the arrayed soul-silver, the flame eagerly kisses the glittering metal and turns it slowly from silver to red.

When the metal starts to go pink, rust-smelling wisps of smoke drifting from its surface, Nahteran is ready with his wind magic. A faint breeze floats around the room, scentless, unlike those coming from the Fiorden and Byrnisian doorways. But when Nahteran moves his hands, it concentrates, becoming a tiny funnel cloud that bears down on the slowly melting silver. It has the effect of a putty knife, smoothing the lumpy, glowing blob of metal out until it resembles a rib, resembles the real phoenix flame armor.

Then Taya hits it with a blast of ice wind, solidifying it again.

We all stop and let the magic die down, staring at what we've created. I'm out of breath, and my heart is beating fast. Looking at the others, I see it's the same for them; Nahteran's face is flushed and Taya's chest is rising and falling rapidly.

"This is going to take for—ev—er," Taya observes between pants.

"We can stay down here all night if we have to," Nahteran says.

He's out of breath too, the magic having taken its toll on all of us, but a strange intensity has come over his face. His eyes are bright, and there's a spark in them, something I don't think I've seen on his face since I found him in Winterkill. It looks like hope.

———

After we assembled the basic shapes of the armor imbued with Byrnisian fire, Fiorden poisoning, or similarly dangerous magic, we melted down the gold and coated the pieces in a thin layer.

Then Nahteran and I huddled close to the lantern and used the points of our daggers to recreate the phoenix flame armor's intricate carvings as best we could; while Taya power drilled the tiniest of holes in the armor and strung it together with copper wire from the supply closet.

By the end of it, we were exhausted. We all had burns on our hands from the fire magic and cuts from getting too close to sharp edges in the imperfect light. All three of us were wilted and short-tempered and annoyed with each other.

But after the last snacks and midnight coffees were consumed, we all stepped back to stare at what we had created and realized—we have something. A decently good counterfeit of the phoenix flame armor. It won't hold up to close inspection, but we don't need it to. We just need the Silver Prince to put it on.

We pack everything up, being extra careful with the real armor, but moving fast. I'm desperate to get back up to my room and get a shower. My clothes are sticking to my skin with sweat, and if I'm lucky I might be able to get a couple of hours of sleep before I have to wake up for breakfast. I imagine Nahteran and Taya feel similarly.

But then a nagging thought sneaks through my sleep-deprived brain.

As Taya and Nahteran turn toward the stairs, I call out. "Wait! Now that we've got something to trade the Silver Prince for Mom, how is it all going to go down? I mean, once he figures out we betrayed him, I don't think he'll let Nahteran escape. And how will we get Mom back to Haven since we're not bringing the real phoenix flame armor with us?"

"You're right. That's not going to work," Nahteran says.

Taya bites her lip, thinking. "I know the Silver Prince's bargain said you had to take armor into Oasis. But if we came up with some plausible reason for it, do you think he would come here instead?"

An unmistakable look of relief flashes over Nahteran's face before he nods. "He wouldn't be happy about it. But yeah, he would, if he thought he would get the armor. Still, though . . ." He squints at me. "Are you sure you want him here? In Haven?"

No. That's almost the last thing I want. It makes my heart feel like it's turned into a block of ice. But it's better than the idea of Nahteran venturing into Oasis alone.

"At least then it would be on our terms."

"We could do it somewhere outside of Havenfall," Taya suggests.

"Past the inn's protection. That way he'll have to put the armor on right away, or he'll get sick."

I turn to her. "That's perfect."

She flashes a tired grin. "Any ideas?"

I think. We'll want it to be someplace we're familiar with—or can get familiar with before tomorrow. It needs to have hiding spots, but also be wide open, so that we can run if need be. And far away from people, so that the Silver Prince can't do any collateral damage.

"How about up in the mountains?" I turn to Nahteran. "Tell the Silver Prince with your mirror that you'll open a doorway at a certain time and place. We'll each wear a piece of the real armor so that we can make a doorway, but keep it hidden once the Silver Prince arrives. We'll wait until he gives us Mom, and then we'll give him the counterfeit armor. We'll activate the magic . . . and . . ."

And what? And then this nightmare will be over.

The Silver Prince has already tried to kill me and take Havenfall. He would conquer the whole damn planet if he could. And he has Mom. We have to end his threat however we can. No matter what it takes.

"Okay." Nahteran smiles, and for a second the shadows play oddly with his face, making him a stranger.

A vicious stranger, just like me.

He reaches into his backpack. "I'll send the message."

THAT AFTERNOON, NAHTERAN, TAYA, AND I climb up the mountain to familiarize ourselves with the spot where we plan to make the trade with the Silver Prince. We haven't heard back from him since Nahteran sent a message with the scrying mirror, but there's little else we can do to pass the time. Already the day is going unbearably slowly.

I thought I was in decent enough shape, but Nahteran and Taya outpace me as we climb. As we near the top, they're twenty yards ahead of me on the path, talking and laughing like we're not about to face off with a supernaturally powerful murderer. As if it's just another day.

I can feel myself getting more scared and irritable with every step. I can almost imagine the Silver Prince standing at the top of the mountain, his pale silhouette scarcely visible against the cloudy sky, flames dancing at his fingertips. He's right there, waiting, but Taya and Nahteran don't see him. I blink until the image disappears, wipe the sweat roughly from my brow. But I can't shake the feeling that we're walking straight into his trap, and I can't do anything about it. I can't stop us.

When we get back to the inn, I excuse myself to go help Willow with dinner, wanting to be by myself for a little while. She puts me to work stuffing and shaping tortellini alongside her, which is more responsibility than I usually get—my cooking skills are minimal enough that Willow usually relegates me to chopping or stirring duty. Which makes me think she wants an excuse to talk to me. It's still a couple of hours before the meal, and the other staff—the Fiorden and Byrnisian pages—are all off doing other chores, so it's just Willow and me in the cavernous kitchen.

"You're distracted today," she remarks, casually glancing at me out of the corner of her eye. Her hands move in a graceful almost-blur, creating a half dozen perfectly formed pasta shapes in the time it takes me to do one, all somehow without getting flour on her blue silk day-dress.

I've wondered, often enough, if she is happy here, happy to spend all her days at the inn. She seems to be, but I'm not sure I would be if I were in her shoes. She's smarter than all the delegates, and everything about her speaks to having had a glamorous past life. Is she like Graylin, content at the crossroads, or like Brekken, who deep down I know never would be?

The question is out before I can think about it. "Willow, if not for Havenfall, where would you be?"

Her hands keep moving, but she turns her head and looks at me in surprise. We've never talked much about her life in Byrn—she doesn't seem to like it, usually changes the subject. But now she just looks at me steadily.

"I would be a nomad," she says. "Out in the wild beyond the walls of Oasis."

"A nomad," I echo. Like Nahteran was telling me about.

She nods. "My standing in the court was already shaky"—she winks, maybe in reference to the affair I've heard rumors about—"but the last straw came when I wouldn't renounce my magic. The Silver Prince requires all his subjects to make that choice. Magic or safety."

I nod. "I've heard."

She pauses her work and turns her right hand up toward the ceiling. A tiny cyclone forms there, a perfectly self-contained dervish. I stare. The breeze coming off it gently carresses my face for a moment before Willow closes her fingers and it winks out.

"I was never very powerful, but all the same, my magic is a part of me," she says, her eyes distant. "So I talked to Marcus about staying here permanently, and here we are."

She elbows me to keep working, the moment of seriousness gone. "So whatever you're plotting, spare a thought for us strays for whom this is our only home."

That last sentence is delivered lightly, a joke, but it lands like an anvil in my chest.

A few minutes later, Willow bustles off to do something else. I continue my slow progress with the tortellini. When I finally have a dozen lined up before me, my phone buzzes in my pocket.

Glancing around to make sure Willow isn't watching, I wipe my floury hands off on my jeans and check my phone. On the lock screen is a text from Taya.

> Hey, Nahteran got a message back from SP. We're good
> to go.

I stare at the glowing words. My heart starts hammering, the bitter taste of fear seeping into my mouth. In my mind's eye, I see the Silver

Prince up on the mountain, just like in my paranoid imaginings earlier. Hands raised, flaming and deadly.

Now, with a few hours' reflection, our carefully wrought plan seems reckless to the point of idiocy. I can't fight for shit. Taya can't control her transformations. I don't know about Nahteran's skill set, but something tells me even if I did, I doubt I'd like our odds. We need more help.

I open the message and type a reply. A thumbs-up symbol. Then,

I was actually just thinking we could use more backup. OK if I ask Brekken?

For a moment after I send the text, there's nothing. Then the three dots that mean Taya's typing. Then nothing again. Finally, the text pops up, shorter than I'd expected from all that typing.

Sure, I guess so.

———

I don't see Brekken at dinner, so afterward, I head up to his room, a Tupperware full of pasta in hand as a peace offering. It's late—I didn't really realize how late until now. I hear him get up, shuffle around, and turn on the lamp. When he opens the door, he's still in the loose short pants and spun linen shirt he sleeps in, like he was about to go to bed. It makes my mouth dry up. He smiles at me—not quite as warm as usual, but I'm just glad I'm getting a smile—and steps back to let me in.

Despite yesterday's horrible news about the trial, our talk seems to have eased the stiffness between us, making things feel almost normal again. Brekken's room, though, is as clean and tidy as if it came out of a home-goods catalog, except where his blankets are rumpled and thrown back, the moonlight slanting over them. I feel my face blush and am immediately annoyed with myself.

Get it together. I came here because I had something important to ask him. Something maybe life-and-death.

"Can I sit down?" I ask, tugging at my sleeves, nervous suddenly.

"Of course. Always."

Brekken pulls out his desk chair for me and sinks down at the edge of his bed. As he does so, his smile slides away, leaving him looking serious. He knows me too well. He knows this isn't just a social call, as much as I'd like it to be.

When I start talking, the story spills out of me in a rush.

I tell him about Marcus's executive decision not to negotiate with the Silver Prince and my unexpected realization that I didn't want to give up on Mom, no matter the risk—and neither did Nahteran. I tell him about Taya's idea of creating counterfeit armor, and yesterday's project, all the molten metal and stolen souls.

But Brekken's reaction isn't what I expected. I thought he'd disapprove. Instead, his face grows more and more expressionless, and his eyes glare harder and harder. By the time I wrap up and ask him to join us for strength in numbers, I'm thoroughly unnerved. It's as if I'm looking at a beautifully carved and painted statue.

And I never expected the words that come out of his mouth next. "Maddie, I can't."

"Um—" I close my mouth and ball my fists on my thighs, blindsided. I look away so that my lip doesn't start trembling. "Okay."

Of course, it's not fair of me to expect him to be my knight in shining armor. Especially not before he leaves Havenfall to stand trial for a crime that was my idea. But it had never occurred to me that he would say no. Shining armor is kind of his *thing*. Or so I thought.

"Think it through, Maddie." Brekken's voice is oddly flat and cold.

He's very still. Even the moonlight seems to have retreated from the room, maybe gone behind clouds. "Training for the army in Myr, they taught us that the top officers never congregate all together in one room. Because it makes them more vulnerable to—"

"To attack, yeah, I get it," I snap. Like the president and the VP and the Speaker of the House or whatever. I read somewhere they never travel on the same plane so that if the plane goes down, the line of succession stands. "You're allowed to just say no, you know."

Because I'm not the freaking president. I'm just a girl without her mom.

"I want you to understand," Brekken says. "If I came with you and the Silver Prince killed me, Graylin would have to go to Fiordenkill to stand trial. If he killed both of us, Marcus would be without his husband *and* his heir. I know better than to tell you what to do, but . . ."

He trails off, and the silence that leaches in is heavy and suffocating.

"But what?" I prompt. My stomach is all knotted. I feel like this conversation is already fractured and headed in a bad direction. But a perverse part of me wants to see it through.

He tilts his head forward, like I really ought to understand without him having to say so. "You're heir to the Innkeeper," he says. "For the sake of Havenfall, for the summit, for everyone, do you ever think of developing just a bit of a self-preservation instinct?"

I dig my nails into my palms. "Is this still about Nahteran? Or do you really think I have some kind of duty to stay indoors where I'm untouchable?" My temper rises. "Maybe I should just lock myself in the closet along with the armor. Too bad I can't fit inside a safe."

"You know that's not what I'm saying," Brekken shoots back. "But also, what if the Silver Prince finds the real armor? You'll have handed your world to him on a platter, and he'll probably kill your mother anyway."

"So what do you think I should do?" I growl. "Just let him have her?"

Brekken doesn't say anything. He doesn't have to. His flat-line mouth and hard eyes say enough.

"She's my family," I say. A bubbling feeling in my chest warns me that the tears are about to make their appearance.

"You have to consider the greater good. What's right. Everyone is family to someone," Brekken says. "You can't make distinctions just because of that."

My heart drops, plummets. "Actually—" I stand up. "I really think I can."

Brekken stares up at me, and I feel a coldness hovering between us. And while I've cried in front of Brekken God knows how many times before, I really, *really* don't want to now.

"Good luck at the trial," I say, and make for the door.

Something stops me, though—seizes me, when my hand touches the doorknob. I can't leave like this.

The trial could go sideways.

This could be the last time I ever see him.

I turn around. "What if . . . what if we said screw the trial?" I ask, tears thickening my voice and blurring my vision.

Brekken tilts his head, his eyes widening and softening a little, but he says nothing.

"The people who died at Winterkill are gone," I say. Each word is painful coming up, like they have thorns, slicing at my lungs and throat. "You standing trial won't bring them back. Myr executing you won't bring them back, if that's what they decide. So why not just not go?" I grip the doorknob tight, willing my words to get through to him. "Our worlds have been allied for centuries. Surely one guy can't just upend that history. We'll talk to Princess Enetta. We'll figure something out . . ."

But my next words die on my tongue, because Brekken is shaking his head.

"It doesn't work that way," he says. "The way Fiordens view honor, Maddie . . . it's hard to understand if you didn't grow up with it, live and breathe it." He draws in a ragged inhalation, and for the first time I see the glimmer of fear in his eyes. "Do you think I want to go, Maddie? I don't. But the peace between our realms is at stake here."

"Stay for me, then," I whisper. "Do this for me."

Pain crosses Brekken's face. "Don't make me choose, Maddie. Please."

I keep my mouth shut. After a tense, painful moment, Brekken rises and takes one step toward me.

"I'll stay," he says, "if you call off your deal with the Silver Prince."

My heart thuds, dull and heavy. Like a stone dropping to the earth. I squeeze my eyes shut. Take a deep, shuddery breath.

"I'm sorry, Brekken," I say once I've gathered myself.

I hope he knows what I mean. That I'm sorry for everything. Sorry I can't agree to that trade. Sorry he has to be the one to stand trial. Sorry for the things I've said tonight, especially—especially if this is the last time.

"Me too," he says softly, and stands still and watches as I go.

22

THAT DAY PASSES IN A blur, and nearly twenty-four hours after my fight with Brekken, the bitter taste of tears is still on my tongue when my alarm goes off in the wee hours of the morning. It's still dark out, the moon shining through my window.

I turn over, my blankets soft and heavy around me, and think grog-gily of him. Something bad happened with Brekken. I wish it was just a dream.

But when I grab for my phone to silence the alarm, I know it's not. Everything comes crashing back quickly. Brekken telling me *no*. Him letting me turn around and walk away.

Knowing I might never see him again.

But I can't cry. I can't wallow. Nahteran, Taya, and I are planning to open a doorway into Oasis out in the mountains at sunrise. We are going to confront the Silver Prince, get Mom back, and then get him to put on the counterfeit armor so that he'll never be a threat to Haven-fall again.

Aided by the adrenaline that surges through my veins at the thought, I roll out of bed, splash some water on my face to wake myself up the rest of the way, and get dressed quickly. Jeans. Tank top. Boots. Dagger. A sweater baggy enough that it'll be able to hide a piece of the phoenix flame armor. I'd prefer not to bring the real armor at all—not let it come anywhere near the Prince—but we'll need it to open the portal to Byrn that will allow the Prince and Mom to come through to us.

I walk quietly down the stairs, not wanting to wake any of the delegates. I meet Taya and Nahteran in the ballroom, where there's a back door where we can exit without being seen by Sal's guards, one of whom is always stationed out front at night.

They're already there when I arrive. They haven't turned on any lights; Nahteran paces, while Taya stands looking out the window in a pool of moonlight. She wears her bomber jacket, and I'm hit with a quick burst of gratefulness that I saved it for her. Nahteran has a canvas jacket on, something else borrowed from Marcus. I can't see in the dimness, but I know they probably have weapons belted to their waists, just like me.

We're all nervous. Tightly wound. I wonder if they, too, thought about saying goodbyes just in case.

Taya hoists a lantern high, the same one she used when we created the counterfeit armor. Now we'll use it to hike the dark and steep trails up to the meeting place in the mountains.

She smiles at me, but it's thin, strained. "You ready?"

"As I'll ever be." I look over my shoulder. "Nate, the armor—"

I don't realize the slip—calling him Nate out loud—until after I've said it, but Nahteran doesn't seem to notice. He has his back to us and is kneeling in the center of the ballroom floor, right in front of where the Elemental Orchestra usually plays.

"What are you doing?" I hear Taya ask as I stare in confusion. "Nahteran?"

He takes a vial of something dark and viscous from his pocket—and smashes it against the floor. Liquid pools around him.

I'm still groggy, too much so to understand what he's doing, but my body reacts right away, spilling a wave of adrenaline and dread through me.

Nahteran yanks up both sleeves and presses his hands to his chest, and a howl of wind sounds around me. The world rocks beneath my feet. Beyond him, the doors to the hallway—to the rest of Havenfall—are closed. Barred shut.

"Nahteran, stop!" Taya cries out.

She's already running to him, almost losing her balance with every step as the floor rolls beneath her feet. The polished oak floorboards snap and bulge upward like we're on the deck of the *Titanic*.

I shrink back against the window, the cold glass trembling against my shoulder blades. The truth slowly sinks in. *What has he done?*

The ballroom floor starts to go transparent, like wood and stone are melting into glass. A hairline crack of light appears and grows.

A hot orange light.

The same light as the one that shines through the Byrnisian doorway.

No. No! Then I realize I'm saying it out loud. Yelling, "Nahteran, stop! Stop this!"

The wind swallows my voice, whisks it away.

I don't think my brother could stop the doorway from opening anymore even if he wanted to. He straightens up, shaking, pale and small against the chaos that has filled the room. The wineglasses that I've spent so many hours washing and drying and hanging whip off their racks and shatter against the wall. The chairs along the side of the room shake and tip over. Paintings and mirrors crash from the walls. I see one slip through the liquefying floor.

Suddenly Taya is there, in the center of the room. She has Nahteran by the arm; she hauls him across the heaving floor to the side of the room where I stand, clinging to the outer wall for support as everything shakes. Nahteran is wearing the phoenix flame armor. Beneath Marcus's coat, I can see one gauntlet on each wrist and the golden breastplate shimmers with a red stain, Byrnisian blood.

I feel like I'm spiraling. Falling.

This isn't how it was supposed to go.

"What is this?" Taya screams, shaking Nahteran by the collar.

He's a foot taller than her, but he doesn't stop her or react. Instead, he just wraps an arm around a pillar to stay upright.

"I'm sorry," he says.

The howling wind steals his words, but I can read his lips.

"The trade isn't supposed to be in Havenfall," I cry, shell-shocked. "Nahteran, what are you doing?"

"They planned this," Taya says furiously, keeping one hand fisted in Nahteran's jacket, even though he's not trying to go anywhere. "You and the Silver Prince. Didn't you?"

He hesitates for a second, and then nods, the motion almost lost in the upheaval all around us. My heart plummets, all the hope and happiness evaporating out of it.

Brekken was right.

Nahteran betrayed us. Again.

Then—

"It's not what you think," he yells.

One of the ballroom windows blows out behind him; he ducks, his arm to his face against the broken glass. Outside, trees sway, caught in the gale. The wind and crashing have intensified so much that when Nahteran speaks again, he has to almost scream to be heard.

"He told me it had to be here in Havenfall, or he wouldn't come. But he doesn't know about the trick armor. This can still work."

"Why didn't you tell us?" I ask, confused and impossibly hurt, so hurt it feels like a void has opened up in my chest to match the one forming beneath our feet.

I can feel the wood changing just like it did in Winterkill, turning honey-soft. The soles of my boots sink down. I see silhouettes beneath the floor, upside-down buildings, metallic and strange against a violently red-and-gold sky.

"Because you might not have believed me." Nahteran stumbles and almost loses his footing as the floor bucks beneath him. "And then there'd be no one to follow the Silver Prince's instructions and he'd kill Mom." He clings to the pillar like it's a life preserver in a thrashing sea. "I swear he doesn't know about the counterfeit. I swear it."

"Shut up," Taya snarls. Her hand whips out to point toward the opening to Oasis, and I see that the nail of her pointer finger has lengthened and darkened, into a blue claw.

"He's coming."

Nahteran blanches and hastily buttons his jacket. I don't know why. It's warm in the ballroom. Too warm. The hissing intensifies, glittering steam rising up from the opening into the air, and the ground shudders, the transparent part spreading until it's almost at our feet. I fling my arms out to keep my balance, and Taya grabs me and hauls me back before I fall over the edge. She drops to her knees, bracing herself against the wall, and I do the same.

A warm, metallic-smelling breeze fills the ballroom. Nahteran is standing, still. His expression a mask, impossible to read, his eyes glassy and his jaw set. His gaze stays fixed on the light in the doorway to Byrn. Its center, where the blood fell, is clear as diamonds. I can see Oasis's buildings and shining empty streets, black shapes in the sky.

Then a figure starts to rise from the opening in the floor. I can see only a silhouette through the dark steam, but I instantly recognize it. I know that pale form, those sharp features and proud posture. I know the Silver Prince.

He steps out into the ballroom, just as calm as if this were another night at the summit, another dance. He wears a crown that I never saw when he was pretending to preserve peace at Havenfall. It's a circlet of black metal with spikes rising straight up. A long, slender white sword dangles lazily from his fingertips. As I watch, frozen, he raises his hand and sends a thin, silent blast of fire at the doors to the hallway. Melting the filigree from the heavy wood—sealing the doors shut.

"Nahteran," he says, his voice rising above the hiss of the doorway as though carried by the Oasis air filling the room. His voice is warm, jovial almost, but it still sends a shiver through my bones. "I am glad to see you holding up your end of the bargain. I confess I wasn't sure if you would."

I shift my gaze to Nahteran, trying to catch my brother's eye. The look on his face is awe mixed with fear. It hurts my chest to see his reaction, which seems like a look forged out of years of history, and not good history.

He told us a minute ago that he was still on our side, but I no longer have faith that that's true. I want to believe it. I just can't. I push myself to a standing position and grab Taya's hand, pulling her up too. The ground is still shuddering, but I want to be on my feet if the Silver Prince comes at us with that sword. I draw my own dagger and grip it tight.

Nahteran stands his ground, stepping away from the pillar and drawing his sword. His other hand is fisted at his side, but his voice is calm.

"But you haven't fulfilled your part yet, Silver Prince," Nahteran says. "Where is she?"

"Ah."

I can't see the Silver Prince's face, but I'd bet anything he's smiling that Cheshire cat smile that I fell for so many times before. He turns back and kneels down next to the opening, the transparent doorway frothing and hissing around him. Reaching down into it, his hand disappears into the floor—and then a moment later, he draws it back out wrapped around a woman's wrist.

And then an arm.

And then Mom.

The Silver Prince pulls her out of the opening like a rag doll and sets her on her feet. She looks uninjured, but I wouldn't say okay. Her face is sallow and gaunt, her hair cropped short. Her clothes are ragged, and there are metal bands around her wrists and ankles—probably enchanted with binding magic. She stands stiffly, like she's been hurt.

But her eyes flash with life. It's strange and jarring to see, when so much else is wrong, when I'm so filled with fear. But a part of Mom is fighting back for the first time in forever, and that gives me just the tiniest spark of hope.

Nahteran looks as shaken as I am. His eyes are fixed on Mom, and he's leaning forward slightly, like he wants to go to her too.

"Mom," he whispers, and my heart splinters. "Are you okay?"

Could he have been telling the truth? That he only coordinated with the Silver Prince because he wanted her back?

The Silver Prince taps Mom's back—a deceptively casual gesture, but Mom stumbles forward from the force of it. I leap to catch her, and as I do—as her weight hits me, making us both stumble back—the Silver Prince seems to notice me for the first time.

And smiles. He sheaths his sword and lifts his hands, palms facing inward. Flames spring up between them, bright and eagerly lapping at the air. My breath catches. This isn't borrowed magic like with the soul-silver. It belongs to the Silver Prince, is native to him. And using it, he will never tire.

"Madeline." The Silver Prince's voice is silky smooth as ever, his manner relaxed despite the chaos all around us. "How nice to see you again."

His voice isn't raised, but somehow it cuts through the wind all the same, like the sound waves are boring a tunnel through the air just to reach my ears. Maybe they are; maybe the Silver Prince's control over the air reaches to a molecular level. I push Mom back behind me. Not that I'm much protection. I tighten my grip on the knife. It isn't magic, but it will have to do.

I won't let fear stop me.

I lunge at the Silver Prince, aiming my knife for his heart. He side-steps, leaving fire in the space where he just stood; my momentum almost carries me straight into it. I jerk to the side and pivot, trying to regain my bearings. I attack again, and the Silver Prince's fist catches me across the face.

Stars bloom in my vision, and my teeth rattle; I stumble back, the world tilting around me.

"Stop!" Taya's scream comes from behind me. "We have what you want! We have the armor!"

I twist to look behind me, and they're there, both of them, Nahteran and Taya, holding each other to stay upright. Nahteran has a gold breast-plate in his free hand, and Taya holds the two gauntlets. Behind them, Mom is looking on in horror, shaking her head wildly, but I know what she doesn't. That the armor is fake. I can tell, the shape subtly off, the carving not as intricate as it should be. But looking up into the Silver

Prince's face, seeing the naked greed animating his features, I know he can't tell.

My mind kicks into overdrive. When Nahteran opened the doorway in the ballroom, I thought everything was ruined. But seeing the fake armor makes me think we still have a chance to pull it off. The words I rehearsed in my head a thousand times yesterday burst from my lips.

"No!" I scream. "What are you doing?" I stagger to my feet, ready to lunge at Nahteran and Taya, to sell the performance that giving up the armor would be the destruction of everything I love.

Turns out I didn't have to fake the fear in my voice, or that I'm on the verge of tears. The ballroom of Havenfall is destroyed all around us. The Silver Prince is here. The world hangs in the balance.

But then—

A great *fwoom* sounds in the air. I turn around to see a fireball hurtling straight toward me.

But before it finds its target—namely, me—something hits my back with the force of a boulder. I go down, hitting the ground and rolling. Blue fur and fire flash through my vision, and the dagger drops from my grip. Taya has shapeshifted and pushed me out of the way just as the fireball flies over, close enough to singe the fur on her spine.

"Enough!" Nahteran cries. He sprints toward the Silver Prince, all the pieces of the counterfeit armor now in his hands. "Take it!"

But just as the Silver Prince is about to claim his prize, Nahteran stops, withdrawing the armor.

Nahteran backs up. "Promise me that no harm will come to them," he says, gesturing at Taya and Mom and me.

"I will make no such promise," the Silver Prince snarls.

He lifts his hands at his sides, flames flickering between his fingers.

A plume of fire rises from his palm, a slender, threatening column like a flaming sword, and lashes out at Nahteran.

Nahteran leaps back, but not fast enough; the fire catches him across the chest and he falls, swearing. I clap a hand over my mouth to hold in a scream. The counterfeit armor almost slides through the floor into Oasis before Nahteran rolls over and grabs it, jumping back to his feet.

"Haven't you learned that all the worlds belong to the strong?" The Silver Prince advances on Nahteran, who scrambles to his feet and backs away, the front of his shirt scorched from shoulder to shoulder. "It is impossible that we should have our new world without injury. It is them or us. Haven't I taught you that already?"

The flames lash out again. Nahteran throws up an arm to protect his face and cries out. The flames pull back and coil between the Silver Prince's hands. Nahteran stumbles, dropping the counterfeit armor to clutch his arm, and I see an angry burn mark running the length of his forearm.

I'm moving before I can think about it, running to pick up the armor. Holding the breastplate in one hand and the gauntlets in another to make it look more real, I advance on the Silver Prince, slow and deliberate, belying the terror battering at the inside of my chest. I realize now it was stupid to expect the Silver Prince would hold up his end of the bargain, to give Mom back without a fight if we gave him the phoenix flame armor. I have to get him out of here before he kills us all and burns Havenfall to the ground.

"Marcus has soldiers," I lie, keeping my eyes locked on the Silver Prince. "They're just on the other side of the ballroom door. If you want to live, take the phoenix flame armor and go."

The Silver Prince grins at me, reaching one graceful arm out toward the armor. "Changed your mind, Innkeeper? Aren't you afraid of what will happen when I have this?"

228

"I'm not the Innkeeper anymore," I growl. "My uncle is alive, no thanks to you. And no, I'm not afraid." They're my first words to him that aren't a lie.

And somewhere, in the background, I can hear pounding. Shouts. Like maybe Marcus is at the door. But all my senses are running together, adrenaline warping my perception. I can't tell if I really hear it or if it's just wishful thinking.

"You will be," the Silver Prince says, and snatches the armor from me.

I freeze, holding my breath, as his grin stretches wider. He lifts the breastplate up and drops it over his head, letting it settle on his shoulders.

Now.

I don't think anymore, my body taking over. I lunge for the Silver Prince and grab the breastplate, working my fingers through the gaps in the metal. I squeeze my eyes shut and call forth all the fire and poison magic in this metal, directing it inward at the Silver Prince's heart.

The Silver Prince screams, a terrible, agonized howl that drills into my ears, overtakes my world, and drowns out everything else. His hands wrap around my throat, closing my windpipe.

Panic, a pure animal panic that I've never felt before, obliterates me. I batter at the Silver Prince's chest, his face, keeping my left hand on the armor to continue pouring our deadly magic into him. But he won't release his grip on me. My eyes flutter, my vision going strange and watery, and then dark at the edges—

Then I'm free. I crash to the ground, gagging, and crawl instinctively away, looking over my shoulder to see Taya crouched in a face-off with the Silver Prince. He has one hand to his chest, and his face looks bruised. Red blood gathers at the corners of his mouth. As I watch, he staggers and falls back, spinning like a drunk.

My heart speeds. The magic is working.

The Silver Prince falls to his knees.

We have him. *It's over.*

But then he lifts his head toward me. His face is sickly white, blood trickling from his mouth and a hatred in his eyes so intense, it roots me to the ground, freezing me where I am on my knees. He raises my dagger from the floor.

It bursts into flame, white-hot like a tiny star trapped on Earth. And then it flies at me.

I can't move. I can't even scream at first; it punches its way free at the same time I feel a blistering heat on my face. The last thing I see before I shut my eyes is the Silver Prince falling forward, face-first. Sinking through the doorway and falling, falling, falling into Oasis.

Someone screams.

I open my eyes. Nahteran is suspended in the air above me, and for the briefest instant I think this is some kind of strange new magic.

Then my brother hits the ground hard on his back, my dagger hilt rising out of his chest.

23

STATIC FILLS MY SENSES. GRAY and buzzing, crowding out the swirling image of Byrn through the doorway, the clamoring wind, Taya's shout
of dismay. I black out for a few seconds, and when I come to, I'm on
my back, looking up at Havenfall's ballroom ceiling. It's caved in at the
northeastern corner, the beams snapped and splintered, a ragged bit of
gray morning sky showing through.

Then I realize the floor beneath me is soft, quicksand-soft. And I'm
sinking. I jerk up with a gasp, tugging my limbs free from the translucent substance of the closing doorway to Oasis.

Mom and Taya are crouched at Nahteran's side. He's unconscious,
and Taya's back blocks most of the sight, but I glimpse the red of blood.
My stomach flips over.

Mom turns to me at the sound I make. Her face is gaunt and grave,
bruised and flecked with dried blood. But I don't know whose blood.

"Maddie, catch," she says, and throws me something large and gold.

I catch it out of instinct, tipping forward with the weight of the phoenix flame armor breastplate. It's warm and thrumming with magic, but spattered with Nahteran's blood.

I shudder, wanting to throw it away from me, but I understand what Mom wants me to do. So I back up carefully, putting more distance between the breastplate and the gauntlets, which are still on Nahteran's wrists.

The farther back I go, the more the room settles. The seething wind dies down, and the floor settles and hardens, the almost-liquid of the doorway reverting to wooden boards. But warped and broken boards stick up at odd angles, the bedrock below showing through in places.

The orange light dims. The window into Oasis darkens and shrinks and shrinks until I can't see it anymore.

Then the wind finally dies down. For a moment, everything is silent, until the door to the hallway gives way with a deafening bang, the heavy wood crashing to the floor.

I whirl around, blinking the tears out of my eyes, to see my uncle rushing through, followed by Graylin and Sal and Willow. They drop the concrete planter they were using as a battering ram—another teeth-shaking impact on the floor—and rush toward us all at once. Marcus makes for me, while the other three converge around Nahteran and Mom.

He's deathly pale, his eyes closed. His chest is rising and falling, but faint and fast, like a bird's. Taya puts pressure on the knife wound with a wad of cloth that's already red around her hands. She determinedly blinks away tears. But I can tell from her face that this isn't good. And Mom. Mom leans over Nahteran, sweat-damp hair falling into her face. For the first time in years, the limp emptiness of her expression is now replaced with a terrible, faraway, lost look.

Back at Sterling Correctional Facility the other week, she told me not to endanger myself by seeking Nahteran out. That he was probably long gone, and she didn't want to lose two children when I got tangled up with the traders too. But all that forced indifference has fallen away now, leaving her broken, carved open. She didn't lose two children. But it's very possible she might lose the same child twice.

Marcus loops one arm beneath my torso and one behind my knees, trying to lift me up. But I pull back. My mind isn't working properly enough to form words, but I don't want him to take me away, I don't want to leave Nahteran. Yet in yanking away from him, a wave of dizziness hits me and I stagger, coming heavily back down on my knees. I belatedly realize the blow to the head I took must have been pretty hard.

A few yards away, Graylin is bent over Nahteran, healing magic shimmering between his hands. Mom is kneeling by his side, oblivious to Sal's attempts to bandage her up as Willow tends to Taya.

But I can't stop myself from staring at Nahteran, that horrible, heartbroken void in my chest yawning open again. He was telling the truth before. He didn't betray us. He did what he had to do to get Mom back. And now we have her. But he might not get to be with her again.

Somehow, we're moving, Marcus helping me stagger over to join the huddle at my brother's side. I can see the magic swirling through Graylin's fingers. But it's not working, or not working fast enough.

I fall down on my knees, reaching out to put pressure on the wound, and something falls out of the neck of my sweater. The jack necklace.

Taya notices it too. "What's that?"

I take it off with trembling hands and show it to Taya. "Soul-silver. I think it's a piece . . . a piece of his soul."

Taya, Graylin, everyone goes very still. For a moment, everything is quiet.

Then Taya says, "Give it to me."

My mouth dries up. I'd completely forgotten about the jack after Nahteran and I discussed it at Winterkill.

I'd need another Solarian, he had said. Another Solarian to restore that fragment of his soul.

Taya takes the necklace in her hands. I'm focused on Nahteran, but out of the corner of my eye I see her lips part and shock and awe register on her face.

"Maddie, it's a piece of his soul."

"What?" Focused as I am on Nahteran, making sure that his chest is still rising and falling, her words don't sink in at first. Then they do. I look up, my breath snagging. "What do you mean?"

She doesn't answer. Just takes a ragged breath. "Maddie . . ."

For a moment, everything else in the world fades away except Nahteran and Taya and me. I watch, not daring to breathe as she pulls the chain from the jack and tosses the former aside. She holds the jack carefully in cupped, bloodstained hands. She squeezes her eyes shut, her face creasing in concentration. And . . .

Something floats up from the metal. Something scarcely visible, hardly more than a shimmer in the air.

I hear myself make some indistinct noise of exclamation, words being far out of my grasp at this point. Taya's eyes fly open and fix on the same thing, the shimmering bit of *something* in the air.

Selu, I think. Soul.

Taya lets the jack, its shine duller now, fall through her fingers to the floor. She lifts her hand and catches the *selu*, wrapping it around her fingers like the palest, most translucent thread. She lowers it to Nahteran's face. She tips her hand down over his mouth, and the translucent light slips from her fingers and between his lips.

My heartbeat fills my hearing, slow and erratic. I'm spent, as exhausted as I've ever been in my life, but also as alert as I've ever been, waiting, hoping for Nahteran to wake up.

His chest reaches the top of its arc and stops.

My heart threatens to break all the way open.

But then he breathes in deeply. His eyes flutter. He shifts beneath my hands, and turns his head to the side and coughs out a mouthful of blood.

I snatch my hands back from his chest, still scarcely breathing. Taya, Mom, Marcus, Graylin, Sal, Willow, and I watch in wonder as the wound from the dagger slowly closes up, his skin repairing itself like new. Bloodied, but unbroken.

Muscle memory from first aid classes at school finally kicks in, and I hastily but gently roll Nahteran over on his side, positioning one arm under his head and one extended outward, holding him up. Then Graylin and Marcus are on either side of me, Willow and Sal standing by with hesitant smiles. And hope starts to trickle back into my heart.

———

Soon, I'm in the covered porch that serves as an infirmary, lying on one of the narrow white-sheeted beds. Nahteran is sleeping in the one next to me. Early morning sun from an eggshell blue sky pours into the room. Half an hour ago, the room felt crowded with Mom, Taya, Marcus, and Graylin all clustered around us. The anxiousness in the air was palpable as they monitored us for signs of downturn. Graylin sat between Nahteran's bed and mine, taking turns pouring healing magic into us both. Nahteran was on the edge of death from getting stabbed, and the jack's magic—getting that piece of his soul back—didn't fix the burns on his arms and chest. I am, according to Graylin, extremely concussed, and my body is covered with bruises from tangling with the Silver Prince. Meanwhile, Taya—who came out the best of us three, though she still

235

needed bandages up and down her arms to cover the bright red burns—caught Marcus and Mom up on what happened.

I can't help but wish that Brekken were here, to hold my hand and distract me from the aching all through my body and the pounding in my head. But he's gone, through the Fiordenkill doorway to stand trial. And more than that, I don't know, even if he were here, that there would be any coming back from the things we said yesterday, as far as our relationship goes. He'll never change his priorities—his duties, his country, the order and safety of the Realms—and maybe it's selfish of me, but I'll never be sorry for trying to save Nahteran and Mom, even though it risked everything else. Even if I had failed, I still wouldn't regret it. I don't know how to bridge that gap with Brekken or how to mend that break.

"Graylin," I mumble, and he turns his head toward me, brow wrinkled with concern.

He reaches out to feel my forehead, but I stick a hand out of the covers to stop him.

"I was just wondering about Brekken. Did he talk to you before he left? Did he rehearse his defense?"

Graylin smiles sadly and nods. "I tried to convince him to let me go instead, but he wouldn't have it, your Brekken. He showed me the speech he was planning to read at the trial. It was good." Graylin lays a comforting hand on my shoulder, his eyes sympathetic. "I know it must not be much help to hear, Maddie, but I have faith. If anyone can win Myr over, it's Brekken. You know he's a charmer."

I smile weakly and nod. I'm not totally satisfied, of course, but I don't have to figure out things with Brekken today. For all Brekken's trepidation about our plan with the Silver Prince, I survived. I have a chance to make things right, now. I just have to hope that Brekken gets that chance too. I want him to be safe and happy no matter what becomes of *us*.

Out of the corner of my eye, I see Taya looking our way, her hair tucked not so casually behind her ear. My heart flips a little. Turns out, shoving away my feelings for her while she was in Solaria didn't make them disappear. But deep down, even if she feels the same way, I know I need to take time to heal from everything that happened with Brekken. I need to focus on my family for now. My newly whole family.

Once Nahteran is out of the danger zone, everyone clears out except for Mom. To give us some privacy, I guess. Mom quickly falls asleep in the chair between our beds. I close my eyes too and let the quiet wash over me. But then . . .

"Maddie." I hear my name, softly. I let my eyes open a crack, not sure if I'm dreaming or not, to see Mom leaning toward me, outlined in hazy sunlight.

Some time has passed, I realize. The sun streaming into the infirmary isn't morning sunlight, but bright midday rays. And Nahteran is sitting up in his bed. He still looks pale and fragile, but he's *awake*.

He smiles weakly at me. "Hi."

Joy lights me up, and I clamber out of bed to give him a hug. My battered body screams in complaint, but I ignore it. Nahteran's alive. That's the only thing in the world that matters at this moment. He's still for a second, like he's surprised, but then his arms come up hesitantly around me too.

"I was just telling Nate—" Mom's voice cracks, and she breaks off, starts again. "I was just telling Nahteran that I'm sorry for not protecting you two from this. Sorry for everything."

I open my eyes to stare at her over Nahteran's shoulder. Protests immediately rise to my lips, and I open my mouth to voice them, but Mom stops me with a shake of her head.

"I thought Cadius loved me. I thought he was different," she says, her voice pulled taut, on the edge of cracking. "I trusted him when I shouldn't have, and I ruined everything."

Nahteran pulls back from me, looking pained. He shakes his head slightly. "I'm the one who should apologize." He takes a deep breath and looks down at his hands. "I worked for the Prince for years. I trusted him. I almost gave him the armor—"

"But you didn't," I cut in. I grab Nahteran's shoulder so he's forced to look up at me. "You were a kid." I turn my gaze to Mom. "And you fought the soul trade. You dedicated your life to fighting it. One mistake doesn't undo that." Tears are welling up inside me, but they aren't tears of sadness, not precisely. Still . . .

I glance at Mom, who was watching Nahteran like a hawk for hours before I fell asleep. Even though Mom is almost entirely still, even bruised and battered and her face lined and heavy with grief—even so, she looks more alive than I've seen her in ten years.

"No more apologies," I manage to get out. "No one's ruined anything. We're all here, we're alive. That's what matters."

I know it can't stay like this, the three of us here in peaceful stillness. When the Silver Prince's lackeys broke into Sterling Correctional and kidnapped Mom, they obviously didn't do her the courtesy of covering his tracks. She's still a fugitive, still wanted, still on death row. We'll have to help her go into hiding, or figure something else out. But at least she's alive. She's alive, and she's going to stay that way.

As it turns out, yesterday was the last day of the summit. I'd completely lost track of the time. Willow supervised the exodus of the delegates through the doorways this morning while Marcus was with us in the infirmary. Somehow, miraculously, the commotion from the ballroom this morning didn't wake the delegates, and the exit proceeded as planned.

By the time I'm feeling well enough to venture out to the kitchen with Marcus at my side, the hallways of Havenfall are shockingly empty and so quiet that I almost think I can hear the yellow sun streaming through the windows. Usually, the end of the summer and the delegates leaving makes me melancholic, the final ritual before I have to climb on the bus back to Sterling and go back to my life. To being Murder Girl again, to being alone every day, to a world empty of magic.

But I don't feel sad this year. Mostly because when I was dozing in the infirmary, eyes closed but not quite asleep, I caught a little of the quiet conversation between Mom and Marcus. I overheard words like *tutors* and *homeschooling* and possibly *SATs*. And *keep the kids together*.

Nahteran and Mom can't go back into the real world, at least not yet. Nahteran is thought to be dead, and Mom's a fugitive. So I have a feeling that Marcus won't make me go back to Sterling. After what happened, he'll probably never let me out of his sight again. And given the choice, I'll always choose Havenfall.

"I've been thinking," Marcus tells me in the kitchen, then trails off. I'm at the worktable, wolfing down a bowl of cereal as fast as I can without my bruised face hurting. My uncle's at the counter, chopping vegetables for dinner. His favorite thing about the end of the summit, every year, is that with all the staff gone, he gets to start cooking again. I look up—thinking, at first, that his voice has just been lost in the loud drone of the window AC unit that he's cranked up. But I see him looking thoughtful, eyes in the middle distance.

"Thinking about what?" I prompt.

Marcus takes a deep breath. "I think we should call off next summer's peace summit."

I stiffen, a half-chewed bite of cereal lodging in my throat. I swallow it down painfully and then stare at Marcus like he's lost his mind. "Cancel it? Why?"

"Not cancel," Marcus says. He tips the cutting board to the side, pushing a pile of carrot slices into a bowl with the blade of the chef's knife. "Postpone it, I suppose." He looks up, meets my eyes. "And instead, call a few people we trust from all the Realms to spend the year here with us. And work together to root out the rest of the soul trade here in Haven, and even in the other realms, since we have the phoenix flame armor. What do you think?"

I'm almost speechless. Postponing the summit, directing Havenfall's resources to stopping the soul trade and gathering the silver? It hadn't even occurred to me that that was an option.

"Why are you asking me?" I manage.

Marcus holds my gaze. "Because I care about your opinion. You're going to be the next Innkeeper, if you still want to be. What we do here affects you." He looks down then, suddenly becomes very still. "Which is something I should have learned a lot earlier. I'm sorry about that."

"It's okay." I sit up straighter, genuine excitement squiggling through me. It's almost an unfamiliar sensation. I've spent so much of this summer being afraid or shoving down my fear. But with the whole year at Havenfall, with the phoenix flame armor and Mom and Nahteran and maybe others too, I suddenly feel like there's nothing in all the worlds we can't do.

"There are things we have to take care of here first," Marcus continues. "The peace treaty, for instance. We still need a few more signatures each from Byrn and Fiordenkill. And we don't have any at all from Solaria."

Momentary panic shoots through me, then embarrassment. In all the chaos, I'd almost completely forgotten about the peace treaty. "But the delegates are already gone. How can we . . ."

"We have the phoenix flame armor," Marcus says with a wry smile. "Willow is going to be going into Byrn with Sal, since it might be unstable after the Prince's death. But if you ask very nicely—and do some self-defense training with Sal—I might let you go into Fiordenkill and Solaria, as long as you take a buddy."

I stare at him, almost too shocked to be excited. Instead, the hope is like a tidal wave on the horizon—only a tiny ridge in the distance now, but growing bigger, closer, and I know it'll be overwhelming when it hits. I could go back to Fiordenkill, not in secret this time, but on a diplomatic mission. I could go to Solaria with Taya and Nate.

Marcus comes around to my side of the counter and leans against it with his arms crossed. His expression is carefully neutral. But no matter how much he tries to hide it, I think he's excited too. I can see the spark in his eyes.

"We need to repair the ballroom, at the very least fix the roof before it rains. Replace those gold plates that mysteriously went missing." He cracks a smile. "And we need a more secure way to keep the phoenix flame armor. I've been calling around. Thinking maybe we could get some kind of built-in vault downstairs, like they have at banks."

"Sounds expensive."

"Very." He massages his temples. "Just one of the very many things you'll have to deal with as Innkeeper." Raising his head, he smiles crookedly at me. "I won't be sorry to pass the mantle when the time comes. But you have a lot of learning to do in the meantime."

I nod, resisting the urge to say something snarky about how I managed well enough before. But I can't stop the grin from spreading across my face. "Just tell me what to do."

"To start with," he says, "I think you should call your dad." He pulls my cell phone from his jeans pocket and comes over to slide it across the table to me. "I mean, finish eating first, but it's past time he heard about Nahteran."

I stare at the phone, my heart thudding. I'm excited by the prospect of sharing good news, but—

"What do I even say? How do I even begin to explain all this?" I gesture vaguely around, trusting that Marcus will get what I'm trying to say.

Oh hey, Dad, remember how your ex-wife snapped out of nowhere and murdered your adopted son? Turns out none of that is true at all. She lied to protect me from the magical bounty hunters who actually kidnapped him and sold his soul to an evil prince. But I found him. Nate is alive and he goes by Nahteran now and is actually a shapeshifter from another world. Oh, and there are other worlds.

Annoyingly, Marcus just says, "You'll figure it out."

When I stare at him incredulously, he adds, "Tell him the truth. Your dad's a good guy; I trust him. Invite him to the inn if you want. I don't think Nahteran will be venturing out anytime soon, so if your dad wants to see him it has to be here."

"Are you serious?" I ask, holding my breath.

Keeping the inn secret has always been priority number one. But how great would it be to bring Dad here? The petty little kid in me wants to see his face when I prove to him I never lied about the magic that lived here, not ever. And the greater part thrills at the idea of having my whole family, here, together, even if it's not forever.

Marcus shrugs. "Tell you the truth, Maddie, I think things are going to get a lot messier from here on out. Harder to keep a secret."

But the way the corner of his mouth curves up tells me he doesn't entirely hate this idea.

"We might as well get ahead of the story."

———

Later that night, I stand up on the balcony where I once poured my heart out to the Silver Prince, and then later begged Nahteran to give our family a chance. This time, I watch the sun slip below the mountains.

I'm alone, but I'm not. Dad is with me, connected through the phone at my ear. Below my feet, somewhere in the inn, are Marcus and Graylin and Willow and Mom and Nahteran and Taya.

They are probably still sitting in Marcus's living room where I left them. There were so many people that Nahteran and Taya and I were relegated to cushions on the floor, the adults claiming the couch. We spent the night playing cards, drinking wine and tea, telling stories, making plans. Together. Safe.

"I'm still not following, Maddie," Dad says, sounding puzzled over the faint tinny buzz of our bad connection. "I'll come to your uncle's place if you want me to so badly. I can be there tomorrow, but why now? And why do you sound so *happy*?"

"I can't tell you on the phone, Dad."

It's too big. Too much.

I let out a laugh of pure exhilaration and hope into the starry twilight. Maybe there's magic in the rest of the world after all. A breeze picks up, lifting my hair, carrying the scents of pine and flowers and running water.

"Let me show you," I tell him. "Come to Havenfall. You have to see it for yourself."

ACKNOWLEDGMENTS

What a wild and strange journey it's been! Writing and launching *Phoenix Flame* through seemingly endless global upheaval was a challenge unlike any I've ever faced, and I couldn't have done it without the most awesome publishing team an author could ask for.

Thank you to the whole team at Bloomsbury on both sides of the pond, including Cindy Loh, Claire Stetzer, Diane Aronson, Erica Barmash, Faye Bi, Phoebe Dyer, Beth Eller, Courtney Griffin, Mattea Barnes, Naomi Berwin, and everyone else who has had a hand in bringing *Phoenix Flame* to the world! I will forever be thankful for your talent, hard work, and enthusiasm. Thank you for loving Maddie, Brekken, Taya, and Nahteran as fiercely as I do.

Thank you to designer Sarah Baldwin and artist Peter Strain for creating the absolutely stunning, gorgeous, showstopping covers of

Havenfall and *Phoenix Flame*. There aren't enough adjectives in the world to do your beautiful art justice.

Thank you to Lexa Hillyer, Lauren Oliver, Lynley Bird, Stephen Barbara, Lyndsey Blessing, Pete Knapp, and everyone else at Glasstown, InkWell, and Park & Fine—I am blessed to have so many brilliant and indefatigable minds on my team! And thank you, too, to Deeba Zargarpur, Alexa Wejko, and Emily Berge—I'm so lucky and proud to count you among my friends.

The best thing about working with books for a living is all the wonderful people I've met along the way. Thank you so much to Elizabeth, Katherine, Jazmia, Patrice, Laura, Arvin, Mark, and all my other friends and colleagues in this wide world of publishing—you make it all worth it.

Thank you to Celine, Liz, Ronnie, Quinta, Emily, Lindsey, and Brent for being lifelines during the great lockdown of 2020 and always. I am so grateful for you. And I know I probably owe you a text.

Thank you to my family for always being my solid rock, no matter what the world might throw our way. Love always!

Read on for a bonus chapter from Nahteran's perspective!

The landscape looked so peaceful. That's what struck Nahteran as Wyoming scrolled by outside the window, Taya in the driver's seat next to him, the mountains a distant presence to their west. Byrn had plains too, but they were the opposite of peaceful, the ground charred and split with the scars of lightning, the sky constantly roiling with fire-laden clouds. Nothing like this, the rolling, scrubby fields interspersed here and there with scrappy trees or clumps of bushes, cows or horses grazing behind wire fences, stretching as far as he could see beneath a lacquered blue autumn sky.

But it seemed wrong somehow, that quiet. He didn't feel peaceful. Anxiety thrummed beneath his skin. He was frightened of where they were going, yet at the same time he felt like there were invisible threads tied to his bones, tugging him forward.

For a few months now, he and everyone else at Havenfall had been tracking down the soul-silver, and one by one, freeing the Solarians bound inside. It was an enormous project, and sometimes Nahteran had to push away his frustration at the slow, careful nature of it. It was a multistep process of finding a trader, learning everything there was to know about them, and only then making a move to recapture the soul-silver.

There were moments when Nahteran edged uncomfortably close to nostalgia for his time in Byrn, a servant to the Silver Prince. When the

Prince wanted something, he wasn't furtive about it. Thunder and lightning would shake the city. People would fall over themselves to bring him what he wanted. Even though Nahteran hated and feared him, being in close proximity to that power was like touching his finger to a live wire and feeling the electricity shoot through. Painful but exhilarating at the same time. Not this slow, careful, gradual work.

He knew if he brought this up to Taya, she would remind him of everything they had accomplished already. The Solarians back at the inn that they had freed from the soul-silver. Some were still healing up in the infirmary, some opted to return to Solaria, some decided to join with Havenfall and were going out on their own missions. Some had been trapped in the silver so long they didn't even understand English. These Graylin took in and tried to figure out a way to communicate through some new, shared language.

As Havenfall's resident Solarians, Nahteran and Taya were the ones responsible for actually freeing the souls from their spellbound prisons. Nahteran still couldn't quite explain what it was they were doing. When he held one of the silver objects in his hands, it wasn't like he could articulate anything about the soul inside. Yet sometimes it was like he could feel a pull, some invisible tether tugging him toward another silver object. When the two pieces were close enough, something happened—a rush of energy, a blinding white light, and then there was a person where there wasn't one before.

A soul, put back together.

But the soul-silver trade had split many Solarians into more than two pieces. Bringing two together would cause the person's body to reappear, but that didn't mean they were whole again. For that to happen, to bring them fully back to themselves, someone had to track down and hunt and bring back each splinter of soul, wherever it was in all the worlds.

Sometimes—often, though it hurt to think about—they couldn't find all the pieces at all. The Solarian would never be whole.

Would that be his own fate? Walking around for the rest of his life with a missing piece, a hollow place, an emptiness that would never go away?

It didn't have to be, he told himself. Not if he and Taya succeeded today.

As if she had heard her name in his thoughts, she glanced over at him from the driver's seat. "Don't look so worried," she said with a light smile. "You'll jinx us."

Nahteran tried to return the smile but it felt forced, and Taya had already turned her gaze back to the road. Around them, only occasional vehicles trundled by: truckers and pickups and minivans. "Of course," he said, trying to keep his voice similarly light. "Nothing to worry about. Not like we're trying to stake out an infamous silver trader or anything."

Sarcasm was not employed in the Silver Prince's court. It was a new skill to Nahteran. But he was learning. Between Taya and Maddie, he had plenty of material.

"Anyway, I'm taking it as a compliment," Taya said. "It means Marcus finally trusts us to do important stuff."

"Or we're just the next best option since Maddie and Brekken are in Fiordenkill." Marcus had been kind and welcoming to Taya and Nahteran, but there was a trace of wariness in how he had kept them so far from many missions outside Havenfall. Taya wasn't part of Marcus's family, and Nahteran was still regaining everyone's trust after abetting the Prince in his effort to get Mom back. For a few weeks after the Silver Prince's attack, Marcus had kept them relegated to the inn. Now, though, as they tracked down more and more leads, more silver traders, he and Taya had been called into the fray. And thank God.

Lately, Nahteran felt like there was an electric current running beneath the surface of his skin. Like if he couldn't be in motion, couldn't take action, it would burn him up from the inside.

Taya shrugged. "Then I guess we better kick ass."

Nahteran swallowed. He looked at her phone, fastened to the dashboard with a stand improvised from duct tape. The cracked glass screen showed a grainy sprawl of fields and straight roads—the landscape around them now—but up ahead, they'd go west into the mountains, where a red star blinked. Their destination.

About a month ago, the name had started tripping out of traders' mouths, helped along by the Heiress's truth serum. Janna Reynolds. It sounded so ordinary, so unremarkable, except for the way the traders said it. With a mix of jealousy and fear. She was a new trader to the scene, and a different kind than Whit and the others—locals who had heard the rumors about magic at Havenfall and decided to capitalize on it, working with unscrupulous delegates from Fiordenkill and Byrn to smuggle soul-silver from those worlds into this one.

No, Reynolds had money. Last week, they'd captured the trader Whit—the one who almost killed Maddie—and brought him to Havenfall, and he told them all about her. Hundreds of pieces of soul-silver lost from Havenfall over the years had ended up in her possession, even though she had never been to Havenfall herself, even though she was human. She had the magic of money, which Nahteran was learning was just as potent as Byrnisian fire. She bought soul-silver from the traders slinking around Havenfall and then sold the pieces at marked-up prices to buyers around the country. She did deals only once or twice a year, but when she did, powerful people flew in from all over the world. How much did she know about the nature of the magic? Nahteran wondered. Did she know that every bit of stolen magic was bought with a living soul?

And one of them his.

That's what he hadn't told Taya, hadn't told anyone. That going through the records, he'd become familiar enough with the trader's notations to start to see patterns. It was a strange thing reading about the splitting up of your own soul into a dozen strands, then used to bind magic to silver. The neat bloodlessness of it all. Ten pieces to the Silver Prince. One piece gone unaccounted for, which Nahteran figured had to be the jack necklace that Maddie wore. And one last piece sold to Janna Reynolds among hundreds of other objects over the years. A silver bangle, binding—appropriately enough—Byrnisian fire magic.

And now they were headed Reynolds's way.

What would it feel like to be whole again?

The opposite of Havenfall, the Reynolds mansion was a low, boxy creation of stone and glass, a jutting presence on the mountainside. They could just make it out from down below on the road. The trees had been cleared away around the house, leaving a ring of violently green, militaristically trimmed grass. The narrow road off the highway where they turned ended in a dead end: a gate, closed and locked by an electric padlock.

Taya parked the car to the side of the road, and they began the arduous journey up the mountainside on foot, under the cover of trees, staying as silent as they could. Taya held out her cell phone, transmitting their location back to Marcus so he would know where to go with Sal and the others tomorrow. It was slow going, and Nahteran was acutely aware of her faraway expression as she glanced around at the trees. How much easier would it be if she could assume her animal form, with its long stride and padded paws?

But he wouldn't be able to keep up. He had never been able to change his shape at will, like Taya and some of the other Solarians could. The best he could manage was getting some scales to rise along his arms and cheekbones, replicating the Byrnisian appearance that he had worn for so many years of his life.

"When you were in Solaria," he asked, "were animal shapes grouped by family?" The real question underneath hung in his mind, a haunting echo. *If I could access my animal form, would it look like yours?*

He kept his voice low so it didn't carry, but he could tell from the slight shift in the set of Taya's shoulders that she had heard him and was thinking about her answer. Strange how little some things could change over the years. He had a hard time thinking of her as his sister; he didn't remember their early years together as well as she did. He knew this was painful to her, but there was nothing he could do about it. But then occasionally there were moments like these when he had a flash of feeling like he was looking in a mirror.

"Not necessarily," she said, and with his brain spinning in double-time anxiety the closer they got to the mansion, it took him a moment to realize she was responding to his question about animal forms. "Not that I saw. It has more to do with you as an individual. You can't guess what someone's shape will be until it comes upon them."

And what if it never does, he wanted to ask, but let it drop. Maybe once they found the bangle and restored the last piece of his soul, he would find out. Maybe it was just that one missing piece, that one empty space, and then it would be there—his true form, his Solarian form.

Maybe those moments would go away. Moments when he felt a yawning gulf of anger and emptiness threatening to swallow his heart.

The trees around them were alive with sound—birdsong, the wind whispering through branches, all the small forest noises Nahteran was used to by now. Yet, the closer they got to the Reynolds mansion—glimpses of blinding glass occasionally flashing through the trees—the more these subsided. In their place, Nahteran could hear the hum of a generator somewhere. One of the traders, interrogated with truth serum, had said that Reynolds operated off the grid—like Havenfall, keeping her place of business secret from the rest of the world. But where the point of Havenfall's secrecy was protection, hers was profit.

There was something else too that was strange, disconcerting. Something else floating toward them.

Music. Classical music, to be exact. It was distant, tinny. Clearly played out of a speaker. But there was a discordant, repetitive note woven through it. A screech—

"An alarm," Taya muttered.

Cold seeped through Nahteran's body. Had they been seen? He stepped closer to Taya, his muscles tensing and his limbs automatically going into a fighting stance. Taya stared intently at the bank of trees, head cocked and mouth flattened into a tight line.

But there was no other sound. Nothing approaching. Nahteran wasn't sure how long they stood there—thirty seconds, a minute, two— but the sound stayed constant: the ornate, fussy music shot through with the insistent squawk of the alarm.

Eventually, Taya took a step forward, and Nahteran followed, his blood rushing in his ears. They got to the edge of the trees and looked out over the unnatural, golf-course-like lawn. Immediately something presented itself as wrong: the number of cars on the gleaming, circular black driveway. There were several, and they were not the sleek things that Nahteran had expected based on the rest of the place. Parked on the asphalt were rugged black SUVs and one motorcycle—not like Taya's but a huge, hulking one, seemingly meant to intimidate. It didn't square with what the traders had said about Janna Reynolds: a cold, ruthless woman who liked to use her money and power to collect beautiful things.

That, and the front door was open. Standing half open, unattended, giving way to a glimpse of an immaculate living space, all stone and glass.

"Maybe she's with buyers," Taya said.

"She's not supposed to be, not today." The thought made sweat start to prickle his hands. He had run over everything in his head a thousand times. Under the influence of truth serum, the trader they had in custody at Havenfall had told them about a deal that was supposed to go down later this week—Reynolds planned to sell hundreds of soul-silver objects for somewhere north of a million dollars. Before that could happen, Marcus, Sal, and volunteers from Havenfall would break in and capture Janna Reynolds and reclaim her vault of silver. But whatever she'd already sold was most likely lost to them. Whit had said that Reynolds didn't keep records of her buyers. With her, enough money bought you total anonymity. If this deal went down before Marcus and the others arrived to stop it, the Solarian souls trapped in the objects could be lost forever.

Including Nahteran's.

"Shouldn't there be guards?" Taya whispered, her dark eyes scanning continually over the mansion and lawn. "It feels like there should be guards. Security of some kind."

Dread seized Nahteran's heart, and before he could think better of it, he stepped out of the cover of the trees onto the grass. The warmth of the sun fell over his face, but it couldn't calm his raging heart, a drumbeat only he could hear.

But nothing happened. Nothing changed. Here, though, he could tell that the alarm and the music were coming from the house. Something inside him tugged him closer, like he was a puppet on a string. He walked toward the front door.

"Nahteran!" Taya scrambled to catch up with him, caught his arm. "We shouldn't do this."

He didn't want to tell her about the bangle, the fragment of his own soul that might be inside this house, might be being bargained over right now. It felt selfish to focus on that when so many souls were at stake; selfish to fixate on it when he was functioning well enough with eleven out of twelve pieces back in place.

But he didn't feel like himself, even if he wasn't entirely sure who his *self* was. His life was better than it had been in years—the Silver Prince was dead, and he was safe at Havenfall, with all the people he cared about around him. Maddie, Marcus, Graylin, Taya, Dad, Mom. And they were making real progress against the soul traders, freeing Solarians from their silver prisons every day. But nightmares still plagued his sleep. Dark feelings courted his mind: anger at Mom because she hadn't saved him from the kidnappers all those years ago. A sick yearning for a taste of the power he'd had at the Prince's side in Byrn. A dread that he was eternally trapped between worlds, not really Solarian and not fully human. People weren't supposed to feel things like this. There had to be something wrong with him, something broken that regaining this last piece of his soul would fix.

"If the buyers are here, we can't let them get away," he hissed to Taya. "We'll never track down the objects if they do. We have to stop them."

Taya's jaw was set, her eyes burning. He could tell she didn't disagree. Still, she said, "There's only two of us. And—"she gestured toward the collection of vehicles on the driveway—"a lot more of them."

"I have these." Nahteran let his hands drop to the two daggers at his waist, touching the hilts to reassure himself that they were still there, though he never left Havenfall without them. "And you're a Solarian."

Taya cracked a smile, though her eyes were grim. "So are you."

"You know what I mean."

Taya sighed. "Fine." She cracked her knuckles. "Let's do this."

As they crossed the lawn, the music crescendoed to a roaring finale—a triumphant clamor of strings and trumpets—and then faded out. But the alarm continued, a screeching backdrop to Nahteran's growing fear. And there was another sound, a low rumble. He realized all the vehicles were still running, empty as they were. Keys dangled from the motorcycle ignition. Whoever they belonged to, they wanted to make a quick getaway.

He drew his daggers, careful not to let the blades rasp against the hilts.

He crossed the threshold into the house, Taya behind him. As they'd seen from outside, it was empty, ominously so, the expensive, minimalist furniture looking like the stage setting for a play. But two things marred the pristine room. The first was a set of muddy footprints across the light-wood floor. The second was a woman, lying on her side at the entrance to a wide, glass-walled hallway, breathing softly with eyes closed. She was middle-aged, with powdery skin, blond hair, and expensive clothes. There was a mottled bruise on her forehead, and her wrists were tied in front of her with duct tape.

"Janna Reynolds," Taya said with distaste. She crouched down and held a hand in front of the woman's slightly open mouth. "She's breathing. I guess one of her buyers double-crossed her."

Nahteran's whole body was prickling with adrenaline; it seemed to surge through his veins with every blare of the alarm. "We should take her back to Havenfall. Maybe she'll cooperate, tell us where she's been sending the silver."

Taya nodded. "But let's deal with them first."

She lifted a hand and pointed down the hallway, where a closed metal door stood that seemed too heavy, incongruous with the rest of the house. At first, Nahteran didn't know what Taya meant, but he held his breath, trying to quiet his raging heartbeat. And then he heard it. Muffled men's voices. Voices and a series of heavy thuds from falling objects.

His heart sped up even more, his mouth growing dry. His mind felt like a tornado, spinning wildly as he stooped to set aside his daggers, pick up the unconscious Reynolds, and deposit her behind one of the couches, where she'd be shielded from the confrontation that seemed about to happen. He clenched his fists, trying to stay grounded, but emotions fogged his mind. Hatred for her and this little empire, hope that he was so close to being whole again, fear that they would fail. When he picked up his daggers again, they were slippery in his sweaty palms.

He could fight, he knew that. So could Taya. But if they failed . . .

A flash of deep blue in the corner of his vision. He turned his head. Beside him, Taya had taken on her animal form, feline body casting a long shadow over the gleaming floor now splotched with mud, her fire-colored eyes burning and lips pulling back to reveal long, sharp teeth. A pang of envy went through him—he wanted that size, that strength; he wanted sharp teeth and claws—but he didn't have time to dwell on it because the metal door burst open, and they were facing down two men, both laden with duffel bags and dripping silver.

Hatred, heavy and poisonous, spread through Nahteran at the sight. The effect of the silver in the sun was almost dazzling. The men's faces were just smears in his vision, but the objects were crystal clear: a silver crown tipped askew on someone's head, strands of necklaces hanging from a meaty fist, a bangle looped around a muscular arm. A bangle. Static filled his head. His body felt like tinder with a matchstick right in front of him, almost close enough to touch.

Everyone exploded into action at once. Taya leaped toward them, a blur of blue fire. The oldest man whipped the crown from his head and hurled it toward the glass wall of the hallway. It shattered, and cracks raced out in every direction. The men scattered, but the older one wasn't fast enough, and Taya slammed into him, snarling.

Nahteran was running, running toward the man with the bangle, but a roaring to his left made him turn his head.

Headlights.

His stomach plummeted. He threw himself backward, hitting the ground just as one of the SUVs ripped through the hallway, bringing the whole thing down in a rain of broken glass. Nahteran curled up to protect his head. Sharp edges bit at his back and arms, but he hardly felt them. As soon as it was over, he jumped to his feet, the taste of iron filling his mouth where he'd bitten his tongue.

Taya and the older man were still grappling on the other end of the destroyed hallway, but the man with the bangle was sprinting toward the waiting SUV, the duffel bag full of silver banging against his back as he ran. Nahteran launched himself forward, his hands closing around the bag's straps. The man shrugged his shoulder out of them, and the sudden weight sent Nahteran sprawling. The bag dropped onto the broken glass, but the man with the bangle on his arm kept running.

Nahteran scrambled to his feet. Before he could catch up, the man threw himself into the backseat and the driver stepped on the gas, cutting a muddy scar through the lawn. The SUV would have to circle the house before making it back to the road, but if the men made it out, Nahteran knew with a deep certainty that he would never see the two again. He would never get back the twelfth piece of his soul.

With a glance toward Taya—who had the older man pinned, silver pieces scattered over the floor—Nahteran left the bag where it was and sprinted in the other direction, toward the driveway, as the SUV swerved across the back lawn and into the trees. Without thinking, he jammed his daggers back into his belt and made for the driveway, sprinting down until he reached the gate. He vaulted over it onto the empty road. The sun was setting, casting everything in a fiery orange light. To his right was a dead end, a rough wall of stone. To his left stretched the road carved into the mountainside. And in front of him was a vast empty space. A metal railing was all that separated the narrow road from a hundred-foot drop into the valley.

The SUV would probably be able to break through the gate, but if he could block the road, the traders would have to stop or go over the edge. He could hear the engine's rumble from above, barreling down the mountainside. He had just seconds before the SUV would hit the gate.

He reached into the inner pocket of his jacket. His fingers closed around something cool and smooth. A silver ingot. It made him feel sick to use soul-silver for magic. Like he was no different than the traders. But he couldn't think about that now. He closed his hand around the ingot and felt the magic inside surge through his veins, reminding him of Byrn, of air that scorched your lungs and orange skies split with lightning.

Fire.

Flames burst from his hands, twin columns of flickering orange, and he spread his arms, sending them arcing out to block the road on either side of him.

The SUV burst through the locked gate. The clang was earsplitting, and bits of metal flew everywhere. Nahteran's vision was fractured, his body aching. Everything was air and metal and scorching heat. He saw the wheels of the SUV veer toward him, and for a second he was sure he was about to die. The traders were going to run him down, fire or no fire.

Then he saw the man's face in the driver's seat, the fear there. The fear of *him.*

The wheels veered away again, squealing. Too fast to stop. The breath vanished from Nahteran's lungs, evaporating all at once, so that the words rising to his lips came out silent, meaningless.

No—

I didn't mean—

But it was too late. The SUV and the traders and the soul-silver they carried went over the edge—the railing snapping like it was made of paper—and landed in a crash of flame far below.

———

Taya found him there, standing at the side of the road, staring at the charred wreckage below. She was back in her human form, sporting a few cuts and bruises, but not too much the worse for wear. She grabbed him, spinning him to check for injuries.

"What happened?" she demanded, concern underlying the anger in her voice. "Not that I couldn't handle that guy, but you kind of left me in the lurch up there."

Nahteran felt like his lungs were full of stones. He couldn't remember how to form words. He pointed down at what remained of the SUV.

Taya followed his gaze through the gathering dark, and he saw her expression grow somber. "Are they . . ."

"Yes."

A moment of silence passed between them. "They were killers," Taya said after a long time. Then, seeming to realize that wasn't helpful, she added, "It wasn't your fault. They could have stopped."

Nahteran swallowed. "I used fire magic. They were scared. And—" His own voice sounded distant to him. "He had a piece of silver on him. A piece with the last part of my soul bound inside." He drew a ragged breath, ashamed to feel tears threatening the backs of his eyes, roughening his voice. "I'll never be—" He couldn't finish the sentence.

He didn't look at Taya, not wanting to move his eyes from the horizon in case the tears spilled over. But he felt her move closer to him, grab his hand. Her grip was warm and almost too tight, like Gretel leading Hansel out of the forest.

"What do you mean?" she asked, a hint of a warning in her voice.

Nahteran swallowed. It was hard to get the words out, but he made himself say them. "I'll never get all of my soul back."

Taya was silent and still for a moment. Then she pulled him away from the ledge, toward the Jeep.

"There's no *never* for us," she said, her tone firm, brooking no room for argument.

She opened the passenger side door and gave him a gentle shove. Numbly, he climbed in as she went around. She sat next to him, but she didn't turn the car on or speak for another long moment. The car's interior lights faded, leaving them in dimness.

"We have scars, sure," she said at length. "We have missing pieces, but who doesn't? I think souls can heal just like skin and bone." She turned on the car, a gentle rumble starting up around them. She backed up, flicked the headlights on, and then turned up the driveway toward the mansion again.

"What are you doing?" Nahteran asked, surprise jolting him out of numbness for a second.

She gave him a look. "Janna Reynolds is still in the house, tied up, no thanks to you. And the rest of the soul-silver. We still have work to do, even if you're sad."

Nahteran exhaled, imagining the darkness going out of him with the air. The hollow, painful wound inside him was still there. He thought he'd have erased it today. Now he knew it would always be with him.

But it had receded when Taya had grabbed him to make sure he wasn't hurt. Still more when she took his hand, talked him down. Maybe the hurt wasn't because a part of him was missing. Maybe he just needed more time. He drew a breath of fresh air.

"Okay," he said, and this time the words didn't feel like broken glass coming out. "Work. Yeah."

"Yeah," Taya agreed, picking up speed as they ascended toward the dark mansion. "There are still a lot of souls up there who need to get freed. You grab them, and I'll talk Reynolds into coming with us."

She turned to him, grinned. "And then let's get home."